Sign up for our newsletter to hear about new and upcoming releases.

www.ylva-publishing.com

ORDER UP

A MENU OF LESBIAN ROMANCE & EROTICA

R.G. EMANUELLE
ANDI MARQUETTE
EDITORS

MENU

INTRODUCTION

"There is communion of more than our bodies
when bread is broken and wine drunk.

—*M.F.K. Fisher*

PREEMINENT AMERICAN FOOD WRITER MARY Frances Kennedy (M.F.K.) Fisher wrote that "our three basic needs, for food and security and love, are so mixed and mingled and entwined that we cannot straightly think of one without the others." When she wrote of hunger, she said, she was really "writing about love and the hunger for it."

Food can and does serve as a way to create connections between people. Whether love, lust, emotional intimacy, or all three, blossom in the act of preparing or eating food depends on the circumstances in which people find themselves, in the pasts they may share, or in the futures they hope to explore.

The two of us have always been interested in food—in creating it, eating it, sharing it. R.G. Emanuelle is a long-time foodie, food writer, and culinary school graduate, while Andi just really likes food and all the things it signals about life and love.

This anthology is our second foray together into the explorations of the sensuous qualities of food and how it engages far more than taste and smell. We had so much fun with our first food-themed collection, the Lambda finalist *All You Can Eat: A Buffet of Lesbian Romance and Erotica*, that we decided to do it again, putting our different perspectives to work to plan another menu that includes a variety of authors who incorporated food, romance, and erotica into their stories.

We purposely left the subject open-ended so contributors could roam freely through time and place and bring their own particular tastes to the table. We required only that the story incorporate food in its romantic and/or erotic trajectory. And, as we did in *All You Can Eat*, we kept the authors' international styles of writing for exotic flavor and some true fusion cuisine.

Readers will find that each story also ends with a recipe. Some of these are whimsical accompaniments that don't require cooking at all—at least not in the traditional sense. We then arranged the menu like a sumptuous meal by heat level, from warm, romantic appetizers to smoldering entrées that build to sizzling desserts.

With that in mind, our appetizer selections—tasty but complex bits to prime your palate for the next courses—include Jaye Markham, who in "Not Spam Again!" takes us to World War II-era London, and the development of a relationship between two women in the Women's Army Corps. Cheyenne Blue brings us to contemporary Australia in "Bunya Bunya," where a trip to southeast Queensland to collect and cook bunya bunya nuts helps nourish a tentative relationship with one partner's mother.

The act of learning to cook French dishes leaves a woman cold at first in N.R. Dunham's "A Twist of France" when she suspects her partner of cooking up something else, while two women discover something more in their friendship in Marie Sterling's "The Way to a Woman's Heart." And in Andi Marquette's "The Secret's in the Sauce," a woman takes a friend to the emergency room after a cooking incident and discovers more than medicine.

Our entrée selections turn the heat up. Some dishes cook at a slow burn, while others go right to boil. We start with Brey Willows' "God's Tamales," in which a chef who shares a meal with a homeless woman in her restaurant kitchen learns the value of connection and lending a helping hand. Lea Daley's "Sweet or Savory" serves up unrequited love that takes a turn for the better, and Liz McMullen tells the story of a woman trying to make an anniversary dinner for her partner that doesn't go according to plan in "Cassidy's Anniversary Caper."

Rebekah Weatherspoon tosses together a group of friends who meet every month to eat and hang out in the "Potluck Club," and in that mix a romance simmers, and in Emma Weimann's story, a woman creates a feast of "Something Salty, Something Sweet" for her partner.

Once you make it to our dessert menu, you'll find a variety of seductive selections that left the stove burning hot. R.G. Emanuelle serves up the first dessert, "Sliced and Diced," which brings two women together in the heat of a cooking competition, the aftermath of which is heat of a different kind. A caterer finds that her neighbor for the summer has some cooking tricks of her own in Cheri Crystal's "Clinch it with Coleslaw." Partners getting ready for a themed dinner party get sidetracked with a different sort of recipe in CK Combs' "Daddy's Hot Appetizer." A cleanse diet goes off the rails into a whole different sizzling hot menu in Jove Belle's

"Honey and Lemon," and Pascal Scott finishes the dessert tray with a morsel called "The Indulgent Chocolatier," her tale of a journalist who interviews a chocolatier and does, indeed, indulge in far more than conversation.

We hope you enjoy the menu, and that reading the selections leads to some cooking of your own, whether in or out of the kitchen. And we hope, ultimately, that you find, as we have, that food is sexy.

R.G. Emanuelle
Andi Marquette
2016

"One cannot think well, love well, sleep well, if one has not dined well."

—Virginia Woolf

APPETIZERS

NOT SPAM AGAIN!

JAYE MARKHAM

THE WOMAN IN KHAKI ON the serving line scooped up a heaping mishmash of noodles, bright orange cheese, and unidentifiable green and brown stuff and dumped the jumble on Nan's plate.

Nan looked up at the server. "What's this called?"

"Goulash, according to Cookie."

"Funny-looking goulash," Nan said.

"The cooks are trying to cover up the Spam. Again. Don't tell anyone," the server said in a loud whisper.

"I'd laugh if I wasn't about to cry," Nan said.

"My mom calls this leftovers," Betty added.

A stocky corporal rushed up and shoved a pan of soft rolls on the counter. "Move along, girls."

Nan sighed. Another meal of mysterious origins here at the mess. On the other hand, at least they were getting three daily meals, unlike when they first arrived in London in 1943. The post for their unit of the Women's Army Corps hadn't been prepared because a Nazi U-boat attack on their convoy sank a Liberty ship carrying food, clothing, bedding, and supplies. Until other supply ships landed two weeks later, the women lost weight on short rations and suffered some chilly nights.

Nan watched as the server plucked two rolls off the pan and plopped them next to the goulash. "Here. The rolls are good, at least." Her dark hair set off her twinkling blue eyes.

"I love rolls," Nan said. Seeing the woman's last name on her shirt above an apron, she added, "Thanks, Private Martin."

"I go by Marty."

"I'm Nan. I haven't seen you before. Are you new?"

"I arrived last week. Usually, I bake and assist in the kitchen, but today a server is out sick. Where do you work?"

"Hey," said a loud voice from down the line. "Leave the socializing for later. I'm hungry."

"Oh, stuff it, McDonald." Nan glared at the taller woman before turning back to Marty. "I'm in the headquarters, a few streets over. Maybe I'll see you again."

"Sure thing." Marty winked, and Nan's stomach fluttered as she turned and accompanied Betty to a nearby table. They tore into their chow, because any minute their sergeant would be yelling to form up outside. While Nan ate, she watched Marty, admiring her high cheekbones, strong jaw, silky brown hair, and stunning eyes.

"Do you think Marty lives in our building?" Nan asked.

Betty nodded as she swallowed. "Yes, on the fourth floor. I saw her on the stairs recently." She gestured toward the entrance to the dining hall where a sergeant stood with hands on hips. "Sarge is waiting."

They lurched to their feet and dumped their dishes, silverware, and glasses in metal tubs at another table before they dashed outside, cramming the remainder of the rolls into their mouths. Another dozen women from the WAC, known as Wacs, joined them as they marched down the street for headquarters, a structure surrounded by five-foot-high walls of sandbags. Once there, they split into two groups. Nan, Betty, and four other Wacs proceeded to a heavy wooden door where they showed their IDs to the Military Police and went inside.

As Nan and her coworkers typed requisitions, orders, rosters, and correspondence for Army units stationed in London and nearby, Nan's thoughts kept wandering to Marty. Something about her, beyond her smile and easy manner, made Nan want to be friends.

"Drat," Nan muttered as she made another mistake. She had to rip out the three sheets of typewriter paper and two pieces of carbons she was working on. After she ruined three sets of paper, she went to the lavatory, where she stood at the basin and washed her hands with harsh soap and cold water. After work, she'd look for hand lotion at a shop on the way to the hotel where they were billeted. Maybe she'd get lucky and find some despite the rationing. Otherwise, she'd have to write Mama and ask her to send a package.

Nan adjusted her tie and pushed her hair behind her ears, wishing for the hundredth time WAC regulations didn't insist that women's hair be worn above the coat collar. She caught herself. She was far better off than the British, who had lost their homes and loved ones. She returned to her desk and Betty glanced up. "The colonel's aide is looking for you."

Nan sighed. "Thanks." She left the clacking of typewriters behind and went to a large office that faced a park, now full of foxholes and sandbags. The sun, the first in a week, streamed in the high windows.

"State your business, Private," a male voice snarled.

She turned and the staff sergeant frowned.

"No lollygagging, girl."

Snapping to attention, Nan said, "Yes, sir. I understand Lieutenant Nelson wishes to see me, sir."

He frowned again. "Females," he muttered in a disgusted tone. "Through the door to your left. Step lively."

"Thank you, sir." Would some of these men ever accept women into the military? She fought an urge to roll her eyes at him and went into the office, where the lieutenant gave her another stack of work to do. She exited, arms bulging with folders, preoccupied with rumors about an upcoming invasion of France. Were some of these files related to that? She headed back to her desk, where she would divide up the work.

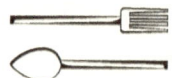

Nan lined up for breakfast before dawn the next morning, hoping for a barrel of coffee. Air raid sirens had sounded throughout the night in another German flyover. Every time the sirens wailed, Nan and her fellow Wacs rushed down dark stairs to the damp basement of their hotel, where they huddled until the all-clear signal. Three times they made that trek. Nan figured she got maybe an hour of actual sleep. She stood, exhausted and irritated, waiting for the service line to open, also delayed because of the raids.

Two female privates hauled an urn of coffee into the eating area and placed it on a table crowded with white porcelain mugs. A cheer went up from the Wacs.

"Thank goodness," Betty said to Nan.

Marty was among the workers, and she bowed to the crowd, while the other curtsied. "Food will be out in a minute, ladies," Marty hollered. Women cheered and whistled.

"Hurray!" Nan shouted.

Marty caught her eye and tapped her forehead with two fingers in a saucy salute. Nan smiled, appreciating Marty's humor. When the line finally opened, Nan decided not to disparage the eggs, once powdered. After all, it was hot food and at least there was catsup.

Marty grinned at Nan. "Good morning, sunshine."

"You didn't get much sleep last night, did you?" Nan asked, noticing the dark circles under Marty's eyes.

"No. We've been here since the final all-clear," Marty yawned. "Pardon me. I'm still waking up."

"You poor dear. We all appreciate you for showing up this morning. I'll bet this is going to be a long day for—"

"Enough with the never-ending devotion. Move along," McDonald growled. "I need to eat."

"Button it." Nan scowled at her before turning back to Marty. "Ignore ol' Grumpy. Thanks again."

"Any time." Marty smiled at her and again, Nan's stomach fluttered and the feeling stayed with her all the way to headquarters, where everything that could go wrong, did. The mimeograph machine jammed, and no one could find the proper tools. A messenger arrived from another office, but with incorrect papers. And finally, the woman in charge of making coffee on a hot plate dropped the percolator. Nan stared as liquid and grounds spewed across the floor. The last of the coffee. Two other women rushed to clean it up.

"I can't think without another cup of java," she said, forlorn. "Betty, please hand me one of those blank requisition forms."

Betty looked at her, sympathy on her face. "Sarge may not be back until lunch."

"I know someone who might do me a favor."

Puzzled, Betty handed her the form and Nan typed up the request.

"If anyone comes looking for me, tell them I'm on a vital reconnaissance mission."

Betty laughed. "Bring back some handsome men while you're out."

Nan waved and left. None of the men she met had appealed to her. Sure, she'd dated a few times before joining the WAC and now in London, enlisted men flirted, whistled, and made cat calls. She sometimes flirted back, and on occasion she joined Betty on double dates, but she never agreed to a second date. She'd rather stay at the hotel and play cards with other Wacs on free evenings.

She headed to the mess once she had the sergeant's signature and sniffed when she got there, hoping lunch wasn't Spam again. She longed for fresh meat. Wacs stood at the large sinks washing and drying dishes. Others opened oversized cans and dumped the contents into huge pots on the stoves. And on a floured wooden table, Marty pressed a cookie cutter into rolled-out dough. A warm spark ran through Nan at seeing her.

"My mouth is watering," Nan said as she approached.

"Oh, geez." Marty said with a laugh. "You startled me." She smiled. "Well, hello. What are you doing here?"

"I'm on official business," Nan said with a serious expression.

"Top secret?"

"It might be."

"How can I help?"

"It's bad. Over at HQ, we're out of coffee and we cannot do important military work without java. Especially not after last night." She held up the requisition.

Marty laughed. "That sounds like an emergency. Ground or brewed?" Marty brushed her hands off on her apron and Nan realized that Marty smelled like vanilla.

"Ground, please. We have a percolator." She handed Marty the form.

"Hold on. Hey, Cookie, I need your okay on this requisition."

The mess sergeant walked over and glanced at the request before adding her initials. "Get her a can, please. I can't leave my cooking."

"Thank you," Nan said, before Marty grabbed her wrist and pulled her along. Nan giggled. "Golly, I must be hungry because you smell good enough to eat."

Pink flooded Marty's face. "Thanks, I guess. I'm making sugar cookies, although they won't have as much sugar as you're used to."

"It doesn't matter. I'll eat any kind of cookies."

"I'll keep that in mind."

Marty brought her to a nearby storeroom overflowing with wooden shelves, many bowing under the weight of large cans of vegetables and fruits, and wooden crates. Stacked bags of beans, rice, oatmeal, flour, and salt lined an entire row.

"Holy Toledo," Nan said.

Marty chuckled. "Pretty swell, huh?"

"It's a small grocery store," Nan said, glancing longingly at a small crate of apples. "Red Delicious. The last time I ate one was in the States."

"Sorry. Those are for the officers' mess."

"Phooey. I'm not surprised they receive all the good stuff. But all this food isn't only for the officers, is it? Why are enlisted having to eat so much Spam when we have this?"

"We weren't resupplied until late yesterday. We're cooking some decent grub for lunch."

Nan read labels as she followed Marty. "Oh, no. Don't tell me there are three shelves of Spam. I want to cry."

Marty chuckled. "Don't worry. Cookie swears we won't serve Spam again for a week. Ah, here's the coffee."

Nan stared as Marty reached for it, noticing her strong hands and forearms as she lowered a heavy box to the floor. The sight made her heart beat a little faster. Marty pulled out a pocketknife and slit the tape of the box to reveal two-pound cans of coffee.

"Here you go." She handed Nan a can and their hands brushed, which sent a warm tingle up Nan's arms and through her body. She started in surprise. Marty's eyes widened.

"Static electricity," Marty said, though she seemed to blush.

"Yes, that's probably what it was. Although, I'm surprised it's that dry in here. Our HQ isn't." Nan tilted her head to look up at her. Marty's eyes reminded her of the blue irises growing back home, and they darkened as she held Nan's gaze.

"You're beautiful with those freckles," Marty said.

Nan grimaced. "Don't tease. I know they're ugly."

"No, they're not." Marty skimmed a finger down Nan's cheek and Nan's breath hitched.

"The neighbor kids called me Spots," she said softly. "I hate them."

"Not everyone has freckles. They make you special and beautiful."

"You're pulling my leg."

"No. I'm not joshing," Marty said, her expression serious. "And your red hair is gorgeous." She fingered a strand before tucking it behind Nan's ear.

Nan swallowed as a shiver ran down her spine at Marty's touch. The room seemed hot all at once. "I—I should be getting back to HQ."

Marty smiled. "Okay." She replaced the box and gestured toward the door. "After you."

Back in the kitchen, Nan signed for the coffee while Marty placed the can in a burlap bag stamped with block letters that said, "Lima Beans." She tightened a string around the top. "Here. No one will try to grab this from you."

"You're brilliant. A perfect camouflage."

"Come on, I'll walk you out."

Nan took a deep breath, crossing her fingers behind her back for good luck. "So... eh... would you like to go to the movies on Sunday afternoon? The Red Cross Service Club for Women is showing a new one from the States."

"I'd love to."

"Swell." Excitement coursed through Nan. "Meet me in our lobby at one o'clock—I mean, thirteen hundred hours." And as she walked back to HQ, her skin seemed to tingle where Marty had touched it.

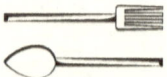

Nan stood in her bra and mud-brown-colored panties, trying to decide what to wear. Yesterday in the serving line, Marty had winked at her and mentioned how much she was looking forward to the film, which only made Nan that much more excited about it.

The door banged open as Betty burst in and glanced at her watch. "Aren't you going to the movies?"

"Yes, but I can't decide what to wear."

"Like we have much of a choice, what with no civilian clothes."

"A lot of the gals will be in trousers so they can sit on the floor in the front, but I think I want to wear a skirt."

Betty sniffed. "Is that perfume?"

"It's a social event. Rules say I can wear it."

"It's terrific." Betty grinned wickedly. "Are you and Marty meeting some guys?"

"Oh, I don't know," Nan said, hastily. "I doubt any guys will notice me."

"Sure, honey. The men outnumber us about fifty to one, but they won't notice little ol' you and your stunning auburn hair." Betty fanned herself.

"I just want to look and smell nice for once," she hedged. She didn't have time to wash it off. She finished dressing and a few minutes before 1300, she walked into the lobby, which was jammed with enlisted men. She stood on her tiptoes and craned her neck, looking for Marty.

"Move it, buster. I'm not interested in you." The crowd parted and Marty emerged. "Whew, here you are," she said, smiling.

"Hello." Nan tried not to think about how sharp Marty looked in trousers but failed. "I'm glad you found me. It's pretty crowded."

"I'll get you through this." Marty took Nan's hand, and Nan's heart pounded at the feel of Marty's grip, warm and firm. She followed Marty, and was disappointed when Marty let go after they got outside.

Bombs had damaged the underground train station near them, so they walked several blocks before finding a battered double-decker bus. They shared small talk as the vehicle made its way around rubble and craters to the ARC club.

"Phooey, another line," Marty said when they arrived. "Or should I say queue, since we're in London?"

"At least the weather's nice." Nan looked around. A sign in a nearby corner grocery advertised Spam. Apparently, it was popular with the English folks. She stifled a groan and looked back at Marty just as the line started to move. Once inside, they found seats near the back of the hall. As the lights dimmed, the opening music of *The More the Merrier* overshadowed the clacking of the nearby film projector. Not usually a fan of crowded spaces, Nan was glad for this one because it meant Marty's shoulder touched hers.

Marty inhaled and whispered, "Swell perfume. What's the scent?"

"Violets. And I hope I'm not crowding you."

"No, but I need to warn you." Marty's breath brushed her ear and Nan shivered. "If there are monsters, you'll need to hold my hand. I get scared."

Nan giggled. "I don't believe you."

"It's true."

"Well, don't worry. I'll protect you."

"I'm counting on it," Marty said with a grin as she grasped and squeezed Nan's hand.

Nan reacted with a flush that spread from her neck to the roots of her hair, and she prayed Marty didn't notice. Fortunately, the movie started and sadly, it wasn't scary, though Marty kept her shoulder against Nan's the whole time. Nan was sorry when it ended. She followed Marty to the tables set up with doughnuts and coffee afterward.

"I loved the scene on the rooftop. It reminded me of our apartment building in New York City," Marty said as they found seats around a long table. One of the women nearby commented to her friend, "Isn't Joel McCrea dreamy?"

Marty shrugged at the remark.

"What do you think about him?" Nan asked.

"He's all right," Marty said with the enthusiasm of someone visiting a dentist. "I liked Jean Arthur's character better. How about you?"

"Oh, she was spunky, for sure," Nan said, glad she wasn't the only one who didn't swoon at good-looking men.

Marty took a bite of a donut and closed her eyes. "Mmm. Is anything better than a hot donut?"

"What about bread fresh out of the oven?" Nan sipped her coffee. "The butter melting as fast as you can spread it."

"Cookies before they cool."

"Hot cross buns with frosting."

"Warm gingerbread."

"Oh goodness, I'm still hungry," Nan said. And for more than food, she realized—like a best friend. But more. But what would more be, she wondered as she watched Marty put a bit of donut in her mouth. These new thoughts were starting to scare her.

"Really?" Marty asked.

"My father says I have a hollow leg. I can eat as much as my brothers."

"In that case, we'd better ask for another plate of donuts. Because all the mess is serving is leftover soup."

"Probably with Spam."

Marty laughed. "I told you, we get a reprieve. I'll be right back with more donuts."

Nan watched her, and tore her gaze away when it wandered down past Marty's waist.

What were these new feelings and what was she supposed to do about them?

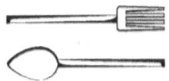

The next few days proved too busy for Nan to socialize with Marty, which might've been good because Nan still was puzzled about why the sight of Marty in the mess line caused flutters in her stomach and an all-over giddiness. Whenever she had a moment, she caught herself thinking about how Marty's eyes sparkled when she joked, and about how her hand felt when she pulled Nan through the crowd and before the movie started. Nan stared at the ceiling of the room she shared with Betty nearly a week after that movie, wondering why she thought more about Marty than any man she'd dated. A knock at the door interrupted her musing.

Nan opened it, and her heart skipped at the sight of Marty. "Hello."

"I'm really glad you're here. May I come in?"

"Um, certainly." Nan stepped aside and Marty rushed in.

"Please close the door," she said, and Nan did.

"I worried you wouldn't be here and that I'd be caught." She unclasped her purse and withdrew two Red Delicious apples. "For you."

Nan stared. "You remembered." Before she thought about it, she pulled Marty into a hug. "You're a sweetheart." She kissed Marty's cheek then pulled away when she realized what she'd done. She chided herself. Women often kissed cheeks. She cleared her throat. "Thank you. You should have one too."

"They're for you. They're a bit bruised. Cookie was thinking of throwing them away, since there wasn't enough for a pie."

"I don't care. Where's your knife? We'll share one now, and I'll hide the other for another time."

Marty took a knife out of her purse and cut away the bruises before she sliced it.

"Oh, this is heaven," Nan said as she bit into a piece. "I can almost forgive having Spam if I got one of these a week."

Marty laughed and took a bite. "Mmm. Golly, you don't know what you miss until it's gone. So how've you been? I haven't had a chance to chat with you."

"They've got us working extra hours. This is the first evening I've had free all week. I shouldn't complain. At least the raids haven't been as frequent, nor have we run out of coffee."

"Well, you know where to go when you do. Do you have some time now?"

"Yes, what do you have in mind?"

"Have you been to a pub?"

"Once, on a double date." Nan hesitated. "I didn't particularly like the pint of bitters."

"You need to try the lager, according to my roommate."

"Well…"

"There's a pub two blocks from here where we can play darts. Please come, it will be fun."

How could she say no to Marty's smile? It made her insides glow like a field full of fireflies. "All right."

"Don't worry. I'll keep you out of trouble."

Nan grabbed her coat. "A little trouble is okay."

"That's the spirit." Marty held the door for her and Nan held her gaze for a long moment, not understanding why she wanted to pull her close and run her fingers through Marty's hair, and feel her lips—

"Ready?" Marty asked.

"Yes." She locked the door behind them, delighting in Marty's closeness and how it felt when their hands inadvertently brushed as they went down the stairs. Why didn't she react this way to a man? Was she one of those women the Army warned about? The kind who like women the way they should like men?

"Come on, slow poke," Marty said. "It's right up here."

Nan quickened her pace. And what if she was? Because it didn't feel wrong. In fact, it felt right. More right than when she tried to feel something for men and didn't.

"Are you okay?" Marty stopped at the door, concern on her features.

"I'm fine. Just thinking."

"We don't have to do this. I just thought it would be fun."

"It will be." Nan smiled at her, reassuring. Everything about Marty felt *right*. "So tell me all about darts. I've heard people can be ruthless."

Marty laughed and opened the door. "After you." She placed her hand at the small of Nan's back and Nan wished she wasn't wearing her coat. The touch was too brief, but they had a while to be together because curfew wasn't for three hours. Surely, she wasn't wicked in wanting to spend more time with Marty, was she? Even if Marty didn't feel the same way, at least she'd found a friend.

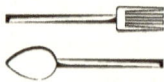

"There's Spam in this, isn't there?" Nan stared at the so-called goulash on her plate. The server shrugged, but she looked sympathetic. "Again?" Nan said.

"Fresh meat is difficult to come by."

"It's not so bad," the woman behind her said as they moved down the line. "Use extra catsup."

"I swear, if this war ever ends, I will never eat another bite of Spam as long as I live." Nan sat down, wishing for another evening like the one she'd had a few days ago at the pub with Marty. She finished eating, and was on her way out the door, when a familiar voice stopped her.

"Hello, Nan. Do you have plans tonight?" Marty stood holding the door to the kitchen open with her foot.

22

"No." She grinned. "Can you come over after you're done? Betty got a weekend pass away."

"You sure?"

"We can play cards." Stepping closer and lowering her voice, she said, "Mama sent me some cookies."

"There's an offer I can't refuse. See you in a bit."

Nan nodded, painfully aware of the sparks bouncing around her chest. She rushed to her room and set up a hotplate and pot. Betty had managed to secure a radio, so Nan turned it on and the sound of big band music filled the small space. It made her a little homesick for the States, but she forgot all that when a knock sounded at the door.

"Come in," Nan called.

Marty entered. "Hi. Sorry it's a little later than I wanted."

Nan took her coat and purse and put both on Betty's bed. "Better late than never. Have a cookie." She gestured at the box on the small table. Marty selected one, bit into it, and moaned softly. "Oatmeal raisin. And they survived the journey here mostly intact."

"I've got hot water for tea. Would you like a cup?"

"Yes, please."

"I don't have any milk, but I do have honey."

"Plain is fine."

Nan handed her a cup. "Let's have a toast. To new friends."

"Here's to new friends." Marty clinked her cup gently against Nan's.

"Have another cookie." Nan moved toward the table just as air raid sirens sounded in the distance.

"Oh no." She put their cups on the table and grabbed a blanket off her bed. "Another night in the basement. And it's so cold down there." The lights flickered and went off and the radio died.

"Unless the bombs come closer, why don't we stay here?"

Nan hesitated.

"The sirens aren't close. We'll move if that changes."

"Okay."

"Come here," Marty said. "The best way to keep warm is to get close. If you're okay with that." Moonlight through a slit in the blackout curtains revealed Marty as she sat down on Nan's bed. Nan's heart pounded hard enough for Marty to hear, she was sure, but she joined her on the bed.

Marty pulled her close, and covered them both with the blanket. Nan forgot to breathe at the feeling of Marty's breasts against her back. Marty tucked her arm around Nan's stomach and pulled her closer.

"How's this?"

Nan inhaled the smell of soap and Marty's unique scent. "Fine."

"If you ever come and visit me in New York after this, I'll be sure to have plenty of blankets around."

"What about just doing this?"

Marty was silent for a moment and Nan bit her lip, hoping she hadn't overstepped.

"That'll work," Marty said, and her breath was warm against Nan's ear.

"Why don't you stay here tonight? There's no telling how long the lights will be out."

"You sure?"

"Yes. Besides, I like you keeping me warm."

"Same here. Good night," Marty said softly.

"'Night." Nan stayed awake a while, the warmth of Marty's body filling her with both comfort and something else. Another air raid siren sounded in the distance and Nan tensed, waiting for the bombs, but none came and she drifted to sleep.

Sometime in the night, she woke to find Marty raining kisses all over her face and neck, while her own hand cupped Marty's soft breast. Marty's lips touched hers and a rush of heat ran down her body. She threaded a hand through Marty's silky hair and kissed her back.

"Oh no." She jerked away.

"What's wrong?" Marty said.

"I'm sorry. Neither of us knew what we were doing. We were asleep."

Marty sat up. "You were sleeping?"

Nan froze. "You weren't?"

"Eh, oh." Marty scrambled off the bed. "I thought you were awake when you, um, touched me. Otherwise, I wouldn't have started kissing you."

"You wanted to kiss me?"

Marty chewed her lip. "Are you gonna be mad and report me?"

"No. No." Nan clasped Marty's hand. "I adored your kisses."

Marty grinned. "I loved you touching my breast."

Nan pulled back the blanket and motioned for Marty. "I'm not sure what to do."

"I have some ideas," Marty said. "Let's start here." And she leaned in for another kiss.

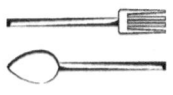

Nan checked her reflection in the small mirror on the wall of her room. Marty would be here soon, and although it had only been last night, Nan ached for her touch again, longed for her kisses, and the feel of her hands on her skin. Betty wasn't due back until the next morning, leaving them one more night together. A siren blasted the air and Nan froze. Not again. A muffled explosion followed seconds later and the glass in the window rattled.

A Wac slammed the door open. "Come on. They're close."

Another explosion shook the mirror off the wall, but luckily it landed without breaking. Nan grabbed a blanket from her bed and followed as bits of plaster drifted from the ceiling. Where was Marty? Nan hoped she was still at the mess hall because there was a basement there. Oh, God. Please let her be safe, Nan chanted in her head as she followed the Wac down the cramped stairs. Soon they were engulfed by a throng of Wacs, all hurrying to get underground. Another explosion seemed to rock the structure and Nan stumbled against the wall. She regained her balance and continued on, coughing in the swirls of dust and plaster.

Finally in the basement, she wrapped the blanket around herself and huddled against a far wall, listening to the muffled thumps of bombs and the eerie wails of the sirens. Thoughts of Marty almost sent her back up the stairs, which she knew was stupid. Some women talked softly, comforting each other. The walls seemed to shake, and Nan closed her eyes tight, willing the bombs to stop.

"Hello, sunshine," said a voice next to her ear.

Nan opened her eyes. "Oh, God. I'm so glad to see you." She pulled Marty into a hug. "I was so worried."

"It's okay. I was finishing up when the sirens started."

Nan wanted to hang on forever, but she released Marty, mindful of their surroundings.

"When this war ends, I want to follow you to New York."

"I was hoping you'd say that." Marty winked and Nan's heart sped up. Nan patted the floor next to her and Marty sank down. Nan drew the blanket around them, glad for the opportunity to feel Marty against her.

"I would've brought the rest of the cookies, but they're upstairs, sadly," Nan said. The naked lightbulb hanging from the ceiling flickered then died, and almost everyone groaned in the dark. Nan felt Marty's lips on hers and she kissed her back, feeling a rush at doing it in a room full of people.

"No cookies," Marty said after a while against her lips. "But we do have this."

"What?"

Marty pressed something wrapped in cloth into Nan's hand. "I brought sandwiches."

"What—"

"Guess."

Nan put the cloth near her face and sniffed. She groaned. "You didn't."

"We'll always have Spam, sweetheart."

Nan laughed and pulled her close. "As long as I'm with you," she whispered, "I won't mind."

SPAM SANDWICHES

One can of Spam
Four slices of bread
Mayonnaise
Catsup and mustard as needed
Lettuce and tomato, if available

Slice the Spam (the thicker the slices, the longer to heat). Place slices of Spam in a skillet, if a hotplate or stove is available. Heat for 5-15 minutes, depending on slice thickness. Toast the bread (if you like) and spread mayonnaise on two slices, one for each sandwich. Place 2-3 slices of Spam each onto the two plain pieces of bread and put mustard or catsup (or both, if that's your personal taste) onto the Spam then add lettuce and sliced tomato over that. Add a slice of bread with mayonnaise to each to top off the sandwiches.

Serves 2.

BUNYA BUNYA

CHEYENNE BLUE

"I'm going back to country," Tianna says. "Want to come?"

We walk along the foreshore at St Kilda. To our right, Melbourne sprawls in a haze of smog. To our left, the quiet wavelets of Port Phillip Bay lap the foreshore. A dog races along the stony beach chasing a seagull.

"Will I be welcome?" I concentrate on my feet, on my one red shoe, one purple shoe. "I'm *gubbah*, a white woman."

She halts, tugs on my hand until I stop too, and we both face the bay, the city at our backs. "You feel it, Jenn. This land is my land, but it's yours too. You belong here. You're a white woman, but you're *my* woman. That makes you welcome."

We are silent, and her hand in mine is rough and dry, and it holds mine so tightly I can't pull away. Not that I want to. Out on the water the ferry to Tasmania makes its stately way to the Heads. "Like a bloody block of flats," Tianna always says about its steep and blocky shape. She leans against me for a moment, and I look down and see her face peering up at me through the mass of dark brown curls. "My woman," she says again, and that settles it.

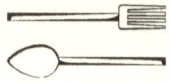

Tianna has told me often of her people. She is Barrangum. Her people come from southeast Queensland—not the tidy areas of the Sunshine Coast where people holiday, nor the hinterland where Green voters attend meditation workshops, and refuse to vaccinate their children, but inland. It's only a couple of hours' drive from the coast, but the land is sparse and drought-ridden, except when it's flooding. The land of contrasts, but all of them harsh.

She's told me stories of growing up on the mission there, a joyless place of parched grass and fibro houses and a *No Alcohol* sign at the entrance. She was happy, though. "It wasn't the worst," she says, with her usual laconic understatement. She ran barefoot, attended the mission school, got her first job in the nearby town, and realised she wanted more. That's when she elbowed her way into university, completed her social work degree, and eventually ended up in Melbourne, working with older Koories, finding them a place to be.

Most people don't know she's an Aboriginal person. She just is. She's paler-skinned than many, and doesn't shout the fact, doesn't drape herself in black and yellow and red, the colours of the flag. She doesn't draw attention to it, even when there are dickheads in the pub banging on about land rights, or making borderline racist comments. She's the eye of the cyclone, and she's as calm and still as stone, while debate swirls about her.

"How can you listen to people saying such stupid things?" I asked her once. She just shrugged.

"Let them be," she said. "They'll learn one day. No point ramming it down their gullets. They'll only choke on the knowledge."

I don't know how she can be like that. I'm the fierce one in our relationship, the one with the causes. Doctors Without Borders, Legal Aid, and of course fighting bonehead politicians in Australia for marriage equality. Tianna just shrugs, like she usually does. "It will come. Like the rains, it will come."

"And then will you marry me?" I ask.

"Of course."

So when she asks me to come to country with her, it is, in many ways, taking me home to meet her family, scattered as they are. Her father is dead, but her mother still lives in the pale fibro house on the mission, where she collects the pension and has a few beers in town. On the drive back to the mission, she has a stubby every fifty kilometres and leaves the empties at the entrance by the *No Alcohol* sign.

I've heard tales of her mother: The woman who was taken from her own mother and brought up in a white household even though she was born in the sixties when you'd think such things had stopped. The woman who found her own way back. The woman who bore five kids and lost three. One dead, one missing, and one who pretends she's Thai and won't come home. The other two are Tianna in Melbourne, and a younger brother who works on a cattle station. Will she see me as a daughter, or will I forever be the woman who keeps Tianna in Melbourne, far from country?

It isn't true, of course. Tianna was living in Melbourne for a handful of years before I met her, and she's been home three times in the two years we've been together. This time, though, is the first time she's asked me to come with her.

"I'll book the flights," she says. "We'll go in January."

"That's an expensive time to travel. All the schools will be on summer holidays." My hands are busy preparing food in our inner-city apartment. Dicing, chopping, frying. The simple food we prefer.

"Has to be then. The bunya nuts will be falling. I need to visit my tree."

I'm silent and I wonder if I've misheard. Tianna sits at the bench watching me. She steals a snow pea from the prepared vegetables and chomps it.

"My bunya tree," she says, when I still don't say anything.

My incomprehension must show on my face, as she says, "Way back when, the only land that Aboriginal people ever owned as individuals was a bunya bunya tree. If you don't know better, you might think it was a hoop pine, but bunyas have spiky leaves, and a domed crown. Every January, the nuts fall. The cone is bigger than your head and twice as heavy. Last year, some tourists parked their car under a tree, and the nut put a dent in the roof nearly down to the floor.

"Every three years there's a big harvest. There's a festival of sorts, but it's a tourist thing now. Not going for that, though. Just going."

"Will you get the nuts from your tree?"

"Yeah. Although it's not really *my* tree. No one knows now who owns what tree, and no one cares. It was the men who owned them, anyway. Not us. But I go because it's time to spend with my mum, preparing, eating. Have you ever tasted bunya nuts?" She looks at me then, back from the faraway place behind her eyes.

I shake my head.

"You wait. Delicious."

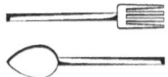

Once we are away from the Queensland coastal strip, the land stretches in front of us. It's all so lush and green by the coast, and even inland the lushness continues, for it's the wet season. But there's rat's tail grass in an unbroken wave by the roadside, and prickly pear chokes the dry forest areas. "Needs a fire through," Tianna says, and presses the throttle so that the rental car surges forward.

We reach her mother's place at dusk, just as the lazy kangaroos stir for the evening, leaping in front of the car in huge bounds. There's a flock of cockatoos in the sky, thick with impending rain.

I ask Tianna what I should call her mother.

"Aunty," says Tianna, and I nod. It's a respectful address, and it's appropriate.

Her mother—Aunty, I must think of her—is small and spreading, nothing like Tianna, who is wiry and intense. Her mother hugs her, murmuring into her hair, and while Aunty's greeting to me is friendly enough, I sense a wariness directed at me, the woman who stole her child away, who keeps her in the city, although that's not true. Tianna keeps herself in the city.

The house is small and untidy, and there are dogs outside, skinny ones with waving tails. They greet Tianna ecstatically, but eye me with caution. A bit like Aunty. We sit at the table and Aunty goes down to the takeaway and comes back with battered fish and chips. We eat with our fingers, and it's like home, all our greasy vinegar-slicked fingers reaching for the last chip.

"We go out to the mountains tomorrow," her mother says, and it's the first thing she's said in a while. "Got the ute packed and ready."

Tianna nods, and her mother goes off to bed, leaving us on the tiny veranda, where we can see the stars, so much bigger, so much more intense than in the city. Apart from the occasional bark of a dog, and the scurry of something small, the night is silent. Tianna goes off to make tea and hands it to me, strong and black. We sit together on the bench, and our free hands find each other across the worn cushion.

"We'll be camping tomorrow," says Tianna. "You up for it?"

I nod, although she can't see me in the darkness. I feel this time together is a test, of our love, of our relationship. How the *gubbah* fits in. I determine that whatever she throws at me, I'll take it without complaint. I don't even make a joke about my hairdryer, although I think it.

She puts her tea down, and leans in and kisses me, and her lips are tart with vinegar, but her breath is the same sweetness it always is, and the way her hand grasps mine and how she pushes herself against me, is the same.

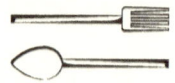

The three of us leave in the ute, which is a new Holden with fresh white paint. We drive for a couple of hours, until the mountains that rise from the plains become closer, and the ute swoops its way up and around the bend, past the

National Park sign. We take a track that's marked for park management use only, and I wonder if we need permission for this, or if they always have permission. I don't say anything.

There's been heavy rain before we arrived, and the ute bogs in the red clay. Tianna and I get out and push, leaving Aunty to burn the clutch, and the ute surges forwards, spraying us with thick mud. I grit my teeth so that I don't complain, but Tianna just laughs.

It seems like a long time before the ute stops—deliberately this time. We're deep in the forest, in a cathedral of trees that reach for the sky. Gum trees mainly, but here, where we stop on the pointy edge of the ridge, there's the spiky dark green trees that Tianna pointed out earlier. Bunya pines—tall and distinctive, with their rounded domes.

Tianna leaps from the ute before it comes to a halt, and turns her face up to the dappled trees. She says something in a strange tongue, and as I approach her, she reaches for my hand, clasps it tight and turns her face upwards again.

Aunty comes up on Tianna's far side and clasps her hand, and says something, and Tianna's hand clasps mine so hard I feel my bones rub together, and Aunty replies, and I can see her looking at me sideways. I don't know what Tianna's saying, but I can hope.

The undergrowth is thick, much of it the hard, scratchy branches of lantana. But there's a deep bed of rotting vegetation and our steps are light on the springy surface. I try not to think of leeches, of ticks, of snakes, and spiders and all the things I don't have to deal with in Melbourne.

Tianna releases my hand and moves forwards, dropping to her knees. She stands, carefully holding a spiky cone. It's bigger than my head, and the segments are loosening.

"Bunya bunya," she says. Aunty nods approvingly and Tianna puts it in the tray of the ute, where it splits and the segments fall apart.

We move around the tree, and find more cones. I pick one up carefully, spreading my fingers wide to bridge the spikes, holding it away from my body. There's another tree not far away, but when I move towards it, spying the bright green cones underneath, Tianna stops me with a tug on my shirt. "That's not my tree," she says. "That's someone else's."

I see Aunty watching me, and I nod, halt my steps. I think that there's no one else here, that no one really owns the trees anymore, and we could take the nuts, more would fall, but this isn't my country. This isn't my tree. I was born in Australia, but right now, I'm as foreign as any *gubbah* ever was.

Aunty nods to Tianna's tree. "You climb? I got rope."

No. Surely not. The trunk is wide and spiky and rough as an echidna approached from the arse end. Tianna's skinny legs and arms will get cut up, scratched to blazes. If she could even get up there. But Tianna's staring up at the tree, considering.

"Nah," she says. "I'll leave it. We got enough. Leave some."

Indeed, we've got seven big cones in the tray. I'm relieved. I won't try and stop her if she does climb, but I'm glad I don't have to watch her embrace the tree.

Aunty nods, moves back to the ute and gets into the driver's seat. I'm surprised. We've been here less than fifteen minutes. I expected more. Some sort of ceremony, some sort of meditation on the land. But Tianna is also climbing back into the ute, taking the cramped middle seat again,

36

where her knees stick up on either side of the gear knob like chicken wings.

"C'mon, Jenn," she says.

Aunty's revving the engine so that it smokes out the back. I don't think they'll leave me behind, but I jump in quicksmart and Aunty revs louder and burns the clutch and the ute lurches back to the dirt trail that leads to the bitumen.

I think we'll camp in the forest, but Aunty drives us in a haphazard fashion down from the ranges, to the plains that stretch to the west. It's hot and dry and the ute smells of stale sweat and hot skin. We drive for an hour, and pull into a pub, a two-storied building with a veranda that lists slightly to one side. The footy is on the telly, and the girl behind the bar serves us a slab of beer to go. Tianna heaves it in the back of the ute, next to the cones. Aunty darts back, pulls out three stubbies and gives one to each of us. The beer is cold and I'm thirsty.

Twenty minutes further on, the corrugated dirt road turns into a track and the track ends at some granite slabs and boulders, and we stop. There's nothing here, apart from the boulders, to distinguish this place from any other that I can see. It looks like grazing land. It's scrubby with patches of brigalow, and the occasional drooping gum. The brown earth is wide between the clumps of grass—the rains can't have fallen on this side of the range. It's dusty, dry, brown, and red. Aunty lowers herself from the ute, and Tianna scrambles out the driver's side, as if she can't wait for me to get out. An empty stubby falls out and rolls in the dirt.

Tianna and Aunty dart around, gathering timber, rolling the swags out of the ute and on to the ground. I stand around, feeling as useless as tits on a bull, while they work. Only now do I see that besides the beer we bought in the pub in the tray of the ute, there's no other food. Except for the bunyas.

"Get kindling," Tianna says, as she passes me, dragging a downed branch of acacia. She drops the branch and it's so dry that it splits and crumbles into a pile of puff-dry wood and white ants. I go for the smaller twigs and branches, treading carefully, as this is snake country. The whole of Australia is snake country, even in Melbourne, where the red-bellied black snakes follow the winding Merri Creek and Yarra River into the heart of the city. Or so I've heard. I've never seen one. But here, the warnings seem more immediate. Aunty drags three more beers from the plastic and hands one to each of us before downing hers in long gulps.

We're on the slightest of rises, the barest of hillocks, and the land stretches wide and red to the west. Far away I can see headlights sweeping along in a straight line. From the speed, it must be the paved road to Dalby.

The small amount of kindling I manage to collect I help push into a pile, and Tianna and Aunty pile the bigger logs on top. Tianna lights the fire, coaxing the dry gum leaves into a tiny flame, which eventually catches, and soon the campfire is ablaze. The three of us sit on a log, in a row, like pigeons on a fence. I'm next to Tianna, and I feel the press of her bare leg against mine. She rolls her stubby between her palms and stares into the flame.

Night comes down abruptly, a stage curtain descending. I'm hungry. I've only had beer since breakfast. I think of the lack of food we have. I'd offer to prepare some, if there was anything I could cook, but there are only the spiky bunya nuts in the back of the ute.

It's this, more than anything, that makes me feel out of control, and unsure. Food is my constant. I love the action of choosing ingredients, of preparing it, cooking it, and eating it. I love how it brings us together, me and Tianna, for she loves it too, and while her cooking is a lot more haphazard than mine, she loves to experiment with how things go together. It was one of the first things we had in common—us, the white girl from the city and the brown girl from the bush.

Tianna and Aunty stare into the fire, which is burning down to red heartwood embers. They don't talk, but Tianna has picked up my hand, and holds it between her dry palms, so I know she's thinking of me.

Aunty rises to her feet, and pokes the fire with a stick. Without a word, she returns to the ute and brings back one of the bunyas and drops it in front of Tianna. It splits, and the fibrous husks fall away from the central core. Tianna bends, and picks up the husk, peels the fibre away to reveal the smooth egg-shaped nut. She tosses the husk into the fire where it flares into yellow flame, and continues stripping the nuts clean.

I mimic her movements and there is soon a big pile of nuts. Aunty, who has been watching us, returns with more beers, and picks up the nuts and tips them into the embers, using a stick to bury them in the heat.

When all the nuts are in the fire, Tianna rises and holds out a hand to me. I stand—stiff from bending, and the lack of back support—and I take her hand.

"We'll be back," Tianna says to Aunty, and hand-in-hand we walk away from the fire.

I follow Tianna, who climbs to the top of one of the granite boulders. From here we can see west, towards the glow of light on the horizon that is the town of Dalby, where all the roads out here seem to lead.

Tianna turns to face me and wraps her arms around my waist. "You okay?" she asks.

I nod. I feel strange—although that is probably from hunger and too much beer—but I'm okay. The silences between the three of us, and the bigger silence of landscape, are sinking through my skin, absorbing me.

Tianna presses her face against my neck, and I feel her breath warm against my skin. "Tell me what you're thinking."

I could tell her how beautiful it is here. How strange. How I'd be so scared to be alone if she weren't with me. That I'm nervous about sleeping in a swag on the ground with all the creepy crawlies and snakes, but instead I blurt, "I'm hungry."

I feel her smile against my skin. "You won't be soon. Bunyas are very filling. Give it another twenty minutes or so."

My stomach gurgles, and she laughs.

Tianna kisses me. Her lips are dry, like her palms, but pliable. She's an active kisser, never one to lie back and receive. So her tongue darts into my mouth, and her hands map the shape of my body, as if she's committing me to memory.

"Mum likes you," she says.

I'm surprised. Aunty hasn't said many words directly to me, and I'm still feeling the vibe that she wishes I were someone different. A bush girl maybe, not a city girl.

"She never says much," Tianna continues, "but you'd know if she didn't. She wouldn't have waited for you to get into the ute, and she wouldn't have handed you a beer."

"That's good," I say. "I was hoping it would be okay."

"She's right." Tianna's short answer is all I'm going to get, but she takes my hand and leads me further onto the rock, so that I can see the sky, the sky we don't see in the city, where the Milky Way sweeps down in a snake trail of glory.

"I wanted you to see this," she says.

"The stars?"

"Yeah, them too. But I wanted you to see my country, where I'm from. You learn this place and you'll know me."

I'm silent. I'd thought I *did* know her. I know her smiles and her short way of speaking. I know her passion for her job, and her bad driving. I know that she avoids the pavement cracks, and eats the crunchy tails of prawns. I thought I understood her.

"You do understand me."

It's as if she's picked the words from my head.

"This, though...this is a part of me that Melbourne can never be."

I'm silent for a moment, absorbing the night, letting her words settle into me. "Are you saying that you want to move back here?"

"No. Not yet. But one day, when I'm old." She turns to face me, and her eyes glitter in the starlight. "Do you think you would want that too?"

When I'm old, she said. When I'm old too. I concentrate on the implication in her words—that we will be old together—and that knowledge feels right. It feels good.

Then I think of the other part of the sentence. Would I want to move here too?

I open my mouth to say that I just don't know, I don't know how I'll be in the future, where I'll want to live, what sort of person I will be, when the ute horn blasts loud into the night.

Tianna's gaze fixes on me for another long moment. "You don't have to answer now." She touches my hand. "Nuts are ready."

She turns and walks back to the fire, leaving me to bob in her wake like a dingy towed behind a yacht.

Aunty has the nuts out of the fire. They're lined up on the granite, shells blackened. A few have exploded and the ragged kernel inside is as black as the outside. There's a container of salt, and a hammer.

I squat on the log and watch as Aunty lines up a nut and smashes it with the hammer. Once the shell is crushed, she digs the nut out with her fingers, a white ovoid, maybe a couple of centimetres long. She pours salt onto the rock, dips the kernel into it and hands it to Tianna, who hands it to me.

It's hot and scalds my fingers. I see Tianna with a second one, and she's chewing it in her asbestos mouth, never mind the heat. I nibble, and it's salty and dense and oh-so-delicious. I eat more, smile, and Aunty hands me another—directly to me this time.

We sit and eat, taking turns to crack the nuts with the hammer, sharing around the kernels. The bunyas aren't like other nuts. They're more like a chestnut. Starchy, not oily, Tianna says, and tells me how one year she made a huge batch of pesto, using bunyas instead of pine nuts, and the ground nuts sucked in all the oil, so that after a day the pesto was crumbly and dry.

I'm completely full and satisfied by the time all the nuts are gone. The slight head spin from too much beer has faded, so that when Tianna hands me another beer, I gulp it in long swallows.

The fire has burned low, and Aunty leaves, slipping silently into the shadows from the fire. I see her humped shape in her swag, her shoulders rising and falling with her breathing.

I yawn, and Tianna notices. Without a word, she goes to our swag and unrolls it. It's not a double, but it's bigger than a single. The night is warm, and the swag will be confining, the heat intensifying in close confines, but Tianna strips back the canvas top, leaving just a sheet to cover us from the night. She strips down to her T-shirt and knickers and pushes her clothes down to the toe of the swag. Once in, she holds out a hand to me.

I don't hesitate. I copy her routine and, clad in only a T-shirt and knickers as well, I wiggle my way beside her, until her hair tickles my nose and she curls into my side. One hand moves under my shirt to cup my breast. Two deep breaths, and she's asleep.

I lie there, surprisingly comfortable, though I can feel the hard rock underneath the thin mattress and Tianna's hard knees digging into my thigh. My mind relaxes, and I think about where I am, and who I am, and who Tianna is.

I like this place, I think. I could live here one day, maybe, in a small town, surrounded by space. Melbourne is so huge, so frenetic. I don't think it's a city to be old in. But it wouldn't be easy, living here. It would be hard and hot and challenging.

I would do it, though. As long as Tianna was with me. White girl and brown, in country. I close my eyes.

HOW TO COOK BUNYA BUNYA NUTS

1. Visit southeast Queensland in January. This is where the trees grow, and this is when the nuts fall.
2. Hunt underneath a tree until you find some cones. You won't miss them.
3. Separate the cone into its segmented husks, and peel back the husk to remove each nut in its shell.
4. Place the nuts in their shells in a pot of boiling water and boil for 20 minutes or so. Then immediately smash with a hammer to remove the kernel.
5. The kernel can be frozen, used in many recipes, or—the best way—toss in a pan with butter until warm, and serve immediately with lots of melted butter and salt. Eat with your fingers.

You can roast them, as Tianna and Jenn did in this story, but the boiling method is more reliable.

A TWIST OF FRANCE

N.R. DUNHAM

TRISH WOKE TO A PAINFUL throbbing in her leg, an incessant beeping in her ears, and the smell of smoke. She was terribly used to the first, but the others probably should've been more concerning. Straining her ears to pick up something other than the smoke detector, she caught snatches of Peggy's voice. She was swearing, but her tone didn't suggest any immediate danger. Fortunate. If she had to flee for her life as the building burned behind them, Trish doubted she'd get very far. Then again, maybe that wouldn't be such a bad thing.

She sighed and hauled herself out of bed then reached for the crutches by the nightstand. The wheelchair taunted her from a nearby corner. Her leg hurt badly enough that the chair was almost appealing. Almost.

Making her frustratingly slow way down the hall, Trish coughed as she breathed in the smoke hovering over the kitchen. She couldn't cover her mouth without dropping one of the crutches. The burn in her eyes didn't have much to do with the polluted air.

At some point while she'd been hobbling her way in, Peggy had shut off the smoke detector. It was now a useless mess of wires hanging off the wall. There was a stack of blueberry pancakes on the counter, and near the stove lay a scorched oven mitt that would need to be trashed. Pots and pans littered the stove and the space around it. Peggy was in the adjoining living room, prying open a window to release the smoke. When she evidently realized Trish was there, her smile was sad and sheepish.

"Hey," Peggy said with a blush and chuckle. "So, this was supposed to be breakfast in bed. Obviously didn't turn out so hot."

"Literally or figuratively?"

"Right. I uh, left the oven mitt on the burner. I was trying to get this all done before you woke up. Must've gotten distracted."

"Happens to the best of us," Trish said, barely caring how flat her voice was. Peg *was* the best. The best person, best anything, to ever fall into her life. And she was a damn good cook. Not a professional by any means, but she did amazing things with food. Things that didn't generally involve such rookie mistakes. Unless, as she said, she was distracted. Or exhausted. Or both.

There was that awkward moment they relived at least five times a day where Trish made her way across the room and Peggy opened and closed her mouth, deciding if she should offer assistance. She didn't this time, and Trish had at least that to be grateful for. Peggy's offers of help were depressing, and a little degrading, no matter what her intentions were.

She seated herself at the table and leaned the crutches against it then watched her girlfriend bring over the pancakes. Plates, silverware, and coffee followed. On her last pass before sitting down, she gave Trish a quick peck on the lips.

"Sorry, babe. I don't know where my head is this morning."

"It's fine," Trish said. She knew exactly where Peg's head was, where the rest of her wanted to be, but she couldn't have that conversation now. It was hard to say which she hated more, the crutches or the cowardice. "Any plans for the day?" she asked once Peggy took the place across from her.

Peggy shrugged, cutting at her food without eating it. "Work switched my day off again, but I have to stay at Simone's. Just for a few hours. You going to be okay here by yourself?"

"Yeah, no problem. Tell Jason I say hi." Jason was Simone's four-year-old son, the one Peg so suddenly and graciously agreed to sit for when his daycare arrangements fell through. Just for a few days, she'd said. That'd been weeks ago. Of course, she was just being kind to Simone, the very blonde, very beautiful, very bisexual woman who lived two floors up. She was also very French. Her personality left something to be desired, but that accent...

They ate. Trish offered to help with the cleanup, but was gently rebuffed. Probably a good thing. The dishes would be in serious danger if she tried putting them away while on her crutches. But if she used the chair, she wasn't tall enough to reach the shelves.

Leaving Peg to deal with the kitchen, Trish went into the living room and dropped onto the couch. She rather hated it in here, but was afraid to do anything about it. Recurring theme in her life, apparently. The walls and mantel were lined with photos and awards, old news articles covering her cycling victories. The awards were mostly first place, but they meant nothing compared to the pictures.

She and Peg on their third date, smiling from the back of some dive bar that'd played great music and served even better food. Utterly unhealthy, everything fried and greasy and delicious. She and Peg on the hiking trail that bordered their old house. The two of them skiing in Colorado, then coming back to the cabin to roast s'mores in the fireplace. Doing a terrible job of surfing in Maui, then dining on the best fish either had ever tasted. Posing like the tourists they were atop the Empire State Building.

Sighing, Trish picked up the tablet she'd left on the coffee table and scrolled through menus and apps until she found what she wanted. The Tour de France was streaming live online. It was an all-boys club for now—the race she cared about wasn't scheduled for a few days, but she had a professional interest. Could she still call it professional after her forced retirement?

Peggy entered a few minutes later and watched over her shoulder. Trish could feel her fighting with herself again. She waited for a gentle lecture on masochism, but it didn't come. Instead, Peggy kissed the top of her head, and ran light fingers through her hair.

"Simone's got a half-day, so I shouldn't be long. Promise to call if you need anything?"

"Don't I always?"

"Never."

Trish chuckled, blinking back tears that Peg might've noticed anyway. "Sorry, was it me who nearly burned the building down?"

Peggy kissed her again. "Not since the last time I tried teaching you to cook, no. Sure you don't need anything before I take off?"

"No," she lied. "Go ahead, I'll be here." After shooting Peggy a glance, Trish directed her attention to the tablet again.

"Listen, why don't you let me make up for breakfast? We'll go out to dinner tonight. Somewhere nice, anything you want."

Trish bit back a sigh. "You know how the leg is. It gets stiff so easily." And it was a nightmare maneuvering the crutches around people and chairs and tables. An embarrassment.

"Right. Maybe another time."

"Yeah."

There was a pause in the conversation.

"Love you, you know." Peggy's words hurt more than Trish's leg had the day it was crushed under that damn car.

"Love you too. I'll see you later."

Peggy kissed her hair again, touched it in a way that might've been hesitant. Then she was gone, leaving Trish among the relics of their former life. She stayed on the couch with her eyes slammed shut for a moment, steeling herself. Then she pulled herself up and crossed to the window that provided a good view of their street. This place was on the first floor, of course. Close to the hospital and her physical therapy appointments. Trish missed the old place, the balcony high above the ground where she and Peg used to sit and drink wine and think of things that were no longer possible.

The announcers helpfully narrated everything she was missing as she waited. She'd planned to be in France for the whole of the race, even if she'd only be participating in one event for one day. La Course was relatively new, progress in the fight to get women competing with the men in the Tour de France proper. Trish was meant to ride on the U.S. team, and she'd been embarrassingly excited about it. Peg had thrown an impromptu party. There'd been too much food, too many drinks, and a fabulous amount of celebratory sex after the guests departed.

So much extra training, so many plans. Trish had been determined to do her best, but even if she wasn't first to cross the finish line, the trip would've been worth it. All that stuff about it being an honor just to compete was great, but she'd had other things to look forward to. In all their travels, she and Peggy hadn't yet made it to France. Trish was determined that they'd make time to see the sights, enjoy the city of romance, sample the decadent food that was so legendary. She hadn't yet figured out how to fit all that into what promised to be a ridiculous pre-race schedule when the car accident made it a non-issue.

Peg had suggested, cautious and half-hearted, that they could still make the trip. Trish could admit now that her response was extra bitchy. For months, the majority of her responses had fallen into that category. She'd been whiney and bitter, full of self-pity. Which was why she was half-listening to the biggest event in cycling in her first-floor apartment while her girlfriend headed upstairs to screw the neighbor. The trip might've been cancelled, but Peggy had still found a way to experience French culture.

Despite being a card-carrying cripple, Trish was not, generally speaking, the jealous type. So when Peg first mentioned sitting for Jason, she hadn't thought much of it. Perhaps she was naïve. Perhaps that car wreck had left her with brain damage too. More likely, she'd been too busy wallowing to notice or care. But again, it had been weeks. Weeks of babysitting shifts at the oddest of hours. It was during one of those, late at night, that Trish had called Peg's cell to see when she planned to be home. Peggy didn't answer, but Simone did. The explanation was that Simone had just walked in, and Peggy had been busy with Jason.

Clenching her free hand against the windowsill, Trish watched, waited, until a car that'd recently become very familiar to her pulled up in front of the building. A tall man with dark hair and a ball cap got out and entered the apartment complex. Trish waited another ten minutes, barely hearing the race commentary that still droned on behind her. Then the man reemerged, carrying a child's backpack. Jason was with him, clinging to his hand. Some of the boy's laughing chatter was audible through the closed window. Seemed his dad was taking him to the movies, and he was quite excited about it.

This was the third time Trish had watched the kid Peg was supposed to be babysitting leave the building. Where was he during all the other times? At a friend's place? With an actual babysitter? Or did Peggy and Simone simply put him down for a nap before going at it?

Trish felt like screaming, breaking things. Slumping to the floor and curling into a ball. But any mess she made would be a bitch to clean, and if she curled up on the floor, she'd likely be stuck there for quite some time. Besides, both of those options seemed pathetically melodramatic, and her life was too much like a bad TV movie already. So Trish very slowly and very carefully made it back to the couch, surrounded by memories of the sport she loved, and the woman she loved more. Forcing her attention back to the tablet, she managed to watch the male athletes bike across France for nearly five minutes before she burst into tears, burying her head in her hands.

The thing that made this already pathetic situation even worse? Trish probably wouldn't have said anything. She'd seen Peggy's alibi walk out the door days ago and kept quiet. She could've continued like that, at least for a little while. Because she was a damn coward, and confronting Peg meant losing her, and after everything else, Trish just couldn't stomach that. She loved Peg too much, too much for her own good. So she might've kept her mouth shut indefinitely.

If Peggy hadn't come home with wet hair.

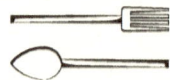

The race was still on, but Trish had long since stopped paying attention. She left the tablet face down on the couch, the play-by-play muffled by the cushions. Having cried herself out, she imagined that she looked even worse than usual. And then Peggy came in hours after that failed breakfast surprise, looking gorgeous as ever with her green eyes and dark blonde hair. Hair that was now closer to brown, and looked slightly damp.

"Hey," Peg said, sounding worn as she hung her coat on the rack by the door. "How's your day going? Have you done your exercises?"

She had, actually. Probably overdone them. A throwback to better days, when her reaction to stress nearly always involved physical activity. Yet it seemed she hadn't gotten nearly as much of a workout as Peg had. "Did you shower at Simone's place?"

Half a second's hesitation, then Peggy was almost, *almost* looking her in the eye. "Yeah. Jason decided he absolutely, positively needed fresh baked cookies and being the sweet little man he is, also decided he should help. Egg, sugar, flour, you name it, it wound up in my hair."

The sheer boldness of it, washing off the scent of sex with barely an effort to hide what she was doing. If she wasn't so sad, Trish thought she'd be impressed. "So, that's what you were doing at Simone's? Baking?"

A frown line formed between Peggy's eyes. "Baking and watching scarily hypnotic preschool shows, yeah. Why?"

She'd skipped her meds today. Peg would be furious if she knew. And how fucked up was it that Trish still cared what Peg thought? The pain in her chest was so much worse than the constant one in her leg when she pulled herself up, nearly losing hold of the crutches as her hands shook.

"Babe, are you...fuck, let me—"

"I saw Jason leave, Peg. More than once. I know he's not the reason you've been spending so much time with Simone."

Peggy, who'd been moving forward to help her, froze on the spot. Her shock gave Trish time to close some of the distance between them. She couldn't get within touching distance. Her leg hurt too much and her eyes burned, and she wanted to stand as tall as she could for this, not take a face full of carpet while she tried to let go with dignity.

"Trish—"

"Look," Trish said, wishing she could hold up a hand without dropping the damn crutches. "I'm not mad about you and Simone. God knows I can't blame you, considering what I've turned into. But, did you have to be so obvious? Lately, at least. I'll admit I don't know how long it's been going on, too much of a drugged-up crybaby to notice. But the last few weeks, were you *trying* to get caught? Because I swear, you could've told me. I'm not...I'm not going to have you stay here and play nursemaid. Not if you can be happy with someone else."

Peggy's mouth dropped open. "You can't be serious. You think I'm cheating on you? With *Simone*?"

"She answered your phone, Peggy! The kid you say you're babysitting isn't there half the time, and now you're showering there too? Not that I don't appreciate you washing off her perfume and God knows what else, but what am I supposed to think?"

There was no immediate answer. Just the sound of Trish's own breathing as she fought past the weight on her chest, and the muted drone of the race. Peggy's eyes were wide and shocked, and they burned into Trish, making her acutely aware of her body's imminent betrayal. Standing tall was all well and good, as long as she didn't have to do it for more than a few minutes.

An endless moment passed. Peggy moved forward again, then stopped. Trish didn't know how she felt about that. Didn't know if she wanted Peg to come closer so she could fall into her arms and apologize for not being enough, or come closer so she could lose the crutches and pound her fists against Peggy's chest, say again that she'd have understood, dammit, if not for the deception.

A moot point, as it turned out. Peggy didn't come forward. "You look like you're going to fall down. Can you please sit instead?"

Trish didn't. She cried. Hot tears she hated more than the ones that came right after the accident, when they told her she may never walk normally again. No one even mentioned cycling. More torturous moments as Peggy bit her lip, looking very much like she wanted to bridge the gap between them. She didn't. What she did do was turn on her heel and walk out.

Trish was left crying and trembling. Probably with her mouth hanging open, but she was in too many kinds of pain to be sure of that. She'd expected Peg to be gone after the confrontation, but not quite so soon, and definitely not so literally. She'd left the door open. Did she expect Trish to come after her? Tall order, that. Except, she really, really wanted to go after her. If only she could do that without falling on her face and breaking something other than her heart.

Trish moved. One step, then two, gritting her teeth with each. The noise from the tablet was suddenly gone. Battery must've died. That left her with nothing except tears and the sound of her breathing. She was working on step three—cursing aloud because why hadn't she just taken the damn pain meds—when Peggy returned. She had a large dish in each hand. Both were covered and looked heavy.

"I really wish you'd sit down," Peg said, depositing the dishes on their kitchen table. Then she was gone again, out the door.

Even through the haze of misery, Trish knew she had to be gaping like a fish at that point. Torn between directions, she eventually crossed to the table. She removed the tin foil covering one dish and found several small pastry puffs. She uncovered the next bowl and saw some kind of stew with a dark broth and what looked like chicken. She was, despite everything, thinking how good the food looked when Peggy returned again, bearing two more covered plates.

"Well," she said, eyeing the uncovered food. "Surprise is a bust anyway. Always so impatient. And stubborn. And other less-than-pleasant things we'll be having a conversation about later. Seriously, will you *please* sit down before you fall down? You're worrying me, and I'm mad at you, and I shouldn't have to be worried about you when I'm mad at you. It's not fair."

Peggy didn't sound mad. She seemed more amused than anything else. Personally, Trish didn't get the joke. Then again, something usually had to make sense in order to be funny. While she was searching for the punchline, Peg disappeared and returned again. Two more plates in hand, and this time she kicked the door shut behind her.

"Stubborn," she repeated, placing the plates on the table. "Fine, then. You can see what came out of all that hot sex I've been having." Keeping one eye on Trish as she spoke, Peggy pointed to and uncovered each dish one by one. "Cheese puffs. They were…puffier when Simone made them, but according to her, mine weren't awful. The stew is *poulet Basquaise.* Chicken, tomato, peppers. Comfort food, apparently, and I figured we both needed some comfort. *Tartiflette.* Potatoes, melted cheese and French bacon. I'm still mangling the pronunciation, but how does anyone go wrong with melted cheese and bacon? *Coq au vin.* More bacon, beef, mushrooms. Julia Child loved it, and I'm not going to argue with Julia Child."

And so it went, as Peggy uncovered scallops, some sort of thin-crust pizza that looked obscenely delicious even when cold and, good God, cream puffs with ice cream sandwiched between them and chocolate sauce drizzled on top. "Peg, I—what the hell?"

"Gifted with words too," Peggy said, a smirk curving her lips. "I was going to wait a few more days, until the women's race was over. Figured you'd be exceptionally down. I know it's not much, but I thought it'd help. Anyway, since we can't make it to France this year, I thought I'd bring France to us. To you."

"Peggy—"

"I was trying to cook for you, you…God you're lucky I'm in love with you. French recipes are new to me, and all that time listening to Simone blab about how much she hates Jason's father." Peggy made a face.

"She was teaching you to cook?"

"Yes, dear. Which was embarrassingly difficult. When Jason was there, all he wanted to do was help, which meant messes and Simone getting distracted and me getting distracted, and not learning a damn thing. When he wasn't there, like I said, all she did was complain about her ex and do very scary things with knives. You thought I was *sleeping* with her?"

"I—you were there all the time, babysitting a kid who wasn't there all the time. You took a shower there."

"Because I was tired and sick of listening to Simone talk, and there was this fucked-up thing with the blender. Not because I was actually fucking her."

It took too long for Trish to process any of this, to form an answer. "And all that food—"

"Practice. I was going to make it fresh on the actual night of the race. She's vaguely curious about why I had to take all this from her fridge now, but not enough to stop getting ready for her date. Some woman she met at a bookstore. Doesn't care why the plan's changed, just wanted me out of there before her girl showed up. Didn't want it to look weird, me being there. Can you please, *please* sit down now?"

Trish nodded, mute. She was both touched and ashamed when Peggy took her arm, helping her into one of the kitchen chairs before seating herself. She leaned the crutches against the table's edge, then wiped her eyes and forced herself to look at Peggy directly. "I honestly don't know what to say. I'm sorry. I didn't think—"

"You thought I would cheat on you, that I could ever hurt you like that?"

Peggy's tone was more hurt than angry, and that made it harder to maintain eye contact. "I thought," she said in a voice Trish barely recognized, "that you deserved better. That you'd figured that out."

The sigh Peggy released was deep and long in the otherwise silent room. "There is no better than you. Not for me."

"Peg, I'm broken. I'm a mess. You shouldn't have to—"

"Stop. I do what I want, and I want to be here with you, even if you're a bit of an idiot sometimes. And you're not broken. You couldn't even walk a year ago. I know you hate the crutches, but give yourself some credit. I do. And I wanted to give you a taste," Peggy shook her head at the seemingly unintentional pun, "of that trip we missed. The one we can still take, as long as you don't give up on yourself or the rehab or...or us."

Peggy took Trish's hands. They stung from gripping the crutches too hard. The cool pads of Peggy's fingers felt like heaven on her skin.

"I don't deserve you," Trish said, sitting forward until their foreheads touched.

Chuckling, Peggy cupped Trish's face in her hands and wiped the tears away. "No offense, babe, but I think we've established that you're no expert on who deserves what. You deserve so much more than you think. That said, you did ruin my brilliant plan and accuse me of cheating on you, so for tonight, you deserve leftovers." Peg stood and went to the stove and began turning dials.

"I just...I don't know what to say."

"You said that already," Peggy replied, rolling her eyes playfully.

"I'm so sorry."

"That's a great place to start." As she spoke, Peg bustled from stove to table, throwing herself into the task of reheating.

"I love you."

"Doing good so far."

"Peg, I—thank you. For everything. You just—you do too much, and I don't know why, and I was so sure you'd realize—"

"You don't know why?" Peggy crossed back to Trish. When their lips met, it was long and slow, and it made Trish's mouth water even more than the delicious scents that were already starting to fill the room. And then Peggy pulled back suddenly, cursing as she rushed back to the food. "Dammit, pay attention when I'm giving you long, heartfelt speeches, okay? And stop distracting me. My French food is still amateur enough without me burning the leftovers."

"Doesn't look amateurish to me."

"You haven't seen the cookbooks. Or Simone's versions."

Trish couldn't help frowning behind Peggy's back. Thank God food was the only thing Peg was sampling from Simone. "And she just offered to tutor you out of the goodness of her heart?"

"I paid her. And I really do have to watch Jason if this date with the bookstore chick becomes a regular thing."

"She asked for money? How much—"

"Shut up. You're worth it. You're an idiot sometimes, but you're worth it. Speaking of, you skipped your meds, didn't you?"

When Peggy turned to look at her, Trish ducked her head.

"Right. Well. Silver lining to you playing the masochistic tough girl, you can have wine with me. We can't have amateur French leftovers without wine."

Within minutes, the apartment was awash in the scent of French cooking. Peg poured something sweet, red, and delicious from a bottle she'd hidden away somewhere. With the wine taken care of, she carefully moved the dishes back to the table. More plates followed, then silverware, and then, finally, Peggy sat down next to Trish.

"Well," she said, raising her glass and inspecting her preparations, "it's not France, but it's not an affair, either."

Trish grimaced. "I'm never going to live this down, am I?"

"God, no. Quit blushing, babe, you haven't had enough wine for that."

"Are you trying to get me drunk?"

"Maybe. Let me know if it starts to work. Now eat before the food gets cold again."

Trish ate, tasting the stew first. The spice of the peppers, the heat of that broth soothing her throat. "God. Peg, this is amazing."

"I doubt that, but—"

Dropping her spoon, Trish reached over on impulse and brushed a finger across Peggy's lips. "Don't. Don't doubt what I tell you. I'm sorry I was stupid enough to do that about you."

"Well," Peggy said, pausing long enough to suck Trish's finger into her mouth and run her tongue over it before continuing, "I'm sure you'll find some way of making it up to me. And technically I *was* being less than honest."

Swallowing hard, Trish didn't bother to respond. There were no words, not when the pad of her forefinger was still warm from Peggy's mouth. That little move quickly started a trend. Soon they were feeding each other more than themselves. Accepting a bite of the tartiflette, Trish closed her eyes, savoring the melted cheese, the contrast of textures as the bacon mixed with the soft cream of the potatoes. When Peg moved on to dessert and tasted one of the cream puffs, Trish hardly felt she had the right to stop her. The moan Peg let out was positively sinful. Trish couldn't resist leaning forward to kiss her, using her tongue to catch a bit of chocolate sauce that lingered on her lips. The noise Peggy made after that had Trish trembling.

"So, how's it taste?" Peggy asked. They were still close enough to breathe the same air.

"*C'est magnifique,*" Trish whispered, "like you."

Peg let out something very close to a growl. "I do love it when you speak French."

"Well, then, allow me to wow you with the last bit that I know. *Voulez-vous coucher avec moi ce soir?*"

"Always." Peg leaned in for a kiss then pulled away, eyes sparkling. "How about now?"

RECIPE FOR HEALING THE HEART

1. Take a cup of suspicion.
2. Mix in another half-cup of doubt.
3. Temper that with the love of a good woman and the desire to bring a smile to a lover's face.
4. Throw in a healthy dash of forgiveness.
5. Mix all ingredients with a solid foundation.
6. Serve hot with your favorite French dishes and French kisses.

THE WAY TO A WOMAN'S HEART

MARIE STERLING

"THE PENGUINS ARE INVADING!"

I stared at my best friend in bafflement. "What?"

"The penguins! They're invading! It's the pengapacolypse!" Caitlin's voice became more shrill with every exclamation. She grabbed my arm, hauled me to the window and pointed down at the parking lot of my apartment building. Sure enough, there was an army of penguins marching in step across the asphalt. "Krill," she stated, suddenly calm. "We need all the krill."

"What is krill and why do we need it?" I asked.

"Krill are tiny shrimp-like creatures and are what penguins eat," Caitlin explained patiently. She opened her mouth again and started singing the chorus to Halestorm's "Here's To Us."

I bolted up in my recliner and gazed around in momentary confusion as my phone kept playing Caitlin's ringtone. I fumbled for the device and swiped my thumb across the screen before her call was sent to voicemail.

"Hello?" I mumbled right before my mouth gaped in a jaw-cracking yawn.

"Are you home, Sarah? Please tell me you're home."

"I'm home," I said through another yawn. "I was just—"

"Thank God. I'll be there in ten minutes." She hung up without a good-bye and I turned to meet the green-eyed gaze of Lily, my cat. She was glaring at me disdainfully, having been unceremoniously dumped from my lap when I woke up.

"Penguins? Really?" I muttered as I stood and stretched, then shambled to the bathroom. A can of Arizona Green Tea made for a full bladder. I laughed at myself as I washed my hands and inspected my reflection. My shoulder-length hair was sticking up on one side from where I had rested my head and it resembled a cockatiel's. A hairbrush fixed that problem but I really couldn't do anything about the red creases on my cheek from the throw pillow. Oh, well.

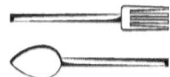

I had left my laptop open to a music-streaming site and "I'm Still Into You" by Paramore was playing as I left the bathroom. I perused the contents of my fridge while singing along and I heard the front door open. I knew it was Caitlin, so I dug around for the last two bottles of pumpkin ale. I had just found them when I heard her footsteps behind me.

"Hi," she said as I opened both bottles and turned to hand her one. She had to reach out and take it from me because I had frozen. She was wearing an old T-shirt that I absolutely loved on her, one that made her cornflower blue eyes stand out even more. She looked especially gorgeous and I couldn't take my eyes off her.

"Do I have a booger hanging out of my nose or something?" Her question brought me out of my daze and I shook my head before taking a drink of beer.

"No. What's the emergency?" I asked after that first glorious swallow. "Doctor Sarah is here to help."

"It's Jamie," Caitlin said with a sigh after a healthy guzzle. She stifled a burp and continued. "I caught her screwing another woman."

I pasted what I hoped was a sympathetic expression on my face while my thoughts spun furiously. *Jamie is a fucking idiot. How could she treat anyone that way? I would never betray you like that.* "You've been dating, what? A month?"

"Dated. Past tense."

"No U-Haul yet?" I teased and one side of Caitlin's mouth quirked up in a reluctant smile.

"Asshole. No, no U-Haul." She flipped her long hair over one shoulder and took another drink. "We had just discussed being exclusive the other night, then I came over to her house and caught her having sex with someone else right on the couch." She sighed and slumped against the wall. I set my beer down and pulled her into a comforting hug.

"Meatball sub therapy?" I asked after a moment. I felt her nod before she let go.

"Oh, yeah. I need your balls tonight."

I chuckled as I grabbed pen and paper to make a grocery list and then placed an onion in the freezer.

"Why did you do that?" she asked.

"It's supposed to help before you chop it. The fumes won't make you cry."

"Good to know. And now I have to make a pit stop before we go."

"Breaking the seal early?" I teased as she walked away. As soon as the door closed behind her, Avril Lavigne's

"Girlfriend" started playing. I rushed over to my laptop and closed out of the site. That song hit way too close to home for me.

I scooped up my purse when Caitlin finished and checked that I had everything I needed, then locked up behind us. We trooped downstairs to the parking lot. Once in Caitlin's SUV, she put in a CD and punched a few buttons. Joan Jett's "Do You Wanna Touch Me" came pouring out of the speakers as Caitlin took off.

Yes, I thought. *I wanna touch you there, and there, and there, and...*I looked out the window, singing softly along, trying not to think too much about where exactly I wanted to touch Caitlin.

Thirty minutes later, I held a box of toothpaste in each hand in the grocery store aisle as I tried to decide between them.

"What does toothpaste have to do with meatball subs?" Caitlin asked as she rounded the corner and placed a package of ground beef and a bag of hoagie rolls in the cart.

"Since I cook with garlic and onions, be happy I'm buying toothpaste," I retorted. I picked a brand and tossed the box into the cart before returning the other to the shelf.

"Why? I don't have to kiss you," she shot back and flounced off.

I stared after her. *If only you would.*

I'd had a crush on Caitlin Archer since we met a few years ago in a cardio kickboxing class. We just clicked, and I almost asked her out, but she wasn't single. By the time things had ended with Caitlin's girlfriend, I was dating someone. Since then, I occasionally detected what I thought might have been more than friendly interest in Caitlin's eyes, but we were never single at the same time. Until now.

I shook my head and wheeled my cart out of the toothpaste aisle and over to the beer section, where I picked up a twelve-pack of a craft beer. Then it was off to collect the rest of the ingredients for the subs. I found Caitlin in the dairy section and then we wheeled to a checkout lane. I had my card out and ready to go when Caitlin lunged across me and swiped hers first. "My therapy, my treat," she said. I knew resistance was futile, so I didn't argue.

Back at my apartment, we cracked open fresh beers and I turned on the oven. As I diced the onion, Caitlin perched on a stool at the breakfast bar and kept me company. I kept conversation light, since it was too early to ask her about Jamie. Caitlin was here to vent, I knew, but she would choose when. In the meantime, she cut a block of mozzarella cheese into cubes.

While I sautéed the diced onions in salt, pepper, butter, crushed garlic, and sherry cooking wine, Caitlin kept up a steady patter of groan-worthy jokes.

"Knock, knock."

"Who's there?"

"Daisy."

"Daisy who?"

"Daisy me rollin', day hatin'."

I threw a wadded-up paper towel at her as we both got the giggles and then turned back to my cooking.

Once the onions were cool, I added some of them to the ground beef, along with Italian bread crumbs, a beef onion soup packet, and various other seasonings. I go with what I call the Mad Scientist Method of cooking and just throw things together. The only downfall is that I rarely write down what all I add, so if I create a masterpiece, it's probably a one-time deal unless I can remember what I did. Caitlin liked to tease me about that, and I let her, because she can get away with almost anything with me.

Once I had everything sufficiently mixed together, I formed shapeless blobs into spheres, dug a hole with my thumb and handed each one off to Caitlin. She pushed a cube of cheese into the hole I had made and reformed the mass into a sphere. Once the baking dish was full, I popped the meatballs into the oven and set the timer.

After washing my hands, I poured a jar of sauce into a pan and set it to heat before adding the rest of the onions to the sauce, along with more sherry, garlic, and whatever else I felt like throwing in. Mad Scientist, at your service.

The timer beeped and I pulled the baking dish out of the oven, then used tongs to place the meatballs one by one into the pan of sauce. Those simmered for a few while I spread foil out onto a cookie sheet and placed two hoagie rolls on top.

"You didn't have a softball game tonight?" Caitlin asked as I worked. The giggles had finally subsided, although my stomach ached a little.

"No," I replied as I stirred garlic powder into softened butter. "The rain last night pretty much took care of that."

"Good. I like having you all to myself." I looked up at the tone in her voice and Caitlin graced me with a beautiful smile. My knees went weak.

"Because of my mad skills in the kitchen."

"Hmm. I bet you have mad skills in other rooms too," she replied and shot me a saucy little wink.

To distract myself, I turned my back and spread garlic butter on the insides of the hoagie rolls, placed three meatballs in the middle of each, and ladled sauce over them. After switching my oven to the broiler setting and readjusting one of the racks, I sprinkled shredded Parmesan cheese on top and placed them inside for a minute or so, grateful for the heat so I could blame my flush on the oven. Once the cheese was bubbling and slightly browned, I took the sandwiches out and plated them.

After we moved to the couch with fresh beers and our hedonistic sandwiches, Caitlin perused my movies for a few minutes before triumphantly holding up *Shrek*. "Do we wanna go green?" she asked.

"Hell yeah," I agreed and she grinned.

"I like how you think." She loaded the movie, settled next to me, and grabbed the remote as I began eating. This sandwich is not for the fastidious diner, so even using a knife and fork, I was glad I had a napkin spread over my lap.

Caitlin gestured at the TV with her fork and a wayward drop of sauce landed on the coffee table. Lily was my girl-on-the-spot, and licked it up before I could say anything. I mock-glared at Caitlin and she shrugged sheepishly before speaking.

"What if Fiona had fancied one of the ladies? Snow White seems like she'd probably be a dead lay, but Cinderella might be fun."

"Snow White would be too easy, anyway. Dead girls can't say no," I pointed out. Caitlin laughed, called me a sicko and kept on with what she was saying.

"She'd have to be home before midnight, though, otherwise you'd just be left with a hot mess on your hands."

"One with a shoe fetish." I sipped my beer.

"That being said, Fiona probably would have lived happily ever after had she just left everyone behind, bought a vibrator, and taught self-defense classes for a living."

"It would've saved that dragon some Farquad-induced indigestion." Caitlin chuckled before suddenly turning to me. "You know what?"

"No. What?"

"Jamie didn't want to venture down south." Caitlin gestured at her crotch. "She refused to, actually."

I gaped at her for a moment with no immediate reply. Caitlin rarely talked about her sex life.

"It was all about her," Caitlin continued. "She didn't care if I got off or not." To emphasize her point, Caitlin chugged the rest of her beer, slammed it down on the coffee table and gave a belch worthy of a frat boy.

"Nice bass," I said and raised my own bottle in salute before taking a drink. Then I stuck my tongue out, touched the tip of my nose with it and waited for Caitlin to look at me again. She did and burst out laughing.

"Look who's well hung," she said

I set down my beer and raised my arms a little.

"Not everywhere. I have small hands."

At that point, Caitlin lost all composure and dashed to the bathroom, yelling she was about to piss her pants.

After she finished in the bathroom, Caitlin veered off to the kitchen to grab fresh beers. I remembered that she had finished hers so chugged mine to catch up. Pleasantly lightheaded, I set my empty down and turned to look at Caitlin as she settled herself on the floor next to me, back propped against the couch, mirroring my position.

"You have always been there for me, Sarah," she said softly. "I don't know what I'd do without you."

I took a healthy swig of beer, mouth suddenly dry. No reply came to mind that wouldn't reveal my feelings, so I kept silent. It didn't matter because Caitlin kept speaking.

"I'm here so often, I should just move in. I already have a key."

I gathered my few wits and gave her a teasing reply. "You know how weird I can get about cleaning. It would drive you crazy." The mere thought of that was driving *me* crazy.

"I'm already crazy. I'm friends with you, aren't I? Lily wouldn't mind, would you, baby?" Caitlin gave me a sexy little pout before she scooped Lily into her lap.

I had resigned myself long ago to residing permanently in the Friend Zone. Hell, I practically owned real estate there. I probably shouldn't have sat so close to her but I couldn't help myself. She was the flame to my moth. I drank my beer quickly while pretending to watch the movie.

"Can I... " Caitlin began to get my attention, then licked her lips. My gaze was stuck on her oh-so-tempting mouth. "Can I crash here tonight?"

"Sure." Plenty of room in my queen-sized bed, and Caitlin had slept there many times in the past. So I'd just suck it up again.

I got up, stretched, and began cleaning off the coffee table. Caitlin helped and I was glad that we were both moving around because then I didn't have to think about how good she looked and how badly I wanted more from her.

I left a T-shirt and a pair of pajama pants on the foot of my bed for her, then went to the bathroom where I brushed my teeth and got ready for bed before changing into my own pajamas. Getting undressed in front of Caitlin when it wouldn't have led to a bedroom activity other than sleeping would have been sheer torture, so I changed in the bathroom.

"Coward," I accused my reflection as I washed my hands. I hoped the sound of running water would drown out my voice. I wanted to say something to Caitlin, to ask her out and make it clear that it wouldn't be as friends. At least then she'd know that I was interested. The worst she could do would be to say no. I hung my head and sighed. That would ruin the best friendship I'd ever had. Dejected, I left the bathroom.

"Your turn," I said.

"About time. What the hell were you doing in there?" she asked as she walked past, the sleep clothes I'd left for her gripped in her hand. While she got ready for bed, I locked up, turned the lights in the common areas off, and switched on both bedside lights in my room. I retrieved Caitlin's e-reader from her purse and set it on the nightstand, then went over to my side. I was settled in and reading my own e-reader when she came into my bedroom.

Caitlin slid under the covers and Lily snuggled between us. We read peacefully for a while and I started to relax. Then Caitlin turned off her light and burrowed deeper under the covers.

"Will you spoon me?" came her soft whisper, and I realized that the whole Jamie thing bothered her more than she let on. "Please?"

"Of course." I turned off my own light and moved close, hoping that my racing heart wouldn't betray my feelings.

Lily seemed to sense that Caitlin needed comfort, because she moved closer and curled up against her belly. A few minutes of arranging and we were set, my arms wrapped around Caitlin as her body warmed the front of mine in more ways than one. Caitlin slid her hand over mine, entwining our fingers and pulling my arm tighter around her.

Silently telling my emotions and my libido to take a hike, I focused on projecting as much comfort and reassurance as I could, since I couldn't allow myself to hope that her gesture meant anything beyond a friend needing some support. As difficult as it had become for me to keep it to myself, Caitlin did not need my feelings piled on top of what she already had going on. After lying awake for what seemed like eons with the fresh, clean scent of her shampoo flooding my nose, I finally drifted off to the sound of her soft breathing.

I woke up the next morning to the smell of coffee and bacon. After a pit stop, I ambled out to the kitchen. Caitlin must've heard me stirring because she had a cup of coffee waiting for me on the breakfast bar. I sat at the same bar stool that she had the night before and took that first heavenly sip.

"Morning," she said.

"Mmm." I grunted back. Once the afterglow from my coffeegasm faded, Caitlin smiled at me, turned the bacon over, and flipped the pancakes that I only just saw. Over the sizzle and pop of the bacon, I heard the bluesy chords of Lynyrd Skynard's "Poison Whiskey" emanating from her phone on the counter.

"I love this song," I commented after another sip. "What's the occasion?" I gestured at the stove.

"A thank you for last night," she replied softly.

Telling her that no thanks were necessary would only spark a debate, so I settled for a simple smile and said,

"You're welcome." Then I smirked at her. "I'd put my balls in your mouth more often if I got breakfast out of the deal."

She laughed as she put butter and syrup on the breakfast bar, then turned around to rinse the bowl she had used for the batter. "Poison Whiskey" gave way to "Faith" by George Michael. Caitlin started shaking her hips just like George had in the video and my gaze went immediately to her ass. She dried her hands on a towel, grabbed plates out of the cupboard, turned around and totally busted me staring at her butt. Caitlin gave me a knowing little smile and I felt my entire face flush. I took a sip of coffee to try and regain my composure. Fortunately, she didn't tease me about it, which would have made it even worse.

Once everything was set out on the breakfast bar, Caitlin sat down to eat with me. I pretended not to notice that she broke off small pieces of bacon and dropped them on the floor for Lily, just like I had pretended not to notice when she'd done the same thing last night with dinner.

"What are you doing tonight?" I asked after a bite of pancake washed down with coffee. "I was thinking maybe a mani/pedi at the mall and dinner at that Mexican place we love. We could make it a total girls' night."

"I can't," she said with regret in her voice. "I have plans."

My heart sank. I had a feeling she was going to see that two-timing über-skank Jamie. *Caitlin,* I pleaded silently, *I'm right here and I would never, ever hurt you like that. Why can't you see me?* "Another time then," I replied as casually as I could.

After breakfast, we lingered over more coffee before we cleaned up. With both of us working, it didn't take long. As I hung the damp dishtowel over the handle of the stove, I thought about how seamlessly Caitlin and I worked together and I knew deep down that a relationship with her could work just as smoothly. In my book, it'd be almost perfect. If only she'd see it.

Caitlin had put on her jeans but still wore my T-shirt as I walked her to the door and pressed a travel mug of coffee into her hand. She wrapped her arms around me in a hug and I pulled her closer without thinking. She felt so good in my embrace that I didn't want to let go, but she eventually extricated herself.

"Girls' night soon," she promised before she left, and I closed the door behind her. Once that barrier was between us, the smile dropped from my face and I slumped onto the couch. Lily padded over and jumped into my lap.

"What am I going to do, Lil?" I scratched the top of her head and worked my way to her ears, neck, and chest. Her purr motor rumbled contentedly while I agonized. "I don't know how much longer I can pretend," I whispered. Lily cuddled closer, then licked my nose. I wrinkled it at her foul kitty breath. "You're right. This whole situation stinks."

I decided to go grocery shopping to distract myself. I had noticed the night before that I was low on or out of a few things. An hour later, after I put away my groceries, I did my laundry and cleaned my apartment, still aiming for distraction. It was almost 4:00 by the time I finally finished, but everything was dusted, scrubbed, vacuumed, fluffed, folded, or in its proper place.

Feeling rather accomplished and smelling faintly of bleach, I indulged in a long, hot shower after which I put on my favorite pair of pajama pants and an old baggy T-shirt before I padded out to the kitchen for some water. Glass in hand, I settled on the couch and snagged the remote. I found the movie *Forrest Gump* and stretched out, blanket over my legs. Lily cuddled next to me and the combined sounds of her contented purring and the rain against my window eased me to sleep. *Me and Caitlin was like peas and carrots*, was my last drowsy thought.

I awoke to a soft hand gently brushing my hair away from my face. I opened my eyes to Caitlin's bright smile and offered her a sleepy one in return, only too aware of her fingertips on my skin.

"Hey," I mumbled around a yawn. "I thought you had plans tonight."

"I canceled them. I can shop with my sister anytime, and I decided I'd much rather spend my evening with you."

My smile widened as I struggled to untangle my limbs from the blanket and sit up. Caitlin was no help as she sat on my coffee table and laughed while I flailed. Once I was finally free, I glanced at the time displayed on the cable box. Almost 7:30 and my stomach's sudden rumble reminded me that I had skipped lunch.

"Have you eaten yet?" I asked on the way to the kitchen. The dismal weather called for comfort food so I started gathering ingredients for grilled cheese sandwiches. I pulled out sliced deli ham, smoked provolone, butter, and the magic ingredient to the perfect grilled cheese, mayo.

"Do I finally get to find out the secret Sarah Hawthorne grilled cheese sandwich recipe?" Caitlin asked. She was standing right behind me and spoke over my shoulder, so close that I could feel her breath on my skin. Oh, God, I loved the closeness, so I didn't move. "Sarah?" Caitlin asked, voice soft, and I started slightly.

"Um, yes." I pretended to roll up invisible sleeves. "Sous Chef Archer, will you please fetch a can of tomato soup from the pantry and get it started?"

"Yes, Chef." She gave me a snappy salute before doing it, and then she poured the soup into a pot, added milk, and stirred slowly. "The secret to the perfect grilled cheese sandwich," I instructed, "is to put the butter in the pan instead of directly on the bread. Assemble the sandwich like normal, adding a little mayonnaise to the inside part of the bread for just a bit of tang."

"You sound like a cooking show. It's cute."

I grinned as I tilted the pan to distribute the butter evenly, then dropped the first sandwich into it. After about a minute, I scooped the sandwich up with a spatula and added more butter before flipping it over. By the time the second sandwich was a perfect golden color to match the first, the soup was ready.

We settled in front of the TV to eat, in poses identical to those of last night. Once again, I pretended not to notice as Caitlin slipped bits of ham covered in gooey cheese to Lily.

Full, but wanting something else, I decided to make hot chocolate. I was stirring unsweetened cocoa powder, milk, vanilla, sugar, half and half, and water together, when Caitlin came in with our dirty dishes. She brushed past me on her way to the sink and my body tingled. I tried not to stare at her and focused on the hot chocolate, pouring it into mugs, with a generous shot of Bailey's before I topped each with whipped cream and drizzled a little chocolate syrup over all of it.

"Are you trying to get me drunk, Hawthorne?" Caitlin eyed me with mock suspicion as we walked back into the living room with our mugs.

"Damn, you're onto me, Archer," I said with a laugh as I settled on the couch while Caitlin wandered around humming along to the movie's soundtrack on the TV. She lit a couple of candles, and looked at me with an expression I couldn't read.

Caitlin joined me on the couch and we sipped and watched the movie. I gathered my courage as I drank, thinking that I couldn't go on like this. It was driving me nuts. *She* was driving me nuts. I finished my drink in one healthy swig, set my mug down, and turned toward her.

"Uh, Caitlin?" My throat felt like it might close up.

She looked at me and before I thought too much about it, I leaned in and brushed my lips against hers in the softest of kisses. My heart pounded and I started to sit back, dreading that I had screwed up everything, but she stopped me, and cupped my face with her palms as she gazed into my eyes for a moment. And then, she kissed me back. Her lips were as soft as I had imagined and her tongue was like velvet as it stroked mine. She tasted of chocolate and whipped cream and Bailey's. She was delicious.

After several long moments, she leaned back with a smile, still cradling my face. Her thumbs gently stroked my cheekbones and I closed my eyes in blissful relief.

"Oh, Sarah," she said softly. "What took you so long?"

THE MAD SCIENTIST'S
MOZZARELLA-STUFFED MEATBALLS

1½ pounds of ground meat (beef, turkey, pork, mixture, whatever you want)

½ cup of breadcrumbs

1 egg

½ medium onion, chopped (optional, as is the sautéing in the story)

1-2 packages of beef onion soup mix (to taste)

Chopped garlic, salt, pepper, Italian seasonings or whatever spices you would like to add, all to taste

1 block of mozzarella cheese, cut into cubes

Preheat oven to 400 degrees F. In a bowl, combine the ground meat with the bread crumbs, eggs, and whichever spices you choose. Add the onions and mix thoroughly. Form into spheres, poke a hole in the side, insert a cube of mozzarella, and reform into a sphere. Place inside a baking dish and bake for 15-20 minutes. I like to place the cooked meatballs in with the sauce and let them simmer along happily for a few minutes. Possible serving options are in sandwiches (like in the story), with pasta, or just by themselves. Enjoy!

THE SECRET'S IN THE SAUCE

ANDI MARQUETTE

"You should've been cooking chile," I said.

Terry looked at me from the exam table in the emergency room. She was sitting on it, her legs hanging over the side. The nurse who'd dropped us off had drawn the curtains around it, so we had a little bit of privacy. "Why?"

"Because it's not an asshole, like your sauce."

"Shut up," she said, but she was smiling. "Given the chance, I'm sure your chile would blurp like my sauce did today."

"My chile never blurps. You should switch your cuisine."

"I'm Italian. Sauce is sacred."

I shrugged. "We should do a study. Find out how often marinara is an asshole and blurps people in the eye, as opposed to chile."

She giggled, which was a good sign because it meant she probably wasn't in much pain.

"Can you see?" I asked.

"Yes. My eye just hurts a little. Like I got dirt in it or something."

I was about to reply when the curtain parted.

"Hi," the newcomer said. "I'm Dr. Barnes." She smiled at both of us and I immediately lost the ability to say anything. Instead, I just smiled back and held Terry's purse tighter. Something about women in scrubs was totally hot, and something about Dr. Barnes made her scrubs even hotter. Kind of sporty. Not much makeup, and dark hair pulled back in a ponytail. She looked like once she finished her rounds here she'd go play intramural soccer somewhere.

"So, Ms. Abruzzo, I understand you got something in your eye," Dr. Barnes said in a soothing professional tone.

I moved aside for Dr. Barnes, who pulled a pair of exam gloves out of the container on the tray next to the exam table.

"Marinara sauce," Terry said.

"And this sauce got in your eye?" she asked, like stuff like this happened every day.

"Yes."

"How?" Dr. Barnes put the gloves on.

"It was cooking on the stove and it blurped."

Dr. Barnes raised an eyebrow.

Oh, God. I'm a sucker for that. "That's the technical term," I said.

Dr. Barnes looked over at me, and I saw that her eyes were hazel before she looked back at Terry. Really expressive hazel eyes.

"Like burped," Terry said. "Only worse. A little bit of the sauce blurped up out of the pot and got into my eye. Like a bad horror movie."

Dr. Barnes smiled, and I felt myself melt a little. "Sounds scary."

Terry nodded. I had to give Dr. Barnes props for approaching this like she would any other situation. I doubted she had many patients who came to her with a marinara injury. She leaned over Terry with one of those bright light things and carefully examined both of Terry's eyes. Then she turned it off and examined her face.

"The good news is, you seem to have gotten it out of your eye," the doctor said, calm and professional. "But it looks like the sauce may have burned the skin underneath your eye." She leaned in closer to Terry's head and carefully held the eyelids of her affected eye open again. "Sorry, but I want to take another look, just to make sure."

Terry muttered something that sounded like "fuck" and what seemed to be another smile tugged at the corner of Dr. Barnes' mouth. That was hot too. It made me think about what a full-blown grin would look like on her. Amazing, I figured.

Dr. Barnes shone the light into Terry's eye, and Terry grabbed my hand and squeezed. Hard. I bit my lip to keep from yelling in pain. Not a good idea to yell suddenly when a doctor was messing around with your friend's eyeball. I gripped the handles of Terry's purse harder with my other hand.

"Tell me again what happened," Dr. Barnes said, all soothing as she removed her hands from Terry's face. I was a little envious of Terry.

Terry sighed with relief and I did too, as she released my hand. "The sauce started bubbling, and I turned the burner down but a blob of it flew out of the pot toward my eye. The next thing I knew, my eye was burning and I freaked out and got to the sink and ran cold water on it."

"On your eye?"

"Well, *in* it, actually." Terry glanced at me and her expression said something like, "How stupid is this, really?"

I smiled, trying to be encouraging, but I was also trying not to laugh. Pretty sure the doctor would not appreciate that. Terry probably would, though.

"That probably helped," Dr. Barnes said, her professionalism making my efforts not to laugh even harder. I cleared my throat and stared at my shoes, which were suddenly really interesting. Doc Martens did not go with the purse I was holding, I decided, and that made me want to laugh even more. I swallowed and cleared my throat again. If I looked at Terry right now, I'd lose it and that would not make a good impression on Dr. Sexy.

"Do you make sauce often?" Dr. Barnes asked.

"I'm Italian," Terry said, as if that explained everything. "And I have a YouTube show. I was making this batch for my new episode."

"Oh?" Dr. Barnes seemed genuinely interested.

"It's called *Delizioso*," Terry said. "Go on YouTube and search that along with my last name."

"I just might."

"And next week I'm having Van on to demonstrate her chile, which apparently never blurps."

Dr. Barnes looked over at me, amusement in her eyes, and I froze. "Really. So chile is a thing with you?" Dr. Barnes said.

"Um," I said.

"It's really good," Terry said, saving me. "Better than good, actually." She smirked behind the doctor's back and I wanted to crawl under the exam table.

"I like chile," Dr. Barnes said, and I swear there was a twinkle in her eyes.

"Well, tune in," Terry said. "I'll post the episode a week from tomorrow."

Dr. Barnes turned back to her. "We'll see. But right now, I'll get you some drops to put in your eye for a couple of days. It seems not much sauce actually got into your eye, which is a very good thing. Your reflexes probably protected you from the worst of it, and the burn on your skin is mild. I'll give you an ice pack to get you home. Do you have aloe vera gel?"

"I do, in my car," I said, and the doctor turned her very professional gaze to me. "I'll, um, make sure she gets it," I said, because I generally get really nervous when women I find attractive look at me.

"Good," the doctor said, and I wrenched my attention from her lips back to my shoes. It had been a while since I'd been knocked off balance by a woman. At least in a good way. She turned back to Terry. "Put a little bit of the aloe vera on a few times a day to help with any discomfort. Take Tylenol tonight and tomorrow if you have any pain from the burn. It'll heal on its own."

"Okay," Terry said. "I will."

"I'll be right back." Dr. Barnes smiled, and pulled her gloves off, and disposed of them in the appropriate receptacle against the back wall before she exited between the curtains. It wasn't a full-wattage smile, but it was pleasant nonetheless. Very.

"She's pretty hot," Terry said with a smirk.

"Yes, well, fortunately for you, she was on duty today. Otherwise, you'd be shit out of luck, marred forever by marinara."

Terry laughed. "Totally worth the trip to the emergency room, though. Especially to see you get all hot and bothered."

"I am not."

Terry snorted.

"What?"

"You're cute when you're hot and bothered."

"Whatever." I leaned against the exam table near her feet, not wanting to discuss Dr. Barnes' attributes, though I could imagine how nice they were.

"Maybe she'll watch you in your upcoming chile episode."

"She's probably busy. She's a doctor and all."

"I think she might be interested in more than your chile."

"Yeah, well, at least my chile isn't an asshole, like your sauce. You should do an episode on that, on asshole Italian sauces. So unlike my chile."

Terry laughed again and Dr. Barnes chose that moment to reappear. She glanced at Terry, then at me, then back at Terry.

"Van says my sauce is an asshole," Terry explained and heat spread up my neck. I shot her a glare behind the doctor's back. "Unlike her chile."

"I'm inclined to agree with her about your sauce. But I can't speak to her chile," Dr. Barnes said, never losing her smooth professional veneer. "Not yet, anyway." She gave me a measured glance and I actually managed to hold her gaze for a couple of seconds before I cleared my throat again and looked at Terry, who was grinning.

Dr. Barnes handed Terry a small bottle of what I guessed were eyedrops. "They're just to alleviate irritation. One or two drops every six hours for a couple of days. You may not need them, but just in case." She handed Terry a business card. "If you have any problems in the next few days, call my regular office. We'll get you in as soon as possible."

"Will do."

"Good. I'll go sign your discharge papers."

"Okay," Terry said. "Thanks, Dr. Barnes."

"You're welcome. Take care." She smiled again, but this time at me. "Let's hope your chile keeps behaving." And then she was gone, but I had a little bit of a flutter in my chest.

"That's your in," Terry said as she got off the table.

"My in for what?" I handed her purse over.

"A date, dumbass." Terry put the eyedrops in her purse. "With Dr. Avery Barnes."

"Oh, hell no. Her name is *not* Avery." I grabbed the business card from her. Yes, yes it was. Avery T. Barnes, MD.

"What's wrong with that?" Terry took the card back. "It's sexy."

"It's a romantic comedy name."

"So? You're kind of a romantic comedy. There are worse things to be."

"True."

I followed her to the main lobby, looking around for a last glimpse of Dr. Barnes, but no luck. Too bad. I waited while Terry was discharged, and then we walked to the parking lot.

"You are such a lesbian," Terry said as I opened the passenger car door for her.

"Maybe I'm just polite, opening your door for you after your traumatic sauce experience."

"Or maybe it's the Subaru you drive. You're a commercial for lesbian stereotypes."

"I thought I was a romantic comedy." I closed the door behind her and went to get in.

"There are lesbian stereotypes in romantic comedies," Terry said as I started the engine.

"Just be glad you had a lesbian stereotype to call today to haul your ass to the emergency room."

"I am. And why the hell do you have aloe vera gel in your car, by the way? Or were you just trying to impress the good doctor?"

"It's in my workout bag. You never know."

Terry laughed. "Thank you for saving me." She squeezed my arm.

"You're welcome. So, are you going to kick this batch of sauce to the curb?"

"Hell, no. I'm going to eat it with extra gusto. No sauce gets the better of me."

I grinned as I turned onto Terry's street. "Please be careful. Wear goggles or something."

"And let the sauce win? Never."

I laughed as I pulled into her driveway.

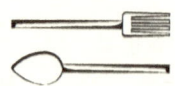

This was my favorite coffee house because it was usually quiet this time of day, and I could get a table in the back, where I would sit and read for a couple of hours. Plus, it was more homey than some of the urban chic places in the city.

Here, the wooden floors creaked and the tables and chairs looked like they came out of a western frontier saloon.

I checked the time on my phone, decided I needed a coffee warm-up, and took care of that before I settled in to continue reading. Coffee at the ready, I sank back into my book, glad I didn't have to work today.

"Hi."

The voice was familiar, but I was not prepared for the sight that greeted me when I looked up from the page.

Dr. Barnes stood next to my table, holding a to-go cup of what I assumed was coffee. She wore faded jeans and a blue tee that had—be still my heart—the original logo for *Star Wars* on it. Her hair was pulled back into a ponytail and sunglasses were propped on her head.

"Uh." Oh, that was articulate. I tried again. "Hi, Dr. Barnes." That sounded semi-coherent.

"It's Avery." She smiled, and my mouth went dry. "Nice to catch you here too." She watched me and I had to make a physical effort not to fall into her eyes again.

"It's close to work. But I'm not working today," I added, as if that was important and not apparent.

"You wouldn't happen to work at the Tattered Cover downtown, would you?"

"I do. I'm a manager."

"I thought you looked familiar when you brought Ms. Abruzzo in last week. How is she?"

"Good. Healed up really well. Do you want to sit down? Unless you have to go." There. Bravado. Specifically designed to ensure I didn't pass out from the all-too pleasurable heat that raced from my chest to my thighs.

"I do. Thanks." She sat down to my left. "Glad to hear the sauce didn't scar Ms. Abruzzo forever."

"Only her pride."

Dr. Barnes laughed and it caused all kinds of fluttery things to happen in my chest.

"So, what are you reading?" She gestured at the book, open beneath my hand.

"A biography of the guy who basically invented Wonder Woman."

"Lepore's book. Just finished it. Really interesting read."

Oh, my heart. She had geek in her. "I'm halfway through, and trying to figure out if the guy truly was feminist. After all, he basically had all these women in his life who pretty much took care of him. There's an element of manipulation there, I think."

"I had the same thought," Dr. Barnes said. "I did enjoy how layered Lepore made the story, though. And how she included the early comic illustrations of Wonder Woman throughout. I'm a huge Wonder Woman fan."

Pretty sure I was about to swoon. Did that even happen these days? Or was that just a nineteenth-century thing?

"I won't say anything else. Don't want to spoil it for you." She regarded me over the lid of her coffee cup as she sipped.

"Thanks. Glad to know you're not one of *those* types."

She grinned and I'd been so right at the hospital. The full wattage of it made me forget to breathe. "So, I caught your chile episode with Ms. Abruzzo on YouTube." She looked at me over the lid of her cup and I wasn't able to respond because I got stuck again in her gaze.

"Thanks for clarifying that yours is spelled with an 'e' on the end. Otherwise, I might've kept thinking you were into Tex-Mex," she added.

"No. Absolutely not," I said, coming to my senses with mock indignation. "It's my modified version of New Mexico-style green chile stew." I paused. "But, technically, it does have some Tex-Mex elements. The chili powder, for example. And maybe more of a tomato base. It's a hybrid, but errs on the side of chile with an 'e'."

"However it's spelled, it sounds delicious."

"It is, if I do say so myself."

"I have no doubt." Her gaze bored into mine and my bravado fled and I sat there like a high school kid, all hormonal and tongue-tied. My palms were even sweating. She smiled. "Any chance I might judge for myself how delicious this chile is?"

I stared, wondering how that would work. "Sure," I finally managed to say.

She waited, another smile flickering at the corners of her mouth.

"Uh," I said after a few moments. "Maybe—"

"You're really cute when you're flustered," she said.

"Excuse me?" Had I heard that right?

"Cute. You."

Lightning bolts zinged down my legs.

"So let me lay this out," she said. "I'm intrigued by a woman who reads interesting books and makes great chile. I'd like to find out what else you read and eventually, how that chile tastes. I'm off this weekend. Any chance our schedules might coincide? Provided, of course, that I'm not being presumptuous about your relationship status."

She waited again and somehow my brain clicked back into gear. "I'm off at three on Saturday."

"So I'm not being presumptuous?"

"You totally are," I said with a smile. "But you're also right. I'm single." And how was it that a super-hot doctor with a geek streak was single too?

She smiled back. "Then could I ask you to dinner?" She raised an eyebrow and my little heart pounded at the sight.

"Definitely."

"Great. So, Van, would you like to have dinner with me Saturday night?" She sounded hopeful and dammit, it was completely endearing.

"I'd love to."

She grinned and I about melted again. "Okay," she said. "Are you a tapas type?"

"Yes." I managed not to faint. Tapas gave her so many extra points. And for the first time ever, I wanted to kiss someone I barely knew.

"Ninth Door okay? On Blake? I can make a reservation."

"Most definitely."

She smiled. "Can I give you my number?"

"Yes." I set my phone up and handed it to her. She gave it back when she was done. "Okay," I said. "Under Dr. Barnes. I'm texting you now so you have my info."

"Avery," she said as I did that.

I looked up at her.

"I'm just Avery. I asked you for a date. Not an appointment."

Oh, God. A melty warm feeling washed over me.

"And I've heard every line there is about doctors," she said with a smile. "So don't even."

"No problem. I'm more interested in your Wonder Woman fascination."

"Good. We can discuss that over dinner. And unfortunately, I have to go run a bunch of errands, as much as I'd prefer sitting here with you a bit longer. But I'll see you Saturday." She flashed me another smile, stood, and walked to the door, but she waved when she got there and I waved back, fully aware of the big, stupid grin on my own face.

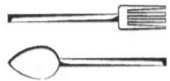

"She asked you out?" Terry stared at me. "Why didn't you tell me immediately?"

"Got busy. And freaked out a little." I looked around the room, hoping nobody could overhear.

"It's about damn time another woman noticed your charms. When is it?"

"Tomorrow." I still tingled at the memory, three days later.

"Oh, my God. Have you picked your outfit?"

I waited for a couple of people to finish grabbing potato chips out of the nearby bowl before I replied. "You're stressing me out. I'm already a nervous wreck about this. You know how I am."

"Okay, okay. I'm just really excited for you."

"Well, be excited quietly, without me knowing."

Brenda came out of the kitchen, wearing her trademark cutoffs, flip-flops, and old Denver Broncos shirt. Though she was pushing fifty, she still retained a lean athleticism. Her short dark hair was speckled with gray, which I thought was sexy. "How are you on drinks? This is a party, after all," she said.

"Fine." I held my beer up. "By the way, I love your house. When can I move in?"

Brenda smiled and gave me a hug. "Plenty of room. I'll let Kathy know so she can get the guest room ready." They had scored a refurbished early 20th-century Craftsman bungalow off Washington Park, a great neighborhood stuffed with a mixture of redone historical homes and newer ones built to capture that flavor without being too obtrusive. If I ever got around to moving out of my apartment, historic building though it was, I'd want a place like this.

"By the way, your lasagna is to die for," Brenda said to Terry. "And Van, your chile is getting rave reviews." She moved past us toward the back door.

"Come on," I said to Terry.

"Hold on." She took the lid off the slow cooker and dipped a plastic spoon into it, blew on the contents, and carefully tasted. "Oh, holy hell. This might be your best yet."

"You think?"

"What did you do? Something's different. Did you use Hatch?"

"Of course. Had a bunch left over from the fall, when I went to New Mexico and bought a bunch. Best to buy chile from the source."

"There's definitely something different in here. It's earthier and richer. You added something. What is it?"

"I did try a different beer. A sweeter porter."

"That's got to be it." She finished the spoonful. "Make it this way for the next food festival and you will be an instant hit." She set the spoon on a napkin and covered the slow cooker again. "Not that it wasn't fabulous before. But this is extra fabulous."

"Thanks. Coming from you, that means something."

She giggled. "This might rival the lasagna I brought."

"Your mystical sauce—asshole that it sometimes is—cannot be rivaled," I shot back.

She leaned over and pecked me on the cheek. "This is why you're my friend. Come on." She pulled me to the back yard. An hour later, I made my way back to the kitchen, nodding and smiling at people I hadn't greeted yet. I tossed my empty bottle into the recycling container then opened the fridge hoping there was another vanilla porter. Lucky me. I popped the top with the bottle opener on the kitchen island. What I wouldn't give for a kitchen like this, with its awesome counter and storage space, gorgeous cabinetry, and tons of natural light. *Some day.* I put the bottle cap in the trash.

"So, I've been hearing rumors that you're responsible for this chile."

Sparks shot down my spine as I turned. "Depends. What kind of rumors?" Thankfully, my bravado had kicked in. But I wasn't sure how long it would hold up, because Avery's hair was down and she was wearing dark blue board shorts with red Hawaiian flower trim, a faded red *Firefly* tee, and battered Converse sneakers. My inner geek swooned.

Avery smiled, and all those flutters from the other day started up. "The best." She held up an empty paper bowl. "And I concur with said rumors."

"Then yes. I'm responsible."

She threw the bowl and spoon away, brushing past me to do it and I managed to remain standing amid faint traces of her cologne. Something sort of crisp and clean, that added to the thoughts I shouldn't be having yet.

"Seriously. That was some mind-blowing chile. Stratospheric."

"Thanks. Glad you enjoyed it," I said, trying to sound nonchalant.

"I'd eat more, but it's all gone."

"Not to worry. I can hook you up."

"Yeah? You don't think that's an imposition?" Amusement danced in her eyes.

"Nope. I'll call you first when I do the next batch." I smiled, hoping I didn't sound like an idiot.

"A secret pipeline?"

"I don't do this for everyone, you know. But you expressed proper appreciation, so you're automatically moved to the top of the call list," I said with mock gravitas and she rewarded me with another smile.

"I'm looking forward quite a bit to that call." She held her hand up. "Don't move."

I froze, my bottle halfway to my lips, and she laughed. "I mean, don't leave. Let me grab a beer." She turned to the fridge and I tried really hard not to stare at her ass and legs. She closed the fridge and opened the bottle. Silently, I rejoiced that she'd chosen a craft brown ale.

"So," she said. "Fancy meeting you here." She put the bottle to her lips and I forced my gaze from her mouth to her eyes. Which didn't help my situation.

"I'd say the same to you. How do you know Brenda and Kathy?"

"I live a few houses down. I moved in maybe two months ago. They made it a point to welcome me to the 'hood, which I really appreciate. New girl and all."

"From?"

"An apartment downtown. Before that, Los Angeles."

I was about to ask more when Brenda came in. "Hey, Avery. Glad you could make it. I see you've met Van. Did you get a chance to try her chile?"

"I did. It could cause world peace to break out." She flashed me a grin and again, I was overwhelmed with an urge to kiss a woman I barely knew. It was crazy and kind of scary, but exhilarating too. I took a swig of beer to keep my mouth occupied.

"I've been saying that for years." Brenda tossed the paper plates she was carrying into the trash. "Come on. I'll introduce you around."

Avery raised her eyebrows at me, questioning, a silent communication and kind of intimate, like we'd known each other much longer. I nodded.

"Catch you later?" she asked me.

"Yeah. I'll be here a while."

"Good." She followed Brenda out of the kitchen, but glanced at me over her shoulder and again, that urge to kiss her washed over me. I set my beer down and started cleaning up in the kitchen, for something to do. A few minutes later, Terry burst in.

"Guess who's here?" she announced, almost breathless.

"I know," I said as I worked the trash bag out of the container. "And no, I don't want to talk about it because it's kind of freaking me out." In all kinds of ways, mostly delicious.

Terry giggled. "Let me know if you need CPR or anything. I'll get her to do it."

"Shut up." But I was smiling. I tied the bag closed and put a clean one in as several other people came in, diverting Terry's attention and I snuck out with the trash

I kept myself occupied with various conversations, but more than once Avery caught my eye and each time, it felt like something arced between us, something hot and fierce and intoxicating.

Nightfall surprised me, because I'd lost track of time. Kathy had started a fire in the portable firepit out back and most of the partiers had gathered there. I made a trip to Terry's car, parked down the block, holding my slow cooker with one arm and carrying a bag with her lasagna tray, utensils, and empty food containers in it. When I returned, Avery stepped out of the house.

"There you are," she said, and something in her tone made me melt even more, because it was genuine and kind of sweet. "I'm headed out and wanted to catch you before I did."

"I'm glad you did." In the dark I didn't feel so tongue-tied.

She moved closer until she was within arm's reach. "Seeing you makes me look forward to tomorrow even more."

Could she hear how loud my heart was pounding? "Same here."

We stood like that in the light from the house's windows, me lost in her eyes, wanting much more but not understanding why or how.

She broke the moment. "I'll see you tomorrow." She moved past me, down the steps to the walk.

"Wait," I said.

She turned.

"I can't let a fellow Browncoat walk unaccompanied down the block."

She laughed. "Spoken like a true *Firefly* fan. I accept your offer."

I joined her, and as we walked, it took all my strength not to grab her hand and pull her close. She stopped at the fourth house from Brenda and Kathy's, another refurbished bungalow, but with bright red trim and lots of plants on the front porch. The light from her porch didn't quite reach the sidewalk, but my eyes had adjusted and I could make her features out in the dark. All I had to do was lean in... but I chickened out.

"You know, you passed my chile test," she said.

"So you have one." The night was cool, but I was anything but.

"Everyone should."

"But you asked me out before you tasted it."

"I asked you out after I'd seen you make it. And I think Terry's a good judge of food. She said it was good on the show, and I went with that."

"Are you sure you trust her? Her sauce can be an asshole."

Avery laughed. Then she raised her hand to my face, tentative. Her palm was warm on my cheek and my heart pounded. More heat spilled down my legs. She leaned in and the touch of her lips on mine was soft and welcoming and much too brief. It left sparks in its wake.

"I'm not usually this forward," she said.

"But..."

She smiled. "I find I have to make an exception in your case." And she kissed me again, and this time her mouth moved harder against mine, hotter and more demanding. My hands found her hips and I pulled her close, and the heat from her body ignited something in mine.

"I'm going to stop now," she said as she pulled gently away. "Because if I don't, I won't be able to." She pressed her lips against my cheek and stepped away. "I might be a little old-fashioned in some ways, because I really want to have dinner with you tomorrow and ask you important questions about your favorite superheroes."

"And then?"

"I'm hoping for a second date."

I grinned. "Done. But I don't bust the chile out until the third."

"An old-fashioned woman like myself." She smiled back at me. "Thanks for walking me home. I'll see you tomorrow."

"Yep." I watched her walk to her front door, and after she unlocked it, she turned and waved before she went inside and as I headed back to Brenda's, Avery's kisses still lingering on my lips, I silently thanked Terry and her asshole marinara. Sometimes the secret really is in the sauce.

ANDI'S KITCHEN SINK CHILE

This is a recipe that is really versatile. You can make it vegetarian or not (pork is quite good), include a variety of different vegetables to your taste, and adjust spice levels to your taste as well. The key is to add spice and beer in layers, after you add the major ingredients. The following includes ground turkey, because that's one of my favorite ways to make it. I don't like to use beans, but you can add them.

1 lb. ground turkey
1-2 tablespoons olive oil
3-5 cloves of garlic, chopped
1 small white or yellow (not sweet) onion, chopped
¼ teaspoon paprika (to start)
¼ teaspoon smoked paprika (to start; optional)
¼ teaspoon chili powder (to start)
1 can diced tomatoes (I like Ro-Tel with green chile)
¼ teaspoon cumin (to start)
¼ teaspoon garlic powder (to start)
¼ teaspoon oregano (to start)
½ bottle dark beer (sweet, smoky porters work best, but if you use a more bitter porter or stout, add ¼ teaspoon molasses to the chile)
2 small potatoes (optional, but it helps give body, especially if you're not using meat)
1 large carrot (optional)
½ roasted red bell pepper, chopped
1 roasted New Mexico green chile (or Anaheim chile), chopped, or 1 small can of Hatch New Mexico green chile
¼ small poblano chile, roasted (optional)

½ large zucchini

½ large yellow squash

1 can beans (black, pinto, red, kidney, or chickpeas)

Brown the ground turkey in a pan with a touch of olive oil if it's already thawed. While it's cooking, you can chop your veggies.

When the meat is done, remove from heat and set aside. Over medium heat, heat 1-2 tablespoons olive oil in 4-quart (or more) soup pot. Add chopped garlic, onion, paprika, smoked paprika, and chili powder. Sauté until slightly browned, about 3-5 minutes. Keep the heat on medium and add can of tomatoes, cumin, garlic powder, oregano, and splash (to taste) of dark beer. If you're using a non-sweet dark beer, add your molasses at this point. Stir to meld ingredients then add cooked turkey and a can of water (use empty tomato can). Add another sprinkle of paprika, smoked paprika, garlic powder, cumin, chili powder, oregano, and splash of beer. Stir and cover and adjust heat to low. Allow to cook for 10 minutes.

Add potatoes, carrot, and varieties of peppers, along with another sprinkle of your spices, and another splash of beer. Cook for another 10 minutes and add zucchini and yellow squash along with another sprinkle of spices and another splash of beer. If you're using beans, add them at this point. Add water as necessary to give you a bit of a broth. This is more of a stew or soup than a chile.

Serve with warm tortillas.

Serves 4-6.

For extra heat, use more chili powder. For less, cut back on the chili powder and green chile and don't use the poblano.

ENTRÉES

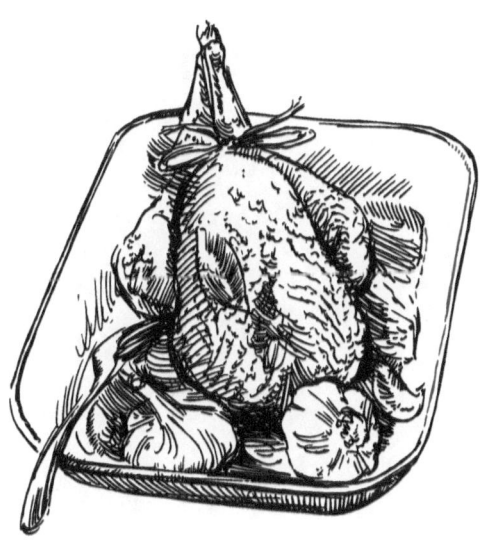

GOD'S TAMALES

BREY WILLOWS

Silence was always louder when the day was over, when Alejandra "Alex" del Olmo turned off the outside lights and locked the front door. The walk back to the kitchen, through the maze of empty tables, now devoid of hungry customers talking about their individual lives, was like suddenly being on an empty freeway. The cacophony of voices, silverware on ceramic, waitstaff and laughter—that was the orchestra playing the score to her work day.

The silence meant the audience had gone home, and she could finally relax. Just Alex and her kitchen. Her home.

She poured herself a glass of merlot and took a slow sip, savouring it. There was still some cleanup to do in the kitchen, though she made sure it was kept clean throughout the day, even if things got hectic. But before she finished cleaning, she wanted to get some prep done. There were several large parties scheduled the next day.

Alex took her time pulling out the ingredients for her special enchilada sauce, as well as the ingredients for the raspberry flan. Large batches of both ready to go meant far less cooking time the next day, and the sauce always tasted better after it had chilled overnight. Alejandra's was one of the best-known Mexican restaurants in the city, and she wanted to keep it that way. She dropped some oil in a massive pot and let it heat before adding enough chili powder to turn the oil a mushy red.

She stopped when she heard voices from the alley behind the restaurant. At this time of night, it was never good when people were in the alley. She turned off the stove, grabbed her extra-large butcher knife, and flung open the back door. She didn't ever need to use it because usually one look, and anyone hanging out in the alley always took off. This time, though, she wished they hadn't, so she could get a piece of them.

Three teenagers were kicking someone on the ground curled in a fetal position, trying to protect their head. Alex swore at them and two ran off, but the third gave the person on the ground a final kick before running after her friends. Alex knelt beside the person on the ground.

"Hey, it's okay. They're gone." She heard soft sobs and realized the figure was a woman. "Come on, let's get you inside and fix you up."

She slowly moved her arms away from her face, and Alex winced. It was covered in dirt and blood, and her lip was cut. "You're safe. Is anything broken?"

The woman moved her legs and arms cautiously. "No, I don't think so."

Her voice was soft and gentle, and Alex liked the timbre. She got to her feet, shying away slightly when Alex tried to help. It was then Alex noticed what she was wearing. Filthy baggy jeans were partially hidden by a ragged sweatshirt four times too big for her. One of her shoes was held together with duct tape. Probably homeless, and they rarely reported harassment or abuse to the police, because they were rarely taken seriously. She could at least clean the poor thing up, though. Alex led the way to the back door, glad the woman followed without further urging.

"Have a seat." Alex pointed at a bar stool beside the sink. "I'm going to get some Band-Aids and stuff."

When she came back, the woman was standing beside the stool. At her questioning expression, the young woman said, apologetic, "It's white."

This young woman, beaten up and homeless, hadn't sat down so she wouldn't get the seat dirty. It made Alex's heart hurt and she was about to tell her it didn't matter, when the woman swayed and went pale. Alex caught her just as she fainted.

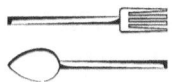

Ruby closed her eyes tighter against the bright fluorescent lights. Something cool and damp pressed against her forehead.

"Hey, there. Welcome back."

She panicked for a moment, unable to remember where she was and who was speaking. *The chef lady. The kitchen.* She breathed easy again. She was safe, for the moment. She opened her eyes and squinted against the light. Her ribs and jaw felt like they'd been in a fight with a brick wall and lost.

"Slowly, *chica*. Slowly."

The chef lady put an arm around her and helped her into a sitting position, and the warmth, the closeness of a caring person, made Ruby choke on emotions better kept locked away. "I'm really sorry. If I could maybe just borrow a rag to clean the blood off my face, I'll go."

The woman looked at her, a perfectly sculpted eyebrow raised. "When was the last time you ate?"

Ruby tried to think. "Yesterday, maybe? No, the day before."

The chef lady placed a gentle hand under her elbow. "Right. Stand up."

Ruby swallowed against the sudden nausea brought on by the motion, and moved away slightly in case she needed to be sick. She prayed she wouldn't. The chef lady led her to a small table off to the side of the kitchen.

"Stay put," she said.

"I really don't want to be any trouble. It's enough you got those people off me—"

"You're not any trouble. What's your name?"

Ruby hesitated, more out of habit than anything else. "Ruby," she finally said. She watched as Alex rummaged around in a fridge and poured something into a glass.

"That's nice. I'm Alex." She smiled and Ruby lost herself for a few moments in it, and in Alex's warm, dark eyes.

"Drink this." Alex set a tall glass of green liquid in front of her.

Ruby looked at it, skeptical. "If you wanted to kill me, you could have just let those guys keep going."

Alex laughed, a full, throaty sound. Ruby liked the way it made her feel. "*Mija*," Alex said, "I've never killed anyone with food, and I don't plan on doing it now. It's a high-protein, high-vitamin juice. It tastes better than it looks."

The truth was, Ruby hadn't eaten the day before yesterday. She hadn't eaten in nearly a week. She'd been unable to get any change on the street and was unwilling to go back to the shelter, which wasn't safe. Vitamins, even in green sludge, probably weren't a bad idea. She tried not to breathe as she drank, but really, all she could taste was apple juice. She relaxed and finished it.

"See? Not so bad." Alex was busy chopping up vegetables and throwing them in a pot. Next to her, she had a pan of something cooking.

Ruby salivated. It wouldn't be good to sit here coveting food she couldn't pay for, though. "Thank you for the drink, I think," she said with a smile. "I'll be on my way."

"Sit. No, actually—" Alex pointed at a door behind Ruby, "Go in there. It's a shower. There are clean clothes too. When you're done, come eat with me. I hate eating alone."

Ruby hesitated. It wasn't like she had any belongings to steal…"Shit. My backpack." She rushed out the back door, Alex calling after her. Ruby nearly wept with relief when she saw her backpack, mostly hidden, next to a dumpster. She didn't have much, but she didn't want to lose what little that was.

"Find it?"

Ruby hugged her bag protectively. "Yeah. Guess they missed it."

"Good. C'mon, I don't want to burn our dinner."

Our dinner. That was a phrase Ruby hadn't heard in a long, long time. And this attractive, warm woman stirred things within that she hadn't felt in a long, long time. But right now, the thought of a shower made her giddy, so, though wary and sure it was all going to go tits up, she followed Alex the chef lady back into the restaurant.

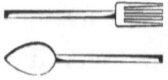

Alex watched as Ruby warily looked into the bathroom before going in. The shower wasn't used all that often, but when she or her staff worked late and wanted to go out after, it meant they didn't have to go home to get ready. Now, she was especially glad that she'd had it put in, and that she had extra cooking togs and towels set aside for when her cooks spilled on themselves. She liked a clean-looking crew, and someone covered in red sauce didn't inspire confidence in the food.

She continued making chicken rice bowls and put a batch of frozen vegetarian tamales in a plastic container. She stirred fresh cilantro into the rice and added a pinch of crushed chilies. Then she squeezed a full lime in and mixed it all together. She put the diced chicken breast in with the red onions and garlic before adding more cilantro and a bit of green chili sauce, along with fresh black beans. In another pan she threw together chopped zucchini, sweet corn, chestnut mushrooms, and a red bell pepper, frying them quickly before adding them to the chicken mixture and letting it all simmer together. She loved cooking, but she enjoyed it even more when she was cooking for someone else. And as unconventional as this meeting was, it felt sort of intimate. She found that she wanted Ruby to feel welcome. And wanted.

The shower stopped running just as Alex finished. She was amazed she'd gotten Ruby to stick around, let alone into a shower. Feeding her was next, if she wasn't completely spooked.

Ruby came out, towelling her hair, dressed in clean, white cook's clothes. They hung on her thin frame. Alex smiled, and was about to ask how she felt, when Ruby looked at her, and Alex stared instead. Ruby's hazel eyes were framed by long, thick lashes and her lips were a delicate pink. Her dark hair reminded Alex of melted chocolate. In another life, she could have been a model. Ruby blushed and Alex realized she'd been staring.

"Sorry. Please, sit down. I hope you like Mexican food." Alex gestured and Ruby moved gingerly over to the table. Alex wondered if she needed to convince her to go to the hospital. "Are you okay, by the way?"

"Fine, thanks. I've taken worse."

"Worse? What the hell is wrong with people?"

"It's a gang thing. They beat up a homeless person to get jumped into the gang properly. The worse the beating is, the higher their credibility." She shrugged, as though it made some kind of sense.

Alex bit back an angry response and said instead, "Well, you're safe now, and it's time for dinner." She served bowls of layered cilantro rice, black beans, spring onions, tomatoes, and cheese. Both were topped with avocado. She decided anything with a sauce would probably be a bad idea for someone who hadn't eaten in a while. This was fairly simple and hopefully wouldn't upset Ruby's stomach.

Ruby sniffed at the dish appreciatively "Are you sure? I mean, this is a ton of food. And—" She frowned and looked away. "I can't pay you."

"Pay me? Who do you think is going to eat all this food? It might as well be you, because I'm not going to be able to finish it. And I really do hate eating alone."

Ruby nodded and licked her lips, staring at the dish in front of her.

"Dig in. Not as good when it's cold." Alex started, and as soon as she did, Ruby dug in with gusto. Alex wondered if she really tasted it, she was eating so fast. "Hey, slow down. You'll make yourself sick. There's no hurry."

Ruby set her fork down, clearly embarrassed. "Sorry. Hungrier than I thought, and I haven't tasted anything this good in a long time."

Alex laughed. "Don't ever apologize for liking my food. I just want to make sure you enjoy it."

Ruby started eating again, slower this time.

Alex watched her surreptitiously. She was dying to know what her story was, but she wasn't about to keep her from eating. Plus, it felt intrusive and Alex wanted Ruby to feel safe enough to tell her story on her own time. For some reason, that was really important. "Are you staying anywhere in particular?"

Ruby glanced briefly at Alex. "Kind of. There are some good underground places, where us housing-challenged people look after each other."

"Underground?"

Ruby finished off her meal, scraping the bowl with her spoon. "Literally underground—the sewer tunnels."

Alex stared. "Sewer?"

"Not as bad as you think. They were carved out of a natural network of caves. So we use the tunnels to get to the caves. There's even running water, from an underground waterfall. It's actually kind of amazing." She stopped talking and stared at her hands, and Alex wondered at a woman like this, who found beauty even in her rough circumstances.

"Would you like more?"

Ruby shook her head. "No, thanks. I would, but I think my stomach wouldn't appreciate it."

They sat in silence for a moment until Alex said, "Is there anything else I can do?"

Ruby looked at her, tears in her eyes. "You've done more for me tonight than anyone has done for me in years. You have no idea how grateful I'll always be that you came into that alley. You're some kind of chef-angel."

Alex grinned, but inside she was heartbroken about Ruby's predicament. Her phone pinged a text message and she remembered she was supposed to be at her best friend's house for a get-together.

Ruby looked at the phone, then back at Alex. She stood. "Really, thank you. I'll just change my clothes and get out of your way."

Alex held up her hand to stop her. "You're not in my way. And do you have extra clothes?"

Ruby shook her head, staring at her feet.

"Wear what you've got on, and stop at a laundromat for your regular ones." She went to the register and pulled out five dollars' worth of quarters, as well as a fifty-dollar bill. "Here's some change for laundry, and a bit more to keep you going."

Ruby stared at the money in Alex's hand, her expression conflicted. Alex realized she may have offended her. She moved past her and set the money in a small plastic bag, along with the Tupperware of tamales.

"I hope I haven't offended you, Ruby. I just want to help out and I'm lucky because I can. I hope that's okay." She offered the bag, and Ruby took it gingerly. "There are vegetarian tamales in it," Alex continued. "That way you don't need to worry about refrigerating them. My grandmother's recipe. You'll love them."

"Offended me?" Ruby's laugh was sad. "After all you've done..." She put the tamales in her backpack. "Thank you isn't enough." She stopped at the door to the alley and looked back over her shoulder. "Could I—do you think I could come back sometime? Just to say hi, not for food or anything." She swallowed so hard Alex could hear it. "You have no idea how nice it is for someone to talk to you, to actually *see* you. To acknowledge that you exist."

There was so much pain, so much sorrow, in Ruby's eyes, that Alex couldn't help herself. She approached Ruby and cupped her bruised face in her hands. "Sweet lady, you're welcome here any time. I'd love your company." Before she could stop herself, she softly kissed Ruby's cheek then pulled away. Ruby's eyes stayed closed for a moment before she opened them and smiled and headed down the alley into the night. With a quick glance over her shoulder and a little wave, she was gone. Alex watched her go and wondered if she'd ever see her again. Her kitchen seemed empty without her and strangely, so did Alex.

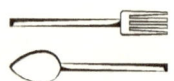

A week went by, and then another. The restaurant was busy, but that was part of Alex's joy, and feeding people was like taking care of family. But every day, she wondered if Ruby would come back, and she hoped she would. At one point, she considered trying to find the underground, but realized, after some research, how ludicrous it would be to try, given the nearly thirty miles of caves under the city.

After nearly a month, Alex's hopes about seeing Ruby again waned, leaving an inexplicable sadness. She hoped like hell Ruby was safe somewhere, and it got under her skin that she might never know. Since Ruby, she paid a lot more attention to the homeless people she saw on the streets, and acknowledged and spoke to them. It wasn't much, but after what Ruby had said, it was something.

One Saturday night, a few weeks after meeting Ruby, Alex was dead on her feet. Every table had been full the entire evening and the staff had been nearly run into the ground. As soon as their basic duties had been done, she sent them home. They'd finish tomorrow morning, and she'd give the kitchen a basic rubdown tonight.

As she cleaned the chrome countertops, there was a knock on the back door, so slight she almost missed it. Alex's pulse quickened at the possibility of who it might be. She opened the door, and stared at the woman outside, dressed in a modest pantsuit, her hair shiny and neat. She looked like a customer, not someone who should be standing in the alley. But when Alex met her eyes, she knew exactly who it was, and she smiled so wide it hurt, surprised at her reaction but welcoming it too.

Ruby held out the neatly folded chef's togs she'd borrowed. "I wanted to return these." Her smile was shy, but her eyes were full of life.

"Wow. I mean…come in." Alex took the proffered clothes and placed them on the counter. "Wine?"

"No, but thank you. Iced tea?"

"Done." Alex took her time pouring, glad for a moment to gather her thoughts. She handed Ruby the glass. "Can you stay a bit? I imagine you've got a story." She motioned toward two bar stools.

Ruby tilted her head slightly in agreement, and seemed to look her over in a way that sparked her insides. They sat in silence and Alex let Ruby take the lead. She finally started talking, so softly that Alex had to lean forward to hear.

"I'd been on the streets a long time. Things were bad at home." She stared into her glass. "The usual story—abusive father, drunk mother. It got bad enough that being on the streets was a better option than being at home."

She looked up and Alex lost herself in Ruby's gaze.

"The thing is," Ruby said, "you have no idea how hard it is until you have to do it. And once there, getting away is nearly impossible. When you haven't showered in God knows how long, no one will hire you and the longer you're on the street, the worse you look, and the less likely someone will take a chance on you. Your world becomes about survival. Nothing else."

She sipped her tea, her hand shaking slightly.

Alex started to respond, then stopped and waited.

"And then," Ruby said, "this weird thing happens. You stop looking for a way out. You accept that this is your life, and you get addicted to the freedom and lack of responsibility. It's almost as hard to get off the streets as it was to be in whatever situation you were in before." She looked at Alex, as though to make sure she was listening.

Alex nodded, encouraging. She liked the sound of Ruby's voice, the way her hands moved slightly as she talked, and the way her eyes were so beautifully expressive.

"So, that's where I was at the night we met. I'd pretty much given up, and was just managing to survive, although I was pretty near the end of that rope."

"I can't imagine."

"You really can't. But the thing is, you also can't imagine what it meant that night you took me in, let me clean up, and fed me. It reminded me..." She cleared her throat and Alex waited as Ruby fiddled with her glass, wiping the condensation with her thumb.

"Of?" Alex asked.

Ruby looked up, as though she was surprised she was talking to someone. "It reminded me I had wanted more, once. I wanted to help people, and make some kind of difference. I left here and went straight to the laundromat. I washed my clothes, and with the money you gave me, I went and bought something really cheap, but kind of professional looking, from the charity shop. I went to an employment office, and I used the address of the homeless shelter. They didn't check, so I went with it. I explained I didn't have a phone, so I'd have to come back." She looked at Alex, her expression worried. "I don't like to lie. But if I was going to make it out, I had to, you know?"

Alex took Ruby's hand, and it was warm and soft in hers. "You'll never find any judgment here."

Ruby smiled, obviously relieved. "I slept in the clothes you gave me, and kept my other clothes nice and clean. And those tamales...they were seriously to die for. If God eats Mexican food, yours would be His choice. I shared one with one of the kids I know who's also sleeping rough. She hadn't eaten in a while." She bit her lip and shrugged as though embarrassed. "Anyway, the next day, I went back to the

117

agency, and they had a posting for me. Just a minor thing—data entry—but I took it and used the bit of money I had left to pay for a spot at the nicer shelter in the city, the one with showers that have locks on the doors. Yesterday, I got my first paycheck, and it means I can afford a cheap hotel until my next one. Then I can look for a cheap apartment. An actual place of my own." Tears welled in her eyes and she squeezed Alex's hand. "Your kindness changed my life. I can never, ever repay you."

Alex sat for a moment, stunned. She hadn't considered the repercussions of that night. She had just wanted to see Ruby again, regardless of her situation. But now, seeing the beautiful, intelligent, and sweet woman across from her, she was overwhelmed.

"Anyway." Ruby stood and took a deep breath. "I'd better get back and get some sleep. I start at seven in the morning."

Alex walked beside her to the back door, unsure what to say, but knowing she didn't want Ruby to walk out of her life. "I wouldn't like that. I don't usually get here until around ten. I hate mornings."

"But you stay till eleven at night. I really admire your dedication." Ruby smiled, a little shy. "Would it be okay if I came back again?"

"Yes!" Alex laughed. "Sorry, didn't mean to be so exuberant. But, yes, please. I'd really like that. In fact, how about Friday? I'm making some huge meals for office work parties, and I'll have a ton left over. Sound good?"

"It sounds great." Ruby leaned forward and gave Alex a soft kiss on the cheek. She whispered, "Thank you for everything. See you Friday."

Once again Alex watched Ruby walk down the alley, but this time, she knew she'd be back. The idea made her breath quicken and her heart swell. She touched her cheek where Ruby had kissed her, and grinned.

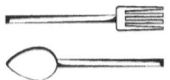

Ruby knocked at the back door, the way she always did. The Friday dinner they'd shared had been the start of something more. A friendship, at the very least. Over the next several weeks, Ruby had stopped by a few times a week, and they'd shared a number of meals and spent long hours talking. She'd never been so comfortable with someone, had never known someone so easygoing and nonjudgmental.

It made Alex sexy, Ruby decided. And sensual and open. And it made Ruby want to share much more of herself, in many different ways. As Alex had talked about her upbringing in a family of nine and her determination to do something that set her apart from her siblings, something she could truly call her own, Ruby had become more and more enamoured of her, and worried at night in her motel room, that her feelings might be a hero worship thing.

But when Alex opened the door this night, Ruby knew it was far more than that. She couldn't stop thinking about her, about the sure way she moved around the kitchen and her strong, elegant hands making art with food. Ruby loved watching her taste the dishes she created just for their time together, and the way she savoured every flavour. She loved Alex's passion, both for her cooking and for the other things she enjoyed.

"Right on time," Alex said as she opened the door. "I'm just about to pull the enchiladas together." She motioned to the bar stool, the same one she'd motioned to the first night they met. "Grab a drink and take a seat."

Ruby shyly pulled the bouquet of flowers from behind her back and handed them over, unable to look Alex in the eye. "To say thank you."

When Alex didn't respond, Ruby looked up and Alex's expression wasn't concerned, or interested, or simply friendly. It was...hungry. Alex took a step forward, her eyes searching and tentative. She paused, then moved in and kissed Ruby. Softly at first, and then with growing urgency.

Ruby wrapped her arms around Alex, pulled her tight. Their kisses were hot and needy. Alex drew Ruby into the kitchen and kicked the door shut behind her, not letting an inch of space creep between them. She pressed Ruby against the shiny chrome counter and traced a line of hot kisses down her neck.

Ruby moaned, her knees weak with desire and the overwhelming feeling of being so wanted by another person. Alex's skin was soft, and she smelled faintly of cinnamon. Ruby planted her feet and twisted so it was Alex pinned against the counter. She slid her hands under Alex's soft sweater, since she wasn't wearing her usual chef's uniform. She caressed Alex's breasts, nuzzled her neck, and lightly thumbed her nipples. She was rewarded with Alex's soft whimper and the urgency with which she pressed against Ruby's hands.

Alex pulled away, took Ruby's hand and led her to the front of the kitchen. She lifted Ruby onto the massive countertop as easily as she would a bag of potatoes. Ruby grinned and raised an eyebrow.

"You get strong working in a kitchen all day." Alex grinned back. "Going to the gym helps too." She slowly took Ruby's shirt off, then trailed kisses over her stomach and stopped to suck her nipple into a hard point.

Ruby arched, needing more and Alex obliged. She gently pushed Ruby down and climbed up beside her. She undid the button and zip on Ruby's trousers and slid her hand inside to cup Ruby's aching center.

"Is this okay?"

"Please. God, Alex. Please."

Alex obligingly slid inside her and Ruby cried out as she held Alex tightly with one arm. Alex took her quickly, and after Ruby came, Alex took her again, slowly and with lingering kisses. Ruby let the tears fall as she came again, never wanting to leave.

They lay together for a little while, holding each other.

"Still okay?" Alex murmured against her hair.

"More than okay. That was..."

"Yeah."

Ruby shifted so she could look up at Alex. "Thank you."

Alex caressed Ruby's face. "For what?"

"For wanting me. For saving me. For making me come that hard." Ruby grinned and wiggled her eyebrows, making Alex laugh. How she loved that sound. "Can I thank you properly?" She started to stroke Alex's stomach, but Alex jumped off the counter with an impish grin.

She held up a dish and dipped her finger in it. Melted chocolate. She sucked it off her finger suggestively. "You know how I love to feed you. Why don't you have dessert while you thank me properly?"

Ruby slid off the counter and moved toward her. Even if it didn't last, it was a hell of a long way from where she'd been. She smiled, hoping Alex could see the desire and trust in her eyes. "I'll spend as much time as I can thanking you in any way you like."

"I hope it takes a long time," Alex said.

"How long have you got?"

Alex smiled. "However long you want."

And then Ruby made it impossible to talk any longer.

THE PERFECT LAZY WOMAN RICE BOWL

Ingredients:

One small can of sweet corn

One tin of black beans

One courgette (zucchini)

Four or five chestnut mushrooms, chopped

One red bell pepper, diced

Fresh coriander (cilantro)

Diced chicken breast (optional—nice without meat too)

One bag of instant microwavable rice (Lime and Coriander or
Mexican are good)

One red onion

Green chili sauce, or a small tin of diced green chilies

One lime

2 cloves of garlic

A dash of chili flakes

1 teaspoon paprika

1 teaspoon cumin

A handful of broken tortilla chips

1 teaspoon sour cream

1. Fry up the red onion, garlic and chicken. Squeeze the lime
juice over the mixture. Stir.

2. Add the courgette, cook until soft.

3. Add the mushrooms and bell pepper. Cook for about five
minutes.

4. Add the beans and sweet corn. Stir it all up. Add the paprika,
cumin, coriander, and chili flakes.

5. Simmer for about ten minutes, stirring constantly.
6. Microwave the rice. Add it to the mixture. Stir it all up together.

Serve with the crushed tortilla chips and sour cream on top.

SWEET OR SAVORY

LEA DALEY

I NEEDED SOME STRAIGHTFORWARD FEEDBACK so I mustered what I hoped was a matter-of-fact tone. "Dykes don't like me."

Delaney didn't even look up from the prefab bookcase we were assembling in my apartment. "But you're a dyke."

"Which makes the situation doubly frustrating."

"*I* like you."

"Well, duh. You're my best friend—you don't have a choice. But seriously, your average dyke doesn't like me."

Delaney studied me for a long moment. "I suppose you're a tad femme-y to hang with the butch crowd—"

"Watch it, woman! Have you not seen me debone a chicken with wicked speed?"

"You have a point. Your knife skills suggest you're a bit too butch for running with the lipstick ladies."

I had to laugh—Delaney never pulled a punch. "I just don't fit in anywhere."

My pal spent more time tightening a screw than was strictly necessary. "I'd put you in the 'Levi's lesbian' category—maybe you should try volunteering at All Out." Which was the storefront theater where Delaney built flats, managed the soundboard, and reluctantly accepted an occasional supporting role. "I think you might find a few friends there. We're just beginning work on a new play—"

"The Siobhan MacFayden piece you mentioned?"

"Yeah, and it's a riot."

I set aside the crumpled instruction sheet, saying, "That's worth considering. But, as a general rule, I'm correct. Dykes don't like me. Consider Corey."

"I'd rather not," Delaney said giving the Allen wrench a vicious twist. My best friend had never liked my long-gone lover. And she'd never made a secret of that.

"No, really. The only place we really clicked was in bed. Corey wanted me... *bad*... but that's all. We had zero compatibility beyond the confines of the nearest mattress."

"And yet that lasted for three years."

"What can I say? I was a fool."

Delaney turned toward me, grinning. And in a flash I saw her with total clarity, as if we were meeting for the first time. She was tall, no lightweight, though every ounce was firm and taut. Her thick, sandy hair was short, very nearly a brush cut. Her hands were strong, with long, slightly blunt fingers. No one would be startled to learn she was a lesbian. But her face was feminine, with high cheekbones and a lush, alluring mouth—something I was sure must annoy her whenever she passed a mirror, but I'd always found it incredibly appealing.

We'd become good friends eons ago at an IT startup, then become inseparable. Even after Delaney took a position with a rival firm, we spent all our free time in one another's back pockets. For nearly a decade, we'd shared everything from homegrown tomatoes to best sellers to the pain of parental loss. We'd seen *Hairspray* at the Fox, worked phone banks for Obama, and even taken an Olivia cruise together, where I'd failed to find romance and Delaney hadn't even seemed to be looking.

Something powerful hit me and suddenly I was breathless, my stomach alive with butterflies as I stared at her. Was I in love with this woman? I thought about it. I'd been called clueless more than once so maybe I'd overlooked the warning signs. To wit: Delaney was always my first choice as a plus-one, the person I'd want to live with on a desert island. I never tired of her company; she never failed to make me smile. What else could that mean? And now here I was, watching her, totally focused on our task, stretching for a tack hammer, broad shoulders flexing under a snug T-shirt. She was a topographical study in womanly anatomy, every swell and curve mapped with absolute fidelity.

The dizzy, electrified feeling racing through me was like being struck by lightning. Or caught in Cupid's crossfire—a whimsical, mischievous, bewildering blow. Because I might be palpitating at the sight of Delaney, who was doing all the work while I sat frozen with astonishment. But that didn't mean anything had changed for her. And we were so damned comfortable as friends—why mess with success? Maybe she didn't even find me attractive. And why would she? Because really—dykes don't like me.

Still, I couldn't quit gaping. I thought I knew everything about Liza Delaney. Now I saw I'd been blind. How had I never registered the exact shade of her flawless skin? Or that look of utter concentration as she worked? Or the expert way that she wielded each tool? And there were other critical gaps in my knowledge. I had no idea how it would feel to run my hands through that dense pouf of hair, nuzzle her neck, or find shelter in her arms. Five minutes earlier, Delaney's wide smile had just been a fact of life. Now it was inexpressibly dear. Never again would I see her merely as my best friend.

I was so distracted that I didn't hear her ask for the Phillips. And when she repeated the request, I passed a standard screwdriver instead. She stopped working long enough to ask, "Are you okay?"

Which made me flush, and the longer Delaney stared, the hotter my face felt. Finally, I managed to say, "I'm a bit short on sleep." Even if that wasn't exactly true just then, I knew it soon would be—after this stunning epiphany, a good night's rest would be hard to come by.

Thanks to Delaney's perseverance, we finished the bookcase just before noon. Once we shoved it in place, I set out tuna salad and tomato wedges. Far from the feast I owed her, but she was scheduled to work at the theater after lunch. At least I had homemade lemon bars on hand, her favorite dessert. I was at the sink peeling carrots, passing them to Delaney for slicing, when she rested her cheek on the top of my head for a millisecond. A commonplace gesture that felt absurdly fresh, ridiculously moving. I dropped my peeler, heard it clatter against stainless steel, and spun toward her.

Delaney regarded me with real concern. I saw green depths in her hazel eyes I'd never noticed before. Then I took in the fringe of dark lashes under level, expressive brows, and those inviting lips. For a fraction of an endless second, I thought she might kiss me. Then I thought I might kiss her.

Instead, Delaney scooped up a bag of chips and a jar of pickles, and I carried our plates to the table. We ate in companionable silence, but all the while my heart was turning cartwheels in my chest. As soon as we finished clearing the table, Delaney grabbed her toolbox and said, "Gotta run, Jess. Maybe you can catch a nap." Then she was gone.

I mooned around my living room, readjusting the furniture, arranging books on the new shelves. The whole time I fiddled, I was compiling lists: What I loved about Delaney. Why a romance with her was impossible. On the plus side, she was bright and laugh-out-loud funny. Kind and thoughtful. Fearsomely competent in all the dykely sports, yet far too courteous to belittle us lesser mortals. And she was a paragon of patience—in fact, maybe she was a little *too* patient.

The cons made a shorter list: I didn't want to ruin a fabulous friendship. I didn't want to make a fool of myself. Delaney had never signaled an interest in more than warm camaraderie. Unless I hadn't been paying attention. Because why else did she spend most of her spare time with me? Why else was she forever trying to ease my passage through life? Why had she used precious vacation time to nurse me through a brutal bout of flu? And why were her gifts always so exactly matched to my tastes?

I surveyed the room. The mirror over the mantel was a gift from Delaney, something magnificent she'd found in a junk shop on Cherokee Street, then fussed over, burnishing the antique frame till it gleamed. Many of my favorite books were offerings from her and most of my plants had started as cuttings from Delaney's luxurious garden. That collection of decorative balls piled in a bowl on my coffee table, one for every special occasion we'd shared? Perfect choices, every one. Delaney couldn't have been woven more thoroughly through my days if we'd lived together.

And now everything had changed in single searing instant of recognition. Maybe all we needed to set our relationship ablaze was the spark I'd just felt? And maybe I should take her up on the idea of volunteering for the MacFayden play? Because the more time I spent in Delaney's presence, the better. Still I decided against mentioning that possibility, in case this wild fantasy evaporated as quickly as it had developed.

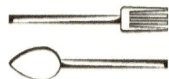

Two days later, utterly devoid of second thoughts, I drove to All Out Theater. From the parking lot, I spotted a rear door propped open to unseasonably warm weather. I stepped inside and looked around. The backstage area was spare and dusty. Stacks of flats leaned against the cement block wall, a Manhattan skyline obscuring an elegant drawing room that overlapped a sun-struck glen. I'd seen all those settings from the cheap seats, could name every play where this scenery had established the mood. I scanned the workspace for Delaney, but she was nowhere in sight. A volunteer in overalls emerged from the wings.

"Excuse me," I said. "I'm looking for the stage manager?"

Scarcely breaking stride, she jerked her head. "Downstairs, last I knew. In the costume room."

I found the stairwell and the costume room, then approached the lone occupant there. A fierce-looking, muscular lesbian flipping through period garments on a pullout rack. I offered my hand. "Jessica Whistler, reporting for duty."

Still intent on her task, the stage manager muttered, "Yeah?"

"I called about volunteering?"

She turned then, and took a long look at me. "Kimber Browning," she replied belatedly, a speculative look in her eye. "Ever used a paint roller?"

"I've revamped my fair share of ratty apartments."

"Let's see what you got," she said with an unmistakable leer. Leaning into the hallway, she hollered, "Stell! Take this gal to the storeroom and set her up to prime those flats!"

Fifteen minutes later, I was on a twelve-foot ladder, loading a roller with white latex, obliterating that glorious golden glen. And steaming a little because Kimber had assigned me the most basic chore, never once asking about more sophisticated skills or interests. So I missed Delaney's arrival, didn't even know she was on site. Until I tuned in to a captivating voice on the other side of the curtain: "Are we still on for tomorrow night?"

"Sure," Delaney replied. "What do you want to do?"

"That depends on whether you're sweet or savory," said the other voice.

"What?"

"We could go to Panache for decadent desserts and classical music, or Torello's for tapas and cava."

"Either sounds fine," Delaney said. "You pick."

"Torello's then—I'm thinking savory's more your style. Is eight good?"

"No!" I wanted to yell down. "She's not available!" But just then the two stepped into view and I saw they were an ideal match. The stranger was nearly Delaney's height, though she was thinner and more wiry. Her dark hair was spiked on top, with crisp geometric designs incised into the shaved sides. A look I couldn't have pulled off in a thousand years. She was cooler than cool—or maybe what I meant was she was über hot. Even worse, she seemed scarily smart.

"Eight's excellent," Delaney affirmed.

"Great," the woman said before she yanked a hammer out of a loop on her pants and started pounding away on some half-finished structure. Delaney watched her for a moment then strolled away. But not before I caught sight of her affectionate wink at the sexy carpenter. Not before I had time to wonder whether she was checking out that sweet little ass.

I swore silently. And the whole time I rolled cheap paint over those enormous flats, a new question about Delaney wove through my mind: was she sweet or was she savory? Now that the issue had been raised, I had to know. But I didn't clamber down from the heights, didn't greet my old pal, until I was sure she'd never guess I had eavesdropped on her conversation.

After rehearsal, I met the entire All Out crew. Including Zev Feinstein, the magnetic dyke with that trusty hammer. She turned out to be an architect by day, the set designer by night. "A pleasure, Jess," she said, extending a hand. "I've heard so much about you. And you must be the fastest painter in the West—you plowed through those flats in record time."

Then she slung her arm over Delaney's shoulder, striking a casual but possessive stance. And yet I liked her. Goddamn it—I liked the woman. Even through my envy, I could see she'd be good for Delaney. Maybe not as good as I would have been, but good.

"Some of us are going for drinks," Zev said. "Want to come?"

All I wanted was to hand in my roller and flee for good—especially since I could see naked lust in Kimber Browning's eyes. I had a sinking feeling I'd have to dodge the stage manager throughout the production. *Serves you right, Jess—you said you wanted to broaden your horizons.* I turned down Zev's invitation to bar hop. But I had a far more troublesome problem just then. If I quit working the show, I'd have to tell Delaney why I'd bailed. If I stayed, I'd be doing grunt work evenings and weekends until the cast took their final bows. And staying the course meant that for nearly two months, I'd have a front row seat to Delaney's developing romance. *Bloody hell!*

Tossing beneath my duvet that night, I couldn't get Zev's intriguing question out of my head: was Delaney sweet or savory? Something I'd never thought to wonder. And I could make the case either way—she was compassionate and considerate; she was wry and salty. It seemed simultaneously urgent that I learn the answer and highly unlikely I'd be able to satisfy my curiosity.

I woke early the next morning, groggy and out of sorts, yet too restless to remain in bed. By six, I'd decided to bake something—my personal way of centering. I thought at first I'd make French bread. Then I imagined kneading that dough, silken and yielding as a woman's breast. Which didn't exactly restore my equilibrium. So I pulled out other ingredients and made a stab at inventing a new Dutch oven recipe. A hardier loaf, something more nourishing, more rustic. Rye bread studded with caraway and chia seeds, I decided. Critiquing the result—not to mention consuming it—would distract me on a solitary Saturday night while Delaney and Zev were doing whatever. A thought that didn't bear consideration.

By evening the rye dough still hadn't doubled in bulk. I dumped it onto a floured cloth anyway, then kneaded it briefly. To my surprise, it felt stiff and leaden, lacking any of the airy lightness I expected. It was, I thought, a faultless match for my sour mood. Googling the problem, I learned that whole grain mixtures rise far more slowly than those made from white flour—plus they require way more liquid. Who knew? I decided to let the dough rise again, then I settled for cold cereal and something vapid on Showtime. Hardly my happiest Saturday night.

Fresh from the oven on Sunday, the rye loaf had an enticingly pungent scent and a delectable crumb. But the recipe undeniably needed fine-tuning. I mixed a new batch, increasing the amount of water, upping the agave nectar to a scandalous level. Setting it to rise, I left home to cram a week's worth of errands into a tiny time frame. I was due backstage again by two.

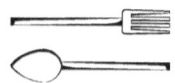

While I waited for a new assignment at All Out, I pretended to watch actors run their lines. But I was actually focused on the soundboard where Delaney huddled with Zev Feinstein. Seemingly in deep discussion about technical matters. Hopefully related to the play. I wondered how long their relationship had been brewing. And why I'd known nothing about it. One thing was depressingly clear: in the future, any and all Delaney time would include Zev. Our

Friday pizza dates, our Saturday movie marathons, our Sunday flea market adventures—Zev would be in the midst of every one.

Or maybe those days were gone. Because the two of them would want private time, and plenty of it. Inevitably there'd be occasions when I would make the assumption I was welcome but they really wanted to be alone. I winced, imagining the furtive exchange of frustrated glances whenever I overstepped my bounds. Maybe it was better to withdraw up front, to accept their invitations just often enough to imply nothing was wrong. Pizza monthly, maybe, rather than weekly. I could join a book club, work longer hours, take up a hobby. Ceding the playing field to Zev without a struggle might spare me a lot of pain. Or maybe I'd just be exchanging one form of hurt for another. *Get used to it, girl!* I admonished myself. At least the brilliant Ms. Feinstein had recognized Delaney's desirability from day one. Did I really think I could call dibs because I knew her first?

When I left that night, I was carrying a long list of props that Kimber had ordered me to procure. How and where, I had no clue. Even worse, I had only the slimmest of budgets to expedite the undertaking. The items included a fainting couch, a mandolin, an elephant gun, and a mounted elk head. Nothing simple. To top things off, I'd watched Delaney depart from All Out with Zev. Who, to my despair, drove a loaded silver Stingray. She was every dyke's dream come true, and my blackest nightmare.

At home, the kitchen smelled of rising dough and I couldn't wait to dive into the latest version of my new recipe. Caraway seeds and agave nectar might sound like an unholy alliance, but when I cut into the weighty loaf the following day, the flavor was a decadent mix of opposites, entirely satisfying. Or perhaps I simply wanted to believe that a heavy dose of carbs was a fitting substitute for eternal love.

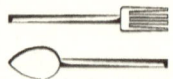

Throughout rehearsals, Delaney and Zev were joined at the hip. I know because I watched their every move. I couldn't figure out why Delaney didn't seem happier, though, why her behavior hadn't changed. Especially since Zev appeared to be over the moon. But, of course, I didn't really know the woman—maybe Feinstein always gave off a heavenly glow, always looked like she'd just won the lottery. No matter how much self-talk I resorted to, I was jealous, jealous, jealous of her in a slow-simmering, despicable way. *Keep your distance*, I chanted over and over again. *No good will come from hanging around them.*

Weeks passed. I discovered a previously unsuspected capacity for acquiring props. I hadn't guessed you could turn up an elk's head on Craig's List. Or that you could barter a loaf of homemade bread for the loan of a silver tea service. Or that an antique store would temporarily trade a Victorian fainting couch for a mention in the program. The props I couldn't beg, borrow, or steal I made by hand, which was surprisingly fun. Better yet, the cast and crew had learned to rely on me, had begun to assume I was a permanent fixture at All Out. And Delaney was right—I fit in with the theater crowd way better than I did with the nerds and coders at work. If I stuck around, I might actually make a friend or two backstage.

But busy as I was, I still had too much time on my hands. Delaney had previously taken up a lot of space in my life. Now I didn't have a clue how to fill all those lonely moments. And that fall, in the privacy of my bedroom, I shed more tears than I'd willingly admit.

From first performance to last, our play was a huge success and everyone's spirits were soaring. Still, I'd decided to bail on the cast party. By then, it was almost impossible to deflect Kimber Browning's amorous advances. And I definitely wasn't up for watching Zev slow dance with Delaney. I pleaded the proverbial prior engagement then made a long overdue trip to visit my parents. So I was the only person on the crew who didn't know that Delaney and Zev split that evening. In fact, with the production a thing of the past, I didn't get clued in until our monthly pizza night, when Delaney showed up at Carraci's. Solo.

"Where's Zev?" I asked as she shoehorned herself into our cramped booth.

"I couldn't say." Delaney's face was carefully composed, uncharacteristically guarded, as if we were mere acquaintances.

"What does that mean?"

"I called it quits."

"But I thought you liked her."

"I do like her... a lot. I just don't love her."

I hoped I didn't sound too snippy when I said, "For someone who wasn't head-over-heels, you certainly monopolized her time."

Delaney looked abashed. "Yeah. Maybe I was trying to convince myself I cared more than I did. And Zev had begun to take things too seriously. Still, I feel like a cretin. She didn't handle it well."

"I can imagine," I said, my mind racing with the implications. "She seemed totally devoted to you." *Now what?* I could hardly seize the moment and confess that I'd fallen for her. That would be crass and insensitive. And it might backfire, confirming that I belonged in the same category as Feinstein—a friend, not a lover. Still I found myself murmuring wistfully, "Did you ever wonder if—?"

Delaney leaned in. "What?"

Too soon! Too soon! my conscience cautioned. "Nothing. Really. Pepperoni tonight? Or sausage and mushroom?"

Everything was awkward with Delaney after that, our contact spotty and disjointed. The months she'd spent with Zev had disrupted all the rhythms in our relationship, allowing an unsettling distance to develop between us. We no longer dropped in on each other, rarely texted, only sporadically phoned. I was irrationally insecure, longing to reach out, but afraid I'd make matters worse. And I think she must have felt a bit sheepish about assuming she could simply reinsert herself into my life. We'd reached a stalemate. Neither of us knew how to bridge the gap, how to reestablish our longstanding patterns.

One Friday night, hoping to kill a bit of time, I mixed another batch of rye dough and left it to rise. The next evening, the seductive aroma and crackled crust of the cooling loaf suggested that I'd finally tweaked the recipe to my satisfaction. Missing Delaney all the while, I sliced the warm dome, slowly and with great precision, as if those mathematically exact divisions could soothe my deepening despair. But when I set out a single plate for one more meal I'd eat in solitude, some internal switch flipped. All at once, I'd had my fill of angst and ambiguity. Shoving the ham and Swiss in the fridge, I scooped up my cell and dialed my absent friend.

"Hey," I said. "Are you home?"

"Yep. Why?"

"I was wondering if you want company."

"Sure. Come on over. I was just about to binge on *Game of Thrones*."

"Wait for me, okay?"

"Don't I always?"

Ragged breath caught in my throat. *Did she? Had she?* Or was I so desperate I was making something out of nothing? *Screw it!* I sprinted for the shower. Then I dried my hair, slipped into a pair of tight jeans, and pulled a clingy sweater over my head. After stuffing the rye loaf into a paper bag, I dashed to the nearest supermarket, where I snatched up fruit, grabbed a round of Gouda, chose the best pinot noir on the shelf, and slung a pricey bundle of all-night firewood onto a conveyor belt. Before I could second-guess myself, I was on Delaney's threshold, the memory of her voice leavening my mood, bubbles of excitement rising through me. Even if this was the biggest mistake of my life, I had to give it a shot. One way or another, I had to know.

When her door swung open, I stepped inside. Wordlessly, I dropped that firewood in the foyer and handed over the shopping bags. As I slipped off my coat, Delaney's quick eyes took in the scoop of my sweater, the fit of my jeans, the look on my face. In the whole whirling universe, the frantic hammering of my heart was the only sound. Crossing my fingers, I stepped closer.

"I'm a very slow learner, Liza Delaney, but I think I've finally realized why I like having you around so much."

She reached for me, drew me against her. "About damn time, Jess. I'd almost given up hope."

Game of Thrones would have to wait. We abandoned the living room for her bedroom, a familiar space that instantly took on thrilling significance. Delaney bent to kiss me, then trailed her tongue along my neck, over a collarbone, down to the swell of my breasts. When I shuddered in her arms, she growled, "How do you feel about hard and fast?"

"Is there another choice right now?"

"Not for me—I've wanted you too long."

She raised my arms, stripped off my sweater, bit the nape of my neck. Then she unhooked my bra and bent to nipples already yearning for those sharp teeth. When my knees buckled, Delaney caught me, cradled me, set me on her bed. I unzipped my jeans and let her whip them off me.

"Jesus God, Jess. You're even more gorgeous than I guessed—"

I pulled her down on top of me, stopping the flow of words with my lips, exploring hers, melting against her, into her. Then I pushed her away, rolled her over, and unbuttoned her shirt. Her breasts were small and firm and irresistible. Delaney bucked under my assault and I halted just long enough to say, "Take off your pants, woman."

She wriggled out of them, exposing a flat stomach, generous hips, a thatch of sandy hair at the juncture of her thighs. "Your choice," I said, voice raspy in my throat. "My hands or my mouth?"

"Both—but not yet." After flipping me, Delaney found exquisite wetness and raging desire. As she slid knowing fingers deep into my core, into my soul, she whispered, "*This* dyke likes you, Jess. This dyke likes you a *lot*." And shining in her eyes I saw everything that was absent when she'd turned her gaze on Zev.

It was long past midnight before we remembered my firewood, the wine, and the food. In the living room, Delaney crouched nude at the hearth, setting logs in place, every detail of her spine highlighted by moonlight through the shutters. Then she rose, enveloped me, and kissed me until I thought I might faint. The heat roaring through me had nothing to do with that flicker of kindling. "Are you hungry?" I managed to ask.

"For everything."

"I'm here, baby. We have time."

"Right," Delaney said, summoning restraint. "Okay. I'll open the wine. You slice the cheese."

Ravenous, we carried a tray into the living room. In the flare of firelight, we tore into the pinot and our snacks.

"This bread is incredible, Jess."

"Thanks, you bum—I invented it while you were messing around with Feinstein. I call it Heartbreak Rye."

But even the best of breads couldn't satisfy our deepest hunger. Soon we were back in the bedroom, gentler by then, more tender. Long before dawn I had the answer to the question that had bedeviled me through so many agonizing hours: my darling Delaney was sweet *and* savory.

HEARTBREAK RYE BREAD

This addictive rye bread is ultra-simple to prepare, but rises for 12–18 hours. It produces a dome-shaped loaf with a crisp crust and chewy interior. Slices toast beautifully.

In a large bowl, mix:
2 cups whole wheat flour
1 cup dark rye flour
½ cup unbleached all-purpose flour
2–3 tablespoons caraway seed
2 tablespoons chia seed (optional)
2 tablespoons ground flax (optional)
2 teaspoons salt
½ teaspoon yeast

Add:
1¾ cups water
½ cup agave nectar

And combine thoroughly. Cover bowl with plastic wrap and set aside for 12–18 hours (overnight is usually sufficient if the room is warm).

Place a large oven-proof pot (including lid)* inside the oven and set the temperature to 425°. Let pot preheat for 45 minutes.
Turn bread dough onto a floured surface and shape it into a ball. Set on a large square of parchment paper and cover with the inverted mixing bowl. Let rise in a warm place for 45–60 minutes.

At that time, reduce oven temperature to 400°. Use the parchment paper to lift the dough and set it inside the heated pot (paper will not burn at this temperature). Cover and return it to the oven, where the dough will bake for 30–40 minutes. Turn off the oven, remove the bread from the pot, and set it on the oven rack. Leave loaf in the hot oven for approximately 30 minutes. Then crack the door and allow bread to cool in oven.

* *I used a 4½-quart aluminum Dutch oven.*

CASSIDY'S ANNIVERSARY CAPER

LIZ MCMULLEN

"Saweeeet." Cassidy mentally high-fived herself for rising before her customary crack of noon. She even made her bed to celebrate the novelty.

This time she was going to have her shit together. She even finished a huge project a week ahead of time so she could take Friday off. Cassidy's boss had looked at her cross-eyed when she handed over the deliverables so early, but today was important. She wasn't going to let anything get in the way of her showing Mazy how much she loved her.

It was their six-month anniversary. *How often does that happen?* "Once in a lifetime," Cassidy said around a mouthful of toothpaste. Cassidy was a consummate flake. Her longest relationship was a whopping two weeks long, and that was back in college.

Cassidy had even managed not to kill the herb garden Mazy gave her on her thirtieth birthday. Mazy was an amazing cook, and actually used the herbs from the garden. She always left little surprises in Cassidy's fridge, claiming she did it so Cassidy wouldn't starve, but Cassidy knew it was more than that. Food was love.

Today was Cassidy's chance to pay Mazy back with her absolute favorite meal: roasted turkey, homemade cranberry sauce, and mashed potatoes with enough butter to make a cow squeal.

"Do cows squeal?" Cassidy asked the delicate stalks of dill she carefully cut from the planter. The rosemary was a little harder to liberate—the stems were thicker and the blades were soft to the touch, but stubborn.

Her cell phone broke her concentration as it growled and barked like a rabid dog. "Oh fuck!" She had chosen a Rottweiler losing its shit barking as a ringtone for her high-strung, bitchy-butchy-bottom of a boss.

Cassidy temporarily abandoned the rosemary battle and answered. After listening to her boss's full-on freak fest for a good ten minutes, she interrupted, unable to contain her horror.

"You stripped the content of Harper's entire website?" The very same website that she designed and handed over with a proverbial bow on top. "How is that even possible?" Cassidy palmed her forehead so hard, she was pretty sure she dented her skull, and she was torn between the desire to vomit up a week's worth of food or curl up in a ball, and sob like a baby. "You can't strip the formatting from the entire site. That tool only works one page at a time."

"I used the strip tool on the back end. I thought I could start over... " Dorian trailed off.

Normally "strip" and "back end" in the same sentence would have tickled her, especially coming from Dorian. "You thought you could recreate nine months of work from scratch? How?" Cassidy paced, and alternately tugged on her hair and bit her lip to keep from screaming.

"I had the PowerPoint you made for the proposal, and um—the File Manager had all the project videos and images files. I tried to use the backup but the file corrupted—"

Cassidy's brain tuned out at "corrupted" and all she could hear was, "Wa womp wawa wa," like she was trapped in a demented version of a *Peanuts* cartoon. She didn't remember squeezing them, but the dill and rosemary were a crushed mess. Blades and delicate fronds stuck to her bare feet and her toes felt fuzzy.

Maybe her boss was wrong. She had to be.

"I'll fix it," Cassidy mumbled. Dorian squealed so loud she had to pull the phone from her ear.

So much for getting a jump on things. The Champagne, lollipops, and unicorns had left the building. First things first. She needed a gallon of coffee, a carton of Tums, and The Force to turn her anniversary around.

The grinding coffee beans made enough of a racket that she indulged her desire to scream some truly masterful curses. That bitchy-butchy-bottom better come through with a whopper of a bonus next month, or it was *on*! The shrill whistle of the kettle was yet another opportunity to get her fuck-my-life shout on. Once her jumbo French press was brewing, she stalked off to the bathroom, leaving a trail of crushed herbs in her wake.

She set the shower to scalding, hopped in, and belted out Taylor Swift's "Shake it Off" while she lathered her hair. Her mood darkened, and "Shake it Off" morphed into a rendition of "Bad Blood" that would have put a drag queen to shame.

Once she dried off, she needed to find some special armor. Her favorite battle T-shirt was so wash-blurred you could barely make out the slogan: *Stand Back! I'm going to do Science*. Black jeans and a broken-in pair of Doc Martens polished off her "I'm going to kill my boss" outfit.

Cassidy papered the wall behind her monitor with printouts of the Harper Industries PowerPoint, along with site map diagrams. They looked like crime scene photos. "Don't psych yourself out, you can do this," she muttered. After an hour of triage in Dropbox, she decided to take a break. It was a quarter to eleven. There was still time to shake her flake reputation and give Mazy the anniversary she deserved, and she'd start by sweeping up the dill and rosemary from earlier, but the greens were too fresh and wouldn't cooperate. "Fuck it," she swore aloud. "I'll deal with that later."

She caressed the blue-glazed planter Mazy made for the herb garden. The surface was rippled but smoother than wood grain. Every time Cassidy saw it, she felt loved, then briefly guilty for never cooking with the now mature plants. She was going to change that, like, yesterday and she'd start by picking whole new herbs for dinner. This time she managed to harvest dill, rosemary, thyme, and basil without incident. She opened the fridge and reached for the turkey. It was solid as a rock. She closed the refrigerator door, and opened it again, willing it not to be true.

"Holy shit. Why the fuck did I buy a frozen bird? Am I insane?" She picked up the fowl bowling ball and plunked it in a pan, nearly denting the rack meant to cradle the turkey an inch above the pan's bottom.

The skin of the turkey was somewhat thawed and didn't protest the olive oil and fresh herb rub she had prepared. Cassidy thought about putting it in the oven now, on really low heat, but the meat would probably dry out near the surface and be raw-as-fuck inside.

The Golden Delicious apple perched on the windowsill taunted her. She was supposed to stuff it inside the turkey to keep it tender and moist. "Christ, how the hell am I going to get the guts out of the bird when it's frozen? You think Elsa makes house calls?" she asked the apple. "Did she even know how to thaw stuff?" Cassidy had never seen *Frozen*, but doubted Disney was going to get her out of this one.

She tried sweet-talking the turkey. "So, I know I'm about to get really personal, and I'm totally sorry for going into your privates and all, but Mazy really loves…" *Sure, tell the dearly departed bird you just want to stick your hand up her butt. Be still her no longer beating heart.*

Cassidy tried tugging the paper out. No dice. Clawing and prodding only produced ooze-covered bits. She did her best Dr. Paul Nassif with some skewers and tongs. No luck. "Fuck fuckity fuck! Guess they won't be hiring me for *Botched* anytime soon."

"Don't. Force. Anything," her PopPop's voice taunted her from the beyond.

"Fine." She huffed and left the mutilated mess, washed her hands, and returned to her office. It was nearly one. If the site was not up as promised, Cassidy could kiss their biggest client goodbye. Theodore Harper was a technophobe, not a surprise for an octogenarian. The man was magical when it came to computers—he could induce error messages even Apple Support had never heard of. The "HTTP 404 Not Found" alert would send him over the edge. It was the internet equivalent of "Your call cannot be completed as dialed, please hang up and dial again."

Cassidy finally nailed down the basic website navigation. Now she had to populate the site with text, images and video. Piece of cake. Cassidy tugged at her hair and regretted it when she found a squishy piece of turkey guts in her bangs. She gagged, ran to the bathroom and...didn't hurl, but it was a close one.

The strains of P!NK's "Slut Like You" trickled into the bathroom from the hall. It was her best friend Lorna's ringtone. Cassidy jogged toward the living room, skidded on dill, but managed to grab her cell without taking a shitter on the kitchen tile. "Huuh-hello?"

"Tell me the truth, do I need to call Lombrusco's?"

"Oh, shit. It can't be three already." Could it? Lombrusco's was the ultimate Italian deli and caterer, though she doubted they could produce what she needed before Mazy got home from work.

"What happened this time, slick?" Lorna's Bronx accent was thick, made worse by her two-pack-a-day habit.

"Dorian managed to strip the coding from Harper Industries' website." She wanted to strangle Dorian, force her to fix this or foist it onto another project manager. But there was no way anyone else could pull this off. "It has to go live by the corporate launch at 8 a.m. tomorrow morning or we're toast."

"Why on *earth* do you let sassy pants touch the files?" Lorna coughed up something that was probably Discovery Channel worthy.

"Still got the flu?"

Cough. Coughity, cough. "Do want me to arrange dinner for you?" Lorna asked, apparently ready to make Lombrusco's an offer they couldn't refuse.

It was three-fifteen. She had to make a choice. "No, I'm going to—"

"You're going to blow off your client for Mazy?" Lorna paused for dramatic effect. "Mama, call off the novenas, I think Cassidy might have successfully removed her head from her ass."

"A lit candle or two can't hurt. But, yeah, I'll text Dorian. It's her mess, she might as well do her own fancy footwork."

"'Atta girl." Lorna hung up. She was polite like that.

Cassidy washed her hands and returned to the kitchen. This time when she dug for gold in the turkey, she felt the innards give a bit. She gripped the waxed paper with one hand and braced her other on the turkey's chest. She tugged, hard. The guts popped out so abruptly that she lost her footing, fell on her ass, and skidded backward into the center island. Cassidy crashed into it with such force, she expected to see cartoon bluebirds tweeting above her head.

Once her brain stopped rattling around, she got up and went for three points and sank the wax papered alien in the trash bin across the room. Cassidy's hands were hazmat worthy, so she scrubbed them while singing a short song her mama taught her to ensure she had washed them long enough. Once her hands were taken care of, she decided to let the turkey sit in the pan while she started on the side dishes. She peeled and quartered the potatoes without incident, then set them in a pot of water to boil. Even the cranberry sauce prep went off without a hitch.

After she set the mixture of fresh cranberries, sugar, and orange zest to cook over low heat, Cassidy went back to her office to continue trying to salvage Harper Industries' website. Her fingers were starting to ache from her rapid-fire keyboard shortcuts, but she was finally making headway embedding the video files.

The smell of burnt sugar and acrid cranberries curled up her nose. "Ack! Why do I always forget when I'm cooking something?" She sprinted to the kitchen. She should have known better and set the timer on her cell phone.

The saucepan was gurgling like a witch's cauldron and the cranberries had popped and splattered the wall, ceiling vent, and stovetop.

Without thought, she grasped the pan handle. "Fuck!" Cassidy yelped and dropped the gurgling pan into the pot of boiling potatoes. Somehow she managed to jump back in time to avoid a scalding splash.

"Holy shit, Cassidy? Are you okay?" Mazy stood in the doorway to the kitchen, her expression caught between shock and barely restrained hilarity. She was wearing grease-stained jeans, a filthy T-shirt, and had a smudge of oil on her jaw. She was the sexiest thing Cassidy had ever seen. Burnt hand forgotten, she headed for her beloved, skidded on herb bits, wobbled a bit, but managed to keep her feet under her.

"Hey, baby," Cassidy said as she went in for a kiss.

Mazy gently held her at bay. "We're both filthy. Let me make sure nothing is going to catch fire first." She seemed utterly impressed with the chaos, but true to form, made sure things were under control. She was practical like that. Cassidy needed more practical in her life. A dollop of common sense couldn't hurt, either.

After she'd checked things over, Mazy shooed her out of the kitchen. "Meet me in the bathroom and start the shower. I'll grab the aloe plant and fix you up when I get there."

Cassidy's hand was throbbing, her head hurt, and she was absolutely filthy, yet she was happy. Really, truly happy. One thing she loved about Mazy was her ability to remain calm. No yelling, no telling Cassidy how foolish or careless she had been, she just took charge and returned the world back to normal.

Cassidy stripped off her shirt and laughed at the slogan, *Stand Back! I'm going to do Science.* Stand back was right, she thought. She had her pants and underwear around her ankles when she encountered a problem. There was no way she could remove her combat boots on her own. They were laced too tightly to loosen one-handed.

"Hold on, I'll get those." Mazy appeared, gracefully knelt in front of Cassidy, and untied the laces. "Lean your good hand on my shoulder while I tug these babies off."

Mazy removed the last of Cassidy's clothes, then whistled.

"Hey, I'm not a sex object," Cassidy teased with mock anger. She looked at her sexy knight in shining armor and blushed. "Well, maybe I'm *your* sex object."

Mazy winked and did her own strip tease, though in a much more orderly fashion. She even folded her filthy work clothes before setting them on top of the laundry basket. When Mazy was nude, she retrieved the aloe plant from the doorway. "Geez, babe, did you have to hurt my favorite hand?"

"Sorry, I wasn't thinking. It all happened so fast."

"Thinking's overrated. Let's get you wrapped up and then we can shower." Mazy cracked open a thick aloe blade and squeezed. The sickly yellow-green sap smelled terrible, but it would work wonders on the burn. Mazy wrapped Cassidy's hand, first in nonstick gauze, then an ACE bandage, and finished by taping a bag around the bandage to keep it dry while they showered.

Cassidy's hand was throbbing, but it no longer felt like her flesh was going to peel clean off, a definite improvement. "Thanks, babe."

Mazy started the shower, then returned to Cassidy's side. "Honey, what the hell happened out there? You're not the best cook, but—"

"I got distracted by work." Cassidy shrugged.

Mazy helped Cassidy in the shower.

Cassidy did her best to keep her hand out of the spray as Mazy soaped up her short hair. Cassidy moaned at the feeling of Mazy's strong fingers as they massaged her scalp. "God, that feels amazing."

Mazy rinsed the shampoo out, then started in with the conditioner. "I thought you were off today."

"I was." Cassidy explained the Harper fiasco.

"Why didn't you just restore from Time Machine?"

Cassidy blinked hard. How could she forget about Time Machine? She jumped out of the shower, skidded on the tiles but kept going. "No way it can be that easy."

"Hey, where are you going?" Mazy scrambled out of the shower.

Cassidy stopped and look back at her. "You're a genius. I gotta see." The hair conditioner stung her eyes, and her hand hurt, but she had to know.

"Here's a towel." Mazy tossed it at her and Cassidy managed to catch it with her good hand before it dropped to the floor. She wrapped it around herself and moved quickly to her desktop. She did her best not to drip her bagged hand on the keyboard as she clicked on the clock icon and entered the Time Machine. Dozens of Finder windows fluttered by on a backdrop of the universe, each new window stacked in front of the last. She selected Thursday's date, and the Finder windows scrolled like an old-fashioned arcade movie reel.

There it was, the Harper project folder in all of its glory. "Hot damn!"

Mazy wrapped her arms around Cassidy from behind. "What do I get for rescuing my favorite damsel in distress?"

Cassidy turned in the circle of Mazy's arms, and used her good hand to draw her lover down for a slow, luxurious kiss.

"That's a good start." Mazy hummed happily against her lips, then broke away when they both needed air. "How about we finish that shower?"

"You could talk me into it," Cassidy said as they returned to the bathroom.

The shower was slow, tender, and beyond sweet, but they didn't get hot and heavy. Mazy said shower sex was far too hazardous, especially with one of Cassidy's hands out of commission.

Once they dried off, Mazy removed the plastic bag from her hand, then kissed her bandaged fingers. "You need to take better care of yourself."

"I know."

Cassidy's stomach growled loudly. Mazy laughed.

"Ugh, I'm starving," Cassidy complained as she toweled off, which was more than a bit tricky one-handed.

"I can help you with that," Mazy said with a sultry tone in her voice.

Cassidy shivered, but took a step back. Mazy was beyond appetizing, but not what she needed at the moment. "Real food," she protested.

Mazy chuckled, "Oh, I know. I brought some food home. Lombrusco's."

Cassidy clapped her hands in happiness, then regretted it. She sucked in a pained breath.

"Hey, hey. No messing with my good work." Mazy kissed Cassidy's injured palm, then wrapped her arms around her. Cassidy sighed, completely content, and allowed Mazy to dress her in a fresh T-shirt and boxers.

"Thank Lorna," Mazy said. "She called from her iron lung to let me know you were experiencing technical difficulties."

Cassidy stiffened. She hated being talked about behind her back, especially when she knew her friend and her lover were right on the money. "Cooking or work?"

Mazy pulled her back into the hug, then massaged the muscles in Cassidy's lower back. Cassidy didn't realize she was stiff until Mazy "Magic Hands" Malone worked a few knots loose. "Does it matter?"

"No. Thanks for everything, baby." She was lucky, and shouldn't go sourpuss, not on their anniversary. "Can I convince you that I'm so pitiful, I need to be fed?" Cassidy pouted and fluttered her eyelashes in a way that she hoped was appealing.

"I'd feed you anyway. I love watching you *eat*."

What started as a shiver became a shudder. Just one word could set her brain into meltdown mode. "Mazy." Cassidy wasn't ashamed of the neediness in her voice. It had been a rough day.

On the coffee table, Mazy set up mozzarella, speck—prosciutto's smoky cousin— seasoned olives, roasted peppers, sundried tomatoes, and other things Cassidy didn't have a name for other than *yummy*.

Two hot-from-the-oven loaves of Italian bread lay snug in paper sleeves. "Mother of God. How did you manage to bring home all the bread you bought?" Bread from Marie's Bakery was irresistible, and the fact that both loaves were intact was a testament to Mazy's self-control.

"Love. True love." Mazy smirked, her brown eyes so damn sexy that Cassidy pressed her legs together briefly.

Mazy raised an eyebrow. She could be insufferable in all the best ways.

Cassidy wiped a runaway dribble of olive oil with the back of her hand, then continued to stuff her face. Even one-handed, she made a huge dent in the elaborate spread.

"I got lucky for sure, but what about the kitchen?" Cassidy asked. That mess needed a Brillo pad, a bottle of bleach, and a blow torch. Cassidy wondered if Mazy could borrow one from the garage.

"There is one good thing." A thoughtful look crossed Mazy's handsome face.

"Oh, yeah?"

Mazy's expression was grave. "You're lucky you didn't do this to *my* kitchen."

"Yes, thank God I didn't do this to *your* kitchen." Cassidy crossed herself twice for good measure, because Mazy's kitchen and her chef's garden were her babies. Heck, she wouldn't even let Cassidy peer closely at her knife collection, never mind do the dishes. Mazy had a system for everything, and if a system got Cassidy out of having to do the dishes, well, all the better.

The fragrance of seasoned olive oil drew her attention back to the food. Cassidy had no idea how hungry she was. She would have made a Hoover vacuum proud. During the chaos of the day, she'd forgotten to eat. It took her a few moments to realize Mazy was not only done, she was watching Cassidy indulgently.

"Are you ready for your present yet?" Mazy asked.

Cassidy smacked her head, then squeaked in pain. "I forgot to get you a present. Well, dinner was supposed to be your gift." Cassidy huffed in frustration, then rubbed her temple with her left hand. "I'm sorry. I wanted today to be perfect."

Mazy leaned over and kissed Cassidy on the nose. "You're perfect."

"Am not," Cassidy said with a pout.

"Imperfectly perfect." Mazy stood, and Cassidy enjoyed the view. Mazy was tall for a woman, and her long, lean legs were nearly as hot as her full ass. It was what Lorna would call "a butt you can bounce a quarta offa."

When Mazy returned with a tiny, navy blue jewelry box, Cassidy felt guilty and more than a little nervous. Six months was pretty damned amazing as far as she was concerned, but marriage? Cassidy was *not* that kind of lesbian. She looked into Mazy's sexy sable eyes. Well maybe she was. She should just open it and stop freaking out.

"Open it up and stop freaking out."

Sometimes Cassidy wondered if she had thought bubbles above her head. She was especially suspicious when her exact words escaped her lover's lips.

"It's not what you think, but you'll like it." Mazy cupped the side of Cassidy's face and kissed her, a mere brush of lips that was over too soon. "Go on, it won't bite."

The hinges on the jewelry box were tight, and creaked when Cassidy opened it. A fresh set of keys rested on the plush cream fabric. The silver key ring was simple yet classy. Cassidy's eyes welled up. She had given Mazy a key to her place early on, but Mazy hadn't reciprocated, and to be honest, at the time she was cool with that. To get the keys now? Cue waterworks.

Mazy gently wiped away Cassidy's tears, and kissed her wet lashes. "I love you, Cassidy, and I want you to know you are always welcome in my home."

Cassidy was trying to stave off the ugly cry, and figured some humor might help her through the ache in her chest. "But not your kitchen."

"Oh for the love of God, never my kitchen." Mazy's grin was lopsided. "I love you, but I love my kitchen more."

Cassidy fake punched Mazy in the shoulder. "Glad you have your priorities straight."

"I do," Mazy replied simply. Never one to do things in halves, she put one arm under Cassidy's knees and used the other to lift Cassidy into her strong, capable embrace. Mazy managed to navigate all the slings and arrows Cassidy created mess-wise that day, even the puddle just outside the threshold of her office.

Cassidy blushed when Mazy placed her on the bed like a conquering hero. Which in many ways she was. "My hero," Cassidy declared without an ounce of teasing.

Mazy looked away for a moment, hiding her flushed face. Her shyness touched Cassidy deeply and she tugged at Mazy's arm with her good hand, and drew her into a sweet, breathless kiss. Cassidy looked up at her lover and said the sexiest thing you can say to someone. "I trust you."

"Oh, Cassidy." Mazy joined her on the bed. They lay side by side. "See, you're perfect. Just like I told you."

Cassidy closed the distance between them and brushed their lips together, then murmured, "So soft."

Mazy hummed in pleasure.

Their kiss was luxurious, passionate and above all else, tender. Cassidy leaned back. "You're perfect too. Happy six-month anniversary."

Mazy smiled. "Next time, we'll cook dinner together."

ROASTED TURKEY

Ingredients:

14 to 16 pound fresh whole turkey

3 to 4 cups homemade chicken soup

½ cup of fresh chopped herbs (dill, rosemary, thyme, and basil)

Salt and pepper to taste

3 tablespoons of olive oil

1 Golden Delicious apple

Directions:

1. Preheat oven to 375 °F.

2. Chop the herbs, then mix with olive oil to create the turkey rub. Add salt and pepper to suit your taste.

3. Remove and dispose of the turkey's innards.

4. Rest the turkey on a rack, within the roasting pan.

5. Rub the herb and olive oil mixture on the turkey.

6. Make shallow slices into the skin of the apple, then insert the entire apple into the turkey.

7. Simmer the chicken soup until it is warm, then turn off the heat.

8. Put the turkey in the oven and periodically baste it with broth from the chicken soup.

9. Bake turkey for 3 to 3 ½ hours (approximately 13 minutes per pound), until the meat thermometer inserted into the thickest part of the breast reads 155 °F.

10. Remove the turkey from the oven and cover lightly with aluminum foil. Let it rest for 15 to 30 minutes before carving.

POTLUCK CLUB

REBEKAH WEATHERSPOON

I FINALLY GET TO REECE'S apartment. I'm really late, but it's okay. I always bring the dessert, so really I can come toward the end of the night, and be greeted like a queen by fifteen drunk femmes craving sweets to go with their booze. There are so many things I hate about social media, but sometimes a Facebook group is so right on the money that you can't say no.

I joined our city's FemmeOnFemme group, hoping to meet a few girls and get opinions on new outfits, but then Allison1 wanted us to get together and Cay suggested we have a potluck, and Reece offered to host it. And then she offered to let us come to her place once a month so we could do it again. Ten months has resulted in some great food, some shitty food, a few new couples, some very sloppy hookups (not me; a few of the other girls), and a group of new friends.

Cay answers the door when I knock and I get a kiss on the cheek, and then a few more, and one-armed hugs and hugs and hugs, as I make my way back to the kitchen. I've brought a two-part dessert with a little assembly required.

Reece is in the kitchen with D and Allison2. I'm happy to see D and Alli2. I give them a squeal and a cheek kiss each.

I can't even look Reece in the eye. The minute I realize she's there, standing next to the fridge with a glass of something sparkling in her hand, my whole face gets hot. And my ears. My fucking ears are hot and my hands are tingling. I clutch my plasticware even harder. Even though I can't really look at her, I see everything she's wearing: green Bermuda shorts, and a pink V-neck and matching sandals. She has a fresh haircut, a nice fade with crisp lines edged above her temple and she's finished the look off with diamond studs in her ears and lip gloss that matches her shirt and shoes. All that and I'm looking at the icemaker instead of her blinding smile with the adorable gap.

"You made it," D says as I move over to greet Reece with a one-armed hug that lasts a little too long.

"It's so good to see you," Reece says under her breath, and it drives me crazy. She gives the best hugs, so I have to force myself to pull away a little. If I don't, we'll be slow dancing or I'll end up just humping her.

We only see each other once a month. She's an attorney and I teach fifth grade at a charter school, and tutor test prep two times a week. Potluck Club is the only dedicated time we all have to see each other, so I know she means it when she says she misses me. She always means it. She's my friend, a good friend. We mean a lot to each other, but I think, sometimes, in completely different ways.

"Likewise," I say 'cause it's safe and "Ohmigod I spent all night thinking about your boobs," might freak her out a little. I extract myself from the embrace I've wanted for the last twenty-nine days and turn back to D. "I did make it!

Traffic was crazy and then there's the part where I left my house, like, five minutes ago." That earns me a few laughs. Reece laughs and I want to die. I still can't really look at her, so I pick a spot just beside her head, but I can tell that she's actually looking at me and she's smiling.

I put my stuff down on the counter. "So I have everything. I just need a knife."

"Oh, here." Alli2 is closest to the utensil drawer so she hands me a knife, but Reece is still there looking at me.

"What did you bring?" D asks as I turn back around and pop the lid on the container.

"Snickerdoodle cake cookies with vanilla frosting." I hear some groans of ecstasy behind me, but I laugh them off. "I think they might be a little dry, but the frosting should solve that problem."

"You said that last time with the cake pops you made," Alli2 says.

"And the time before with the brownies," D throws out there.

I turn and flash them a little smile. "Listen, I just likes my shit moist, okay?"

"Oh, we know you do." Alli2 laughs. "I'll be right back. Bathroom."

"I'll come with you," D says. "I have to go too." As if Reece has multiple stalls in her one-bedroom. They both disappear, leaving me alone with Reece, and I don't know what to do.

When I first saw her picture online, I did a triple take. Reece Farrell is so beautiful, she seems fake. Not fake, stuck up or disingenuous, but fake like there is no way sperm and egg actually come together to make human beings that gorgeous in real life. And I've seen her without makeup. When I'm makeup-free, I look like my grandma after a few drinks. Reece looks like she's advertising one of those makeup cleansers.

I'm not the only one who finds Reece attractive, not by a long shot, and I'm not the only one who's madly in love with her. Raquel asked her out right when Potluck Club started, but they only lasted a month. Raquel dumped her, which made no sense to me at the time, but it turns out they actually made a terrible couple and decided just to be friends. Allison1 had a crush on Reece for a few weeks, but changed her mind when Meesha asked Allison1 out instead. They were moving in together in a few weeks. All the other girls at least hold some type of lusty admiration for Reece, but like me, I'm sure they keep their thoughts to themselves. And that just leaves me and my fantasies about what it would be like to Potluck and Chill with Reece.

I take the knife and start scooping icing into the decorative bowl that fits snugly in the center of the decorative platter I may have purchased just for Potluck Club.

"How have you been?" I ask Reece. I know she's still behind me, and I can be normal with her. I'm great at being normal with her, though the looking at her part is hard. And the not drooling part. And the part where I wish she would ask me to marry her so we can adopt matching Pomeranians and start a black lesbian book club.

"Good," she says, her voice bright and light and beautiful. I wanna kiss her so freaking bad. "So, I had a funny conversation with Meesha before you got here."

"Oh, yeah? What were you guys talking about?"

"Meesha told me what you said."

"Told you what?" I ask as I finish arranging the cookies that are actually perfectly moist around the bowl of icing dip.

"She told me what you told her the last time you guys were over."

I turn and finally look at her perfect face. She's sporting this flirty, kinda knowing smile, but I have no fucking idea what she's talking about. I got pretty drunk at the last meeting of Potluck Club. So drunk that Raq drove my car home with me in it. And I talked so much shit during the party, like about how Cay isn't actually cooking anything, just reheating stuff she finds in the frozen section of Vons. I also told Meesha how much I now love Brussels sprouts, thanks to Allison1's dedication to reinventing the vegetable in different ways every month. And then I—

"She told me that you think I'm cute, but you were too afraid to say anything."

"I—I didn't mean it like that," I say with the most neurotic laugh ever as I turn back to my cookies and icing. "I mean, we all think you're cute." More neurotic laughing. I'm gonna throw up. "Why do you think we all come to your house? It's not for the food." Hahahahahahahaha.

I've told Meesha a lot in the last few months. I think out of the whole group, she's my best friend, but here's the thing that Meesha doesn't know. She doesn't know that my last girlfriend was my first. She doesn't know that my ex is the kind of person who has followers, not friends. Hangers-on that are so afraid of her that they go along with everything she says. Shana was nice in theory, and she was nice to me, at least while we dated, but she has one of those personalities that feels cruel if you cross her.

167

I thought we broke up because she wanted things that I didn't want, and then she told our friend horrible things about me and she also told them I'm terrible in bed, that I'm a horrible kisser. Why my kissing skills have any bearing on maintaining our friendship, I'll never understand, but my sudden loser status means that I am the part of the former pair that is to be left in the dust. At one point, I was so mad that I got up the nerve to confront Shana about it, and she told me it was true. I'm an awful kisser and bad in bed.

I thought she was just being cruel at first, but then something in her tone changed and she told me she thought I would get better and she knows how shy I am and she didn't have it in her to tell me she wasn't enjoying our intimate naked moments together. And then she brought up specific instances, like how when I got up the nerve to go down on her that Fourth of July in the park. I thought I'd exhibited some of my best tongue work because it only took her, like, three seconds to come. But she'd faked it so I would stop. I've never made her come, she tells me. She just used my hand or my mouth, or my leg or my pussy to get her off the way she liked. She thought it would hold her over, but it didn't.

So that's where my head was really at when I told Meesha I have a crush on Reece, but I didn't tell her that. I pulled her aside in the hallway beside the bathroom—that's why D and Alli2 went together; it's a great gossip hallway—and told her how hard it is for me to be around Reece and that I probably shouldn't be drinking, but my crush on her is so massive and out of control, I'm liable to say something that will scare the shit out of her and have me effectively expelled from Potluck Club forever.

"Oh, okay," Reece says, and laughs a little again. And this is why I like her. She knows I'm gonna vomit all over this dessert if she keeps pressing the issue. I'm anxious all the time and very shy. Teaching is easy because I love my kids and they love me because I'm nice and I don't yell like the other fifth grade teachers. Kids are easy, other adults are hard.

Meeting the girls online helped me open up because I could delete my awkward responses before I hit send. But having new friends or a job I like doesn't change the fact that I can feel Reece looking at me still, or the fact that my ears and my chest and my face feel like they are on fire.

"Well, if you know anyone who has a real crush on me, let me know. This life as a single lady lawyer isn't as exciting as it looks on TV."

I turn around, my platter of treats gripped in my hands. "All set."

Reece just smiles and leads me out to the living room. The girls rush me and I barely get my hands back as I set the platter down on our little buffet table. Fiona sees that I still don't have a drink of my own and quickly helps me remedy that situation. I pound the Champagne while Fiona watches and laughs then refills my glass. I make my rounds, catching up with everyone as I stuff my face with mini quiche and stuffed mushrooms and little pieces of spicy fried chicken that Sarai brought. They're delicious, so I eat five or six more, before I gently steal Meesha from the chatter and herd her toward the bathroom. I might be a little drunk again, but I need some booze in my system to confront her properly.

I close us in the bathroom and she smiles at me. "You look so cute. What's up?"

I look down at my dress. There's a little spot of sauce on my boob. Meesha hands me a piece of toilet paper before I can freak out about that too. "Crap. Thanks."

"So, what's up? Are you drunk again?"

"Yes, but that's not why we're in the bathroom. You told Reece?"

"That you have the heavy meat sweats for her? Yeah."

"Oh, my God. I get here and that's the first thing she says to me."

"Did she tell you what *she* said to *me*?"

"No."

"She said that she likes *you*. She thinks you're cute as hell. She brought you up. I was just confirming facts on this situation I know to be true."

I sigh and sink down on the tub. This should be good news. This should be great news. It took me a long time to get over Shana. I should be ready to date again. I *am* ready to date again. But I can't pretend for one second that I am ready to date Reece.

"Why aren't you out there talking to her? Why are we in here?"

I feel like I'm going to cry and I'm sure it's written all over my face. I'm almost twenty-seven. I shouldn't be weepy and nervous over the idea of telling someone how I feel about them. Meesha sits down beside me and takes my glass out of my hand.

"What's going on?"

I tell her about Shana and everything that Shana said after we broke up.

"That sounds like utter vindictive bullshit to me."

Meesha might be right, but Shana was already in my head. I would diiiiiiiiiie if I actually got a chance with Reece and it turns out she thinks I'm just as lousy at all things sex.

"I just feel like a fucking idiot," I say.

Meesha rubs my back. "Have you tried the kabobs Cay brought? She didn't cook them, but she brought them."

That brings a smile back to my face. "Yeah, I had two."

"We're all proper pigs. I love it. Here's what we'll do now. We'll go out there and I'll create some type of diversion and we can act like this sad bathroom session never happened, and then later I'll tell Reece she should back off maybe until you're ready." She says it in a rush, like her mouth is trying to catch up with her brain.

"No, don't do that. I mean, go for the diversion, but don't say anything to Reece. I'll talk to her." And I will. I just don't know when. I follow Meesha out, and she starts screeching about how good all the food is and it makes me smile. The rest of the night is fun. Laughs, booze, food. My cake cookies are a hit. Next month I'll have to do something more. Reece and I carefully avoid each other. It's not cruel, just cautious. I'm afraid I'll say something stupid and she's afraid she'll scare me away.

I'm sober enough to drive home, and after I wash my face I get online and see the little green dot next to Reece's avatar. I feel like I have to say something more.

> *Thank you for having us over again. And sorry I'm the most awkward person ever.*

She messages me back right away.

*You're not awkward at all. You're adorable.
And I host because I can't cook.*

*It seemed like a no brainer to have you guys
bring me food every month.*

I think back and realize I've never seen anything but
take-out containers in her fridge. As hostess, she just offers
to provide the alcohol. I've never questioned it.

I can't really cook either.

*You sure about that? Those cookies were
freaking delicious.*

*I can bake. Baking is different. The last 8
times I tried to do anything that resembled
putting a real meal together have turned out to
be complete disasters. You'd be horrified if you
knew how many hard-boiled eggs I eat per week.*

*Doubt it. My body is 90% pizza and Thai
food.*

I add an *LOL* and then *One of us should learn how to cook.*

We could learn how to cook together.

I see what she's getting at, but I don't know how to
respond. I must be taking too long in Internet time because
she messages me again.

That was me asking you out.

I don't take much time when I reply.

Why?

Because I like you a lot, Talia.

You might not want none of this. I'm a bad kisser.

>: (Says who?

My ex.

Did your ex ever tell you how she liked to be kissed?

It's a good question and the answer is just a little disturbing.

No.

Did you tell her how you like to be kissed?

No. We never had that conversation.

Sounds like the communication there was bad. Maybe don't take her word on your kissing skills. And come over tomorrow night for dinner.

Okay, she's really asking me out. Reece. Reece is asking me out. There go my ears again, and I think I'm going to gnaw a hole in my bottom lip.

Okay. I'll be there. What are we cooking?

Hmmmm. Let's see.

We spend the rest of the night sharing links to recipes and laughing about how bad we'll surely fuck them up. After a while my heart stops beating out of my chest and my ears stop overheating and I'm just talking to Reece and I love it. We decide we should make dinner and dessert together. I'll get the ingredients for my cake cookies. She only got two during the party. She'll make meatball sandwiches.

The next night when I arrive, I actually look Reece in the face. Still so pretty with that cute-as-hell gap in her smile, but I really look at her. I get a cheek kiss that smells faintly of tangerine, but no hug, which is fine. I just need to focus on breathing. It's nice that she's happy to see me.

I hold up the bags I've brought as she ushers me to the kitchen. "I hope lemon cake is okay this time. I wanted to try something a little different."

"Lemon is great. I started on the meatballs." I step onto the kitchen tiles and look around the bright room. She more than started. There are two dozen neatly formed meatballs resting on parchment in the center of her small island.

"These look amazing."

"Let's just hope we don't burn them."

"Then we'll have lemon cake dinner."

I set my bags down, but before I can get everything set up, I feel Reece behind me. I turn around slowly and there she is, dressed down this time, just a T-shirt and skinny jeans, but she still looks amazing.

"I'm glad you came," she says. "But I was wondering if we could get one thing out of the way first. You have to tell me how you like to be kissed."

I look at her lips, wonder if they taste like tangerine too. All of this is a little too good to be true, but my common sense tells me not to blow it. This is Reece. Reece, who is a good friend, and Reece, who asked me out and stayed up almost all night with me laughing about the dumbest things. Reece, who always welcomes me into her home with good hugs and great friends and equal parts silliness and tenderness. I like Reece, plain and simple, and I don't want to screw this up.

"I don't know," I say. "You've never kissed me."

"Oh, that was smooth." She smiles. "I like to be kissed slow. Lots of tongue, though. Lots."

I'm sweating and my ears are hot again. "You might have to show me."

Reece comes close and gently backs me against the counter. She kisses me, nice and slow, and even though it takes a few seconds, there's definitely some tongue. I don't know if this is what she means by lots, but I like it. I kiss her back just as slowly, trying to match her pace and every move. She does taste like tangerines. It's her lip balm and, God, her lips are so smooth. More smooth than my ears are hot. Or my face, my chest, my thighs. I feel myself slipping, my enthusiasm getting the best of me. I lean in closer to her, and then closer, and then I pull away.

175

We're both out of breath.

"What's wrong?" she asks.

"Nothing. I just—I didn't want to swallow your face."

"Not to worry," she says, her gaze drifting down to my lips before she focuses back on my eyes. I can see just how brown hers are. "I liked what you were doing."

"Did you wash your hands before you came to the door?"

Her smile. The gap. So cute. "Yeah. Why?"

I grab her hand and pull her back to the living room "I can't hook up around food. It's unsanitary."

She practically cackles, but doesn't resist.

We're the couch together and I kiss her this time, pausing a moment to ask her one thing. "Please tell me if I'm doing something wrong."

"I will," she says. "I promise."

She kisses me again and then the kissing turns into something else. She's pushing me back against the cushions and sliding her hand up my dress. She's rubbing me and rubbing me over my underwear and I'm so wet it's almost embarrassing, but just almost because I don't want her to stop. I never want her to stop. I grab her wrist and show her what more I want, and I can feel her smiling against my lips.

"Am I doing okay?" she asks, and I realize she's taking my forcefulness as course correction, but it's not. Oh, God, it's not.

I shake my head and flop back, rolling my shoulders. I still have my hand around her wrist. "No, no. You're too perfect, I just—I get excited."

"I'm just teasing you, Tal," she says, but then she pulls away. I watch as she stands and gets completely naked and I'm completely okay with it. She's my height—average— but in the way that I'm average everywhere else, she's soft and round, her brown skin this perfect shade of sun-kissed and god-loved. I think she intends to climb back on top of me, but that won't do. I take her hand and gently shove her down so she's occupying my seat on the couch and then I sink between her legs. I think maybe at first I have something to prove, but I don't. I loved Shana once and now I like Reece. I think I could love her too, so when I gently spread her thighs and take in the damp curls that greet me, I see that there's nothing to prove. I just want to make her feel the way she's made me feel. And I want to taste.

I'm so glad when I do. She's so wet, and so sweet and tangy, practically gushing as I move my fingers around. I look up and her eyes are closed, but she's making this sound. It's the best sound. I could listen to it all night. I'm all fingers and tongue, fingers and tongue, asking her every so often if she likes what I'm doing, even though I'm able to admit that I'm not exactly skilled, I'm just doing what feels right. And she nods frantically, she begs me not to stop.

I think she comes. (I do want to slap Shana for that. She was a damn good faker.) Reece's leg shoots out over my shoulder and her thighs tense against my hands and she groans in a way that is not entirely human. Before I can really understand what's happening, she leans forward and cups my face and kisses me, hard this time, not soft, but with lots of tongue. I think she might eat my face, but it's a completely fitting end to my short life. Talia Winters. Educator. Amateur Baker. Swallowed Whole By The Beautiful Hostess of Potluck Club.

Reece pulls down the straps of my sundress and my bra and frees my tits and then we're both on the floor and shoving the coffee table out of the way. She leans down and tries to devour me some more. She's rough, but holy shit it feels so good, the way she's gripping me and licking and biting at my nipples. I think I might come just like that, just that way, my shoulders press into her light beige carpet, my dress around my waist.

But her other hand finds its way up my skirt again and she looks up at me.

"How many fingers can you take?" she asks through her own panting.

This is not the time for me to try and do logistical math, but I offer my best answer. "Three, maybe. Four."

She just smiles and goes back to sucking my nipple between her plump tangerine lips. She's so slick about it, so smooth and effortless, but she goes from one finger to three and the difference feels so good, I come a little. A slight shiver shoots through my pussy, sending more shivers all over my body. I want more of that. Much more. She can tell. Reece relinquishes ownership of my boobs and we're kissing again, and I'm riding the shit out of her hand. When I come I think I see the other side. There are angels and my other grandma is there giving me a thumbs-up and all of my old cats are just happy to see me.

Finally, I come back to myself, but I'm not done. I pounce on Reece and we are just sloppily riding each other into the carpet. My underwear is still being held to the side by my determined buttcheek and my dress is all in the way, but we don't care. It's been forever for me and I don't know how long for her and I've been wanting this with Reece for months, and I don't know how long she's been wanting me, but we don't let up until we know we're both being ridiculous. We need food and fluids.

I flop on the carpet beside her. "We should have cooked *before*. I'm starving."

She lightly pokes my ribs. "I didn't give you enough to eat?"

"Oh, wow." Her laugh makes my ears hot again. "What do you think will take longer, ordering pizza or actually getting up and starting the sauce and finishing those meatballs?"

"Don't care," she says and she scurries to her feet and finds her phone. "Thank God for delivery apps."

I move back to the couch and fix my clothes as her thumbs move across the screen. Eventually one of us is gonna have to learn how to cook.

MEATBALL SANDWICHES:
THE EASY WAY

You'll Need:
1 lb. ground beef
1 lb. ground pork
1 lb. ground lamb
Bread crumbs
Parmesan cheese
A "splash" of whole milk
1 jumbo egg
Italian seasoning
Salt
Pepper
Olive Oil
Sauce from the jar (I said the easy way)
The crusty bread of your choosing
Sliced provolone cheese

Preheat oven to 400 degrees F.

Combine all the meat, the bread crumbs, parmesan cheese, milk, egg, and seasonings in a bowl. Mix thoroughly. Spend the next 40 minutes regretting all of your life choices as you roll the mixture into two-inch balls. Fry meatballs in olive oil. Set aside on paper towels to drain extra grease, then add to sauce from the jar. Slap as many meatballs that will fit on your crusty bread, cover with sliced provolone cheese. Slide into the oven for 4 minutes or until cheese melts. Enjoy!

Make 4 to 6 sandwiches.

SOMETHING SALTY, SOMETHING SWEET

EMMA WEIMANN

New England, Summer 2001

VERA YOUNG SIGHED AND WIGGLED her toes. A whirlpool was one of the finest inventions ever, especially if situated outside and far, far away from prying human eyes.

Being someplace where nobody demanded anything from her was just what she needed. The whiny cicada song had a mellow quality tonight, helping her to let go of all the shit that had happened at work these past weeks. She enjoyed how the water's warmth seeped into her bones and made her drowsy. Finding time to take a break was a luxury in her life, since there was no doubt she was an adrenaline junky. Being a partner in an international law firm was something she enjoyed but ever since meeting Maddy, her priorities had slightly shifted. Work wasn't everything anymore.

Maddy, whose legs were longer than Route 66 and whose tongue was sharper than the kitchen knives she used as a chef. Maddy, who had brought new joy and meaning to Vera's life. Maddy, who had planned something special for the first evening of their vacation.

Yes. Life was good.

Vera put her head back and closed her eyes, letting the memory of their afternoon together wander through her mind—the long walk, the wonderful picnic, the kissing... Thinking about the teenage-like foreplay they'd had in the car earlier made her horny. Well, hornier than she had already been.

Being able to enjoy the slow, dull pulse that bordered on an ache around her clit was wonderful—simply because she knew that later tonight she would enjoy slow sex, teasing sex, wonderful "let's take all the time in the world" sex. Making love with Maddy was fun. They had brought a bag full of Maddy's toys, some of which they'd never used before. The thought increased the pulse between Vera's legs. A lot.

"Hey." Maddy's soft voice caused a shiver of delight to run down Vera's back.

"Hey, yourself." She drank in the sight of the woman who had stolen her heart.

Dressed in blue jeans, a dark blue button-down shirt, and moccasins, Maddy looked as comfortable in her skin as any human being possibly could. She had aged more than well, and nobody guessed her to be in her mid-fifties. Maddy's gray hair accentuated light blue eyes that always reminded Vera of a perfect summer sky.

"It's time. You can come...inside," she said with a teasing smile, holding out a fluffy bathrobe and a towel.

A tingle raced through Vera. She knew that smile. It was a promise that made her dash out of the whirlpool and nearly fall over her own feet. "I'm really looking forward to see what my personal chef has come up with."

"It's only going to be a secret for a few more moments."

Maddy began to move the towel over Vera's back, her arms, her breasts, making her skin tingle and her insides melt.

Something warm unfurled in her belly and bloomed and spread between her thighs. "You're getting me all wet." Vera's voice sounded rough to her own ears.

"No, I'm helping you get dry."

"That is only true for certain parts of my body." She took the towel out of her lover's hands. As much as she enjoyed this… "If you don't stop we may not eat at all." She was hungry—for both sex and food. "Something makes me think that I need to stock up on energy."

"You may be right." Maddy's smile bordered on evil. "But we'll have a light dinner. Sex on a full stomach is no fun."

Vera sucked in a breath. "We'll have sex." In the most possible dramatic way she put a hand over her heart. "Oh, my."

"Only if you want to."

"If we must, we must." With a laugh, Vera put on the bathrobe.

They entered the cabin together, holding hands.

A whiff of something that smelled of herbs drifted through the air. Vera frowned. The dinner table in the living room was empty, except for the colorful flowers they had picked this afternoon. There were no candles, no soft music playing. Everything looked exactly as it had earlier.

"I want this evening to be something very special for you." There was a slight nervousness in Maddy's voice. She turned towards Vera, never breaking the physical connection between them. "And we'll start in the kitchen."

"You're so mysterious."

She chuckled. "I try my best."

Following Maddy into the kitchen, Vera breathed in the wonderful aromas. A bottle of white wine stood on the well-worn wooden table. Both glasses were already filled. But neither cutlery nor plates were in sight. This was really not at all what Vera had expected.

"Please sit down."

She didn't need to be asked twice, her stomach growling in anticipation. Maddy was an awesome chef.

"Not on the chair."

"But—"

"On the counter."

Vera stared at the counter. It had a stone top and surely would be an uncomfortable, cold place to sit.

"I adore you." Maddy stepped behind Vera and kissed her neck. "And tonight I want to pamper you...and turn you on at the same time." She nipped at an earlobe, before placing feather-light kisses on Vera's neck.

Vera's breathing quickened. "All right."

"We'll eat three courses and all of them contain ingredients that are known as aphrodisiacs." Another nip. This time a bit harder. "And I want to find out if the tales are true."

Shit. This was going to be one evening of sweet torture.

"Come on. I'll help you."

And then, for the first time in her life, Vera found herself on a kitchen counter, dressed only in a bathrobe. Her prim and proper friends would be scandalized.

Maddy put a glass of wine into her hand. "To you, to us, to this weekend, and to life together."

The words were perfect, as was the wine, which had a slight velvety taste.

"The first course was an easy decision." Maddy went to the oven and took out a tray. "The starter is steamed artichokes with lemon-pepper butter." She put the tray down on the counter, together with a basket of white bread, and a small dish filled with some kind of dip. "Did you know that in the Middle Ages women were forbidden to eat artichokes?"

Vera stared at the feast. The smell made her mouth water. "Really?"

"Yes, due to its aphrodisiac qualities." Maddy chuckled. "It was Catherine de' Medici who broke the gender barrier for us. She loved artichokes. And a king."

"I always liked her. Though I would have preferred for her to love a queen. She really missed out."

The skin around Maddy's eyes crinkled as she smiled.

Vera loved every single one of those wrinkles. They were sexy. Her lover was sexy and it didn't matter one bit that there was an age difference of over fifteen years and a lot of grey hair between them. "Come here."

Without hesitation Maddy closed the distance. There was nothing hurried or demanding about their kiss. It was tender, so very tender and promising.

Tracing her tongue around those soft lips, she cupped Maddy's face in one hand. A quiet moan was her reward. "I'll never get enough of you."

The air was charged between them and all Vera wanted was to skip the damn menu and drag her into the bedroom. They could eat later.

"I know exactly what you're thinking about."

Vera grimaced. "That obvious?"

"Yes." Her eyes shone.

"Would it be a bad idea?"

"Any other night, no. Tonight, yes."

"I think the food is working already and I haven't had one bite yet." She let her head fall onto Maddy's shoulder.

"Good. But how about giving it a try, first?" With a smile, Maddy picked a small artichoke up and dipped it into the lemon-pepper butter before holding it out to Vera. "Open your mouth."

She did and groaned. Heaven. This was heaven on her tongue. What a delicious taste, received from those long fingers that knew exactly how to comfort her, to guide her, to play her in the most intimate moments.

Out of reflex, she took Maddy's hand. Then she put those fingers against her mouth. One by one, she sucked in Maddy's index finger, her middle finger, and her ring finger, lathed them with her tongue, and gave each one a parting nip between her teeth.

"You're—" Maddy swallowed hard, "you're not supposed to lead tonight."

"Oh. All right." With a tinge of regret, Vera let go of her hand. "You're the boss."

"At least for now." She winked. "I do have plans for you tonight." With those words Maddy slowly opened the bathrobe.

Vera sucked in a breath as cool air hit her sensitive skin. With fascination she watched how her lover dipped a finger into the lemon-pepper butter and then coated one of Vera's nipples with the lukewarm butter, never breaking eye contact. Her fingertip circled the hardened nipple then darted across the top of the sensitive nub.

"Oh. . ." A glowing flow of heat was running through her blood.

The finger was replaced by a warm, wet tongue and Vera wanted to come right there on the counter. Her whole body pulsed. She ached to grind against Maddy, who chose that moment to break the contact and let go of the nipple.

"No!"

For a moment that felt like an eternity they didn't talk, the only sound filling the kitchen heavy breathing and the ticking of a clock on the wall.

"Yes, sweetheart. Slow. Remember, it's all about being slow tonight." Maddy brought her lips so close to Vera's that it was almost a kiss, but instead of closing the tiny gap that she had left between them, she said softly, "Slow."

"Bitch."

"Maybe, but I'm your bitch."

And there was that smile that Vera adored.

"The main dish won't take long. Why don't you lie down on the sofa and listen to some music. But no touching yourself."

Vera blinked. "You want to get rid of me?"

"On the contrary. But I need to focus on the next course before I invite you back."

Disappointment battled with curiosity. "Then help me down, please."

"It will be my pleasure, m'lady."

Vera walked out of the kitchen with the most provocative hip roll she was able to produce, taking her still half-full wine glass and Maddy's laughter with her. Her whole body was thrumming and she honestly wanted nothing more than to orgasm. But she had received orders. The question was, what else would Maddy serve—for dinner and later, after they had eaten the food?

With a sigh, she lay down on the sofa and closed her eyes. Her whole body was hot and the wetness between her thighs was nearly embarrassing. Sweet torture was probably the best description of what had happened so far.

"Are you relaxing?" Maddy called from the kitchen.

"Yes." She closed her eyes and tried to guess from the sounds exactly what was happening in there. Cutlery. The oven door. What would the second course bring? She sniffed the air. The aromas that were hitting her nose were spicy... maybe fish?

Footsteps approached the sofa.

She opened her eyes.

"Hey, stranger. Are you ready for the next course?"

"Yes." Vera took the outstretched hand and let herself be pulled up. "That was fast."

"It will still be a few minutes, but I didn't want to leave you alone for so long." Maddy planted a soft kiss on Vera's lips. "Have I told you lately how much I love you?"

"You have. I think in the few months we've been together, I've heard it more often than in the nearly fifteen years I was married to Peter."

"Stupid fool. And lucky me."

It wasn't often that Vera thought of her damn marriage anymore. She had been so unhappy, so alone, and so cruel to others back then. Her past had been a time of anger and bitterness, leaving her to think that happiness was a lie. Until

Maddy had appeared and hugged the unhappiness right out of her. "You saved me."

"No," Maddy said. "You saved yourself."

Vera laughed. "Okay. You saved my employees."

"From the bitter witch?"

"Yes, from the bitter, wicked witch."

"I don't think I ever met her. All I met was a wonderful lady with very good taste in food and the nicest laugh I'd ever heard."

"You're delusional."

"No, but I fell in love the moment I saw you."

Vera produced an unladylike snort but otherwise kept quiet. For her, it had been a longer journey. Back then, she wasn't ready to trust anyone and had never thought that the person who would melt her heart and show her true love would be a woman. A woman who had courted the hell out of her.

An alarm went off in the kitchen.

"Ah, the next course is ready. Come on."

Maddy removed a tray of oysters from the oven. This time there were plates and cutlery on the kitchen table. Vera rubbed her brow. She loved oysters. She really did. But she had been looking forward to more foreplay on the counter, to those wonderful long fingers on her—and maybe in her. Eating the main course at the table was somehow... so mundane.

She sat down on a chair and this time Maddy didn't stop her. Well, all she could do was sit and wait for what would happen. She tried to keep the smile on her face while staring at the food.

"I'm sure you've already heard that oysters are considered an aphrodisiac." Maddy smiled down at her.

"Yes."

"One of the reasons is that they are slippery and sensual. Another is that they are able to change their sex from male to female and back."

That was indeed new to Vera. "So they can be male and female, not male or female?"

"Yes. It's said that oysters understand both the feminine and the masculine experience of love. I know how much you love them and that's why we're having New Orleans baked oysters tonight." She put a finger on Vera's nose. "By the way, this is a creole dish and full of delicious spices."

"How do you eat those?" She had only ever had them raw.

"I'll show you in a minute. But first you have to get up, please."

Ah. So there was something more creative to this course than baked oysters. Vera happily rose from her chair.

Maddy took the bathrobe's belt into her hand. "I think that you'll enjoy the oysters a lot." Her voice was low and sexy.

Vera shivered.

"But first things first." Maddy opened the belt and let Vera's bathrobe fall open. "So beautiful and mouthwatering."

Vera's breath quickened as, once again, the evening's cool air hit her skin.

"This time I need more skin." And with that, the bathrobe fell to the floor.

Standing naked in the kitchen before her fully dressed partner was not something Vera felt totally comfortable with. On the other hand, she couldn't deny how turned on she was and how much she wanted to be taken. Right here. Now.

But Maddy didn't touch her. "Sit down, please." She pointed at the table. "The main course is served and we don't want to eat it cold."

With a titanic effort, Vera didn't use the curse that was sitting on her tongue but instead carefully sat down, flinching slightly when her naked bottom hit the cold wood. It really was a good thing that this cabin was so secluded. Just the thought of someone walking in on them... Her, naked on a kitchen table. She couldn't contain her laughter.

"Hey. What is that about?"

"Can you—can you imagine if anyone saw us like this?"

Maddy smiled. "Oh, I can easily imagine how jealous most people would be."

Vera frowned.

"Do you know how many would love to change places with me?"

She could feel the blush on her face. "I don't think—"

"So many people don't even dare to fantasize. Right now, we're living a fantasy." With those words she leaned forward, carefully cupped Vera's breasts, and whispered in her ear, "I want you to know that I have a hard time coming up with reasons why we shouldn't skip right to dessert."

"Yes, why don't we?" Vera's stomach tightened in the most pleasant way.

"Patience, love. I want you to be so turned on for dessert that you can't think straight anymore."

With a wink, Maddy let go of Vera's breasts, picked up an oyster, and slurped it down in much the same way one did with the raw ones. Then she licked her lips, her eyes never leaving Vera's. "Delicious."

Vera bit her lip in an effort not to moan, barely resisting the urge to cross her legs to stifle the throbbing in between. This was cruel. Really, really cruel.

"It's your turn." A small smile. "With the oysters."

"You're lucky that I love you," Vera said with a shaky voice. Then she copied what Maddy had done. The oyster's texture was different but the spices didn't take away from the delicacy. They increased the fun and put fireworks on Vera's tongue. Just the way she liked it.

"And?"

Vera noticed the red tinge of Maddy's cheeks. To realize that she wasn't the only one being affected made her feel a lot more relaxed. "This is good." She slurped down another. "You've really done your best to pamper me tonight."

Maddy winked. "That's true. But we need to prove that these foods really are aphrodisiacs." She slowly brought her hand up and ran a finger over Vera's cheeks and lips. "So moist."

The kiss that followed was more of a brush. Vera got lost in the moment and in the touch.

Once more Maddy slowly broke their connection.

For a moment they just looked at each other. Vera took in the wonderful blue of her lover's eyes, the small scar on her upper lip, and the mischievous smile that was playing around that kissable mouth.

Then Maddy's hands were covering Vera's breasts and next her world was nothing but hands and lips and tongue on and in places that were never mentioned over the kind of dinners she usually had. In between they fed the oysters to each other until they were gone and Vera was a throbbing and whimpering, yet happy, mess. This was absolutely the most fun she'd ever had over shellfish.

"I really don't want to stop, but there is more to come." Maddy's full lips were parted as she took deep breaths.

As much as Vera wanted to kill Maddy for stopping once more, she was curious as to how this would continue. "I—" she cleared her throat. "I fear that whatever is coming next will kill me. Though I have no idea how you could top what you've already served."

"First of all, you have to stay undressed for the next course."

Vera lifted her eyebrows.

"Shall we relocate to the bedroom?" Maddy held out her hand.

"All right." Vera linked their fingers with Maddy's and followed, her knees weak. She had no idea what would come next. Well, dessert…usually. But how?

The bedroom was warm and the huge bed was empty, except for two cushions. The blanket sat on a chair close by.

A wave of excitement rushed through Vera. This looked really promising.

"Please stay here for a moment. I need to get something out of the other oven." With those words, Maddy disappeared.

There was a second oven?

It didn't take long for her to come back with a bowl full of something. "This is not dessert." She picked something out of the bowl. "Please open your mouth for me."

Vera did and groaned. The mixture of sweet and salty was like nothing she had ever tasted.

"Those are bacon-wrapped figs. Their harvest was celebrated by the ancient Greeks with a wild, sexy ritual. Figs are associated with fertility and while I don't expect you to carry my children after tonight..." she wiggled her eyebrows, "I liked the idea of the wild, sexy ritual a lot."

Vera took another one in her mouth, hand-fed by Maddy. It was as good as the first, if not better.

"When I was thinking about what to prepare for dinner, I immediately knew that I had to have these as part of the meal. Wanna know why?" Her voice had gone even deeper than usual.

Vera's heart raced faster. "Yes."

"They are salty and sweet and their taste reminds me of you when I lick you."

"Oh, God," Vera moaned. The fluttering in her stomach spread throughout her body and right into her pussy.

"And now I'll serve dessert but I'll be the one doing the eating." Maddy laughed, a low, throaty chuckle.

Vera's breath caught in her throat. She was shocked at how aroused she was. This wouldn't take long. Not at all.

Maddy stepped closer, wrapping her hands around both of Vera's wrists, their bodies ever so slightly touching. "I love you."

No matter how often she heard those words, she would never get tired of them. "I love you too."

Maddy pressed her soft lips against Vera's. The kiss started off light, tentative even, nearly innocent until Maddy coaxed Vera's mouth open, teasing tongue against tongue before withdrawing.

With shaky legs, Vera found a comfortable place on the bed.

"Now it's my turn." Within moments, Maddy's clothing was scattered across the carpet—button-down shirt, trousers, socks, panties, and bra, all tossed on one pile.

Vera couldn't help grinning as she leaned back. As much as she would have enjoyed a nice, slow striptease, realizing that she wasn't the only one who couldn't wait anymore to feel skin on skin caused a shiver of delight to run down her spine. Maddy was so beautiful. Breathing deeply, Vera let herself fall backward.

In two steps, Maddy was straddling her on the bed. She slowly ran her fingers up Vera's body, from hips to stomach to chest, letting her fingertips graze past her breasts and then went the whole way down again. "I love how you react to my touch." Her thumb slowly circled Vera's clit.

The place between her thighs was an ocean and the ache building inside her nearly made her forget her own name. She moaned and moved, trying to create more friction, more pressure, more anything.

Maddy's fingers dipped into her wetness, started moving slowly, providing shallow thrusts that made sure she wouldn't be able to make it more than thirty seconds without coming.

Vera trembled, her hand making a fist on the sheets.

"You're beautiful." Maddy stopped moving her fingers.

Vera opened her mouth to protest. Her heart was racing and her clit was aching and she needed—

"And now I'm going to taste and savour you. Just like I would with a really good dessert."

The first bold stroke of Maddy's tongue over Vera's throbbing clit nearly was her undoing.

Maddy stopped. "Not so soon. I want this to last a little bit longer."

Vera choked back something between a sob and a scream. "I hate you."

The only reply she got was laughter. Maddy continued stroking her clit with her tongue, but this time the touch was feather light, barely there, teasing her until she wanted to cry and beg.

Vera closed her eyes, bit her lip, and tried to regain her composure, without much success.

"I need more access, honey," Maddy said.

Not wasting a second, Vera curled her right leg over a strong shoulder.

"You taste so good." Maddy hummed while her hands pushed Vera's legs wider to give herself more room, before she started again, with a slow rhythm and a tortuously languid pace.

Whimpering and whining in bliss, Vera weaved her fingers into Maddy's hair and pulled her tighter against her. Within moments, she had lost track of everything in the world except Maddy's touch. "Please," she begged between labored breaths, half-afraid that Maddy was going to stop again.

Her hips involuntarily twitched forward, once, twice and her lover met each thrust willingly. The waves of pleasure crested and crested. And this time Maddy didn't stop.

Vera tumbled over the edge, an explosion in her brain, and a cry on her lips.

As if coming through a daze, she became aware that her legs were unlocked and Maddy's warm body was half on top of her.

Maddy pressed her lips to Vera's forehead. "So, so beautiful."

Vera opened her eyes. Maddy held a glass of water for her that seemed as if she'd magically produced from somewhere. She took several long sips before she was able to croak, "That... this evening...you are the most erotic, wonderful thing I have ever experienced."

Maddy wiped her mouth. "I have some more crazy ideas."

"Yes?"

"Yes." She kissed Vera, who tasted herself on Maddy's mouth. It really was a combination of something sweet and something salty, just like the bacon-wrapped figs had been.

Maddy pulled the blanket from the chair and motioned for Vera to get closer.

She did and leaned her head against Maddy's shoulder and the puffy pillow behind her. Maddy tightened her arm around Vera's waist and it didn't take long until Vera drifted in a state between sleep and wakefulness. She just needed a short break before she would show Maddy that two could play the teasing game.

Maddy pulled Vera tighter against her. "Will you marry me?" Her voice was a whisper, soft and full of desire.

"You...What?" Vera wasn't sure that she'd heard correctly. There was still the sound of waves in her ears from the mind-blowing orgasm she'd had only moments ago. And she was already half asleep, maybe—

"Will you marry me?" It came out in a rush. Maddy took a deep breath. "I know that I'm much older. And I'm aware that this will not in any way be legally binding. But I love you and I want to spend my life with you. I want to make you happy. And try out every aphrodisiacal food in the world with you."

Vera turned around in Maddy's arms. "You really want to marry me?" She couldn't believe it.

"Yes, ma'am."

"You, Maddy Fisher, are the most romantic person I have ever met in my life. And, yes, I will." She moved her hand between her lover's legs and found the wetness she had expected. "But only if I get the dessert this time."

BACON-WRAPPED FIGS

(Served as entrée for four people/five bacon-wrapped figs for each person)

10 fresh figs
10 strips of bacon

Instructions:
1. Preheat oven to 350°.
2. Line baking sheet with foil.
3. Cut the figs in half.
4. Cut the bacon to fit the figs.
5. Wrap one bacon slice around each fig half, and secure with a wooden toothpick.
6. Place figs on baking tray and into the oven for 6 to 8 minutes until bacon is cooked
7. Serve warm.

DESSERTS

SLICED AND DICED

R.G. EMANUELLE

RHEA TAPPED HER FOOT WITH such velocity that the others eyed her with obvious annoyance. She cracked her knuckles instead, but that didn't seem to go over very well, either.

The wait to go in front of the cameras seemed like an eternity. The four contestants for *Sliced and Diced* paced, texted, and did whatever they could to distract themselves. Or maybe they were trying to focus.

Rhea's phone vibrated. She pulled it out of her back pocket and looked at it. It was a message from her sister: *Good luck! You're going to burn them!* Rhea sent a message of thanks, then put her phone back in her pocket. The digital clock on the wall counted down to show time, and her guts did a routine not unlike the last time she had really bad fast food. Her arms began trembling and she hoped she'd get through this day without humiliating herself.

She turned to the door and met eyes with one of her opponents, a tall woman, her back straight and her jaw set. She looked serious and formidable.

The other two contestants included Tim, twenty-something, who seemed brash and arrogant. Rhea knew the type—talented and technically adept, but lacking the vision and diversity that comes with experience. John was perhaps in his forties. She knew his type too—well rounded and skilled, but insecure about going up against the new guard.

Rhea knew that feeling well. In her late thirties, she wasn't too far behind him.

The other woman—Rhea thought her name was Anya—appeared confident, maybe a little audacious, but she also glanced at the clock. They all did. In just a few minutes, they were all going to go out in front of cameras to prove their culinary merit for a $20,000 prize. Even the most die-hard competitor would sweat.

The stagehand gave them the five-minute warning. Rhea's stomach lurched, and the others didn't look as though they were faring much better.

Finally, they were given their instructions: When you hear your name, turn the corner, walk down the corridor and onto the set, and get into position behind a work station.

Rhea seriously considered bolting.

Then she heard her name. Nerves and pride propelled her around the corner. She went to the third work station, and a moment later Anya took the fourth. At least Rhea wasn't the only female contestant. On the other hand, Anya was very attractive, and very distracting. Rhea swallowed. Time to focus.

The hostess of the show introduced herself and ran down the rules, even though they had already been fully informed. There were baskets at each work station containing the secret ingredients required for the first round. From these, they had to create an appetizer for three judges—all renowned chefs—and a presentation dish for the cameras. Upon the signal, they all opened their baskets and pulled out the items.

"Time starts now," the hostess announced with flare, and the four chefs began scrambling for equipment and additional ingredients.

Rhea worked furiously to get her dish completed in the allotted time, and before long her head was pounding and her face was slick with sweat. She had probably never moved so fast in her life.

And just like that, their time was up. She looked at the clock, not really believing that twenty minutes could possibly have passed that quickly. She let out a deep breath and wiped her brow, confident in her plate's appearance. But when she looked over at Anya's plate, she knew she was facing fierce competition. The competitors stood in front of the judges, explained what they had made, then marched out.

Back in the green room, they sat at a stainless steel prep table. Urged to chat for the benefit of the cameras there, the men went on about how they thought they'd done a good job.

Throughout, Rhea kept looking at Anya and realized that despite the intense competition, she was having thoughts that didn't have much to do with food.

"We all did a good job," Anya said. "It's going to come down to something small."

Rhea remained silent. She was having some sort of hot flash but she didn't know if it was nerves, the hot lights, or being around Anya, who was just Rhea's type—and the type she never got. Tall and trim, Anya had green eyes that seemed to spark under the lights. Her spiky hair was dark at the roots but tinged blond at the tips. Lesbian chef haircut number one. And it was really sexy on her.

The stagehand opened the door to bring them back. They waited just outside the green room until the signal to go back on set. Rhea stood right behind Anya, her face at the level of the back of Anya's neck. A sliver of skin showed just below her hairline and Rhea had the urge to kiss it. Instead, she let her gaze wander down Anya's back and shoulders. Her arms were tight in the jacket, a sign of regular workouts, and Rhea wanted to run her hands down both.

When they were back on the set, they lined up for their evaluations. The judges asked each contestant why they were competing. John said he was competing for his family. Tim wanted to open a restaurant. Rhea was next. She, too, wanted to open her own place, a French-style café that featured organic, locally sourced products. That would require a lot of capital. But she also wanted to prove to herself that she was worthy of this industry. She had never won anything in her life and had never really received any special recognition for her cooking, so this win would give her the confidence she needed, and that's what she told them.

Then it was Anya's turn. "I'm competing because my wife, Claire, who died last year, really wanted me to do it. So, I'm doing it for her. And I want to start a scholarship in her name." The looks of sympathy on the judges' faces, the tears in the eyes of one, reflected exactly what Rhea was feeling.

The judges gave their assessments of the dishes, and then it was time to reveal who would be leaving. The hostess lifted up the lid on the presentation plate. It was Tim's. Rhea let out a quiet sigh of relief, but there was no time for celebrating. The entrée round began and the three remaining contestants moved to their stations and opened their baskets. Again, it was a race against the clock and Rhea could think of nothing for the next thirty minutes but getting something prepared. Sweating, her heart slamming in her chest, she dashed around madly, trying to get her dish completed on time. Once again, time was called and Rhea, Anya, and John threw up their hands.

"I think it could go any way, at this point," John said in the green room. "You guys were good."

"I've never been so stressed out in my entire life," Rhea said.

Anya and John nodded.

"Good luck," Anya said, and it sounded like she meant it.

Back in front of the firing squad, Rhea hoped that John would be the one to go. She clasped her hands behind her back and squeezed until her fingers hurt. The evaluation period seemed endless but when the hostess revealed the plate to go, it was John's. His shoulders slumped, and he waved half-heartedly as he left the set.

Rhea and Anya stood face to face in front of the cameras and looked into each other's eyes. For all the world to see, they were competitors, staring each other down before the battle. But for Rhea, it wasn't a stare-down. She dove into Anya's eyes and melted there. And she found something there that was more a glimmer of an invitation than a challenge.

Rhea thought about Anya's wife and that maybe she should throw the competition. Even as she opened her basket and pulled out kumquats, Fruit Loops, and yak butter, she considered Anya's admirable goal. But when the hostess said,

"Time starts now," all noble thoughts flew out of her head. She immediately fell back into competition mode.

As she prepared her dish, she had a vague sense of Anya moving around at the next station. Every time Anya brushed past her to get an ingredient from the pantry, Rhea could feel the heat from her body and it made her tingle. She kept reminding herself that they were in a hot kitchen, busting their asses in a cooking competition. Of course it was hot.

Forty-five seconds to go. Rhea's temples pounded. She got her desserts on the plates, and as the clock ticked the last five seconds, she sprinkled nuts over each.

"Time's up," the hostess said.

Rhea and Anya stepped back from their work tables. Rhea looked at Anya's dessert and her confidence wavered when she saw four beautifully composed kumquat *tatins*. She thought her own Napoleons had worked well but wasn't sure if they were good enough to win. For the last time, they waited in the green room.

"Wow," Anya said. "That was intense."

"I know." Rhea was exhausted and could barely think straight, but the adrenaline in her body made her feel high and alive.

"You're tough," Anya said with a smile.

"You too."

"I really like what you did with the Napoleons. Really nice presentation too."

"Thanks, but I thought yours was better. Cleaner and simpler."

Anya smiled and Rhea felt her insides tighten. She shook off any thoughts that there could be anything between them. What could she offer that would compete with the memory of a woman who'd been so loved that Anya was creating a scholarship in her name? For all the great qualities Rhea might have, she didn't think she could ever measure up.

"Are you nervous?" Anya asked after a while.

"Yeah. You?"

"Sure. But, hey, we made it to the final round." She grinned and it was infectious. Rhea grinned back, though she bounced her knee crazily while Anya closed her eyes and bowed her head on her cupped hands. Rhea wondered if she was sending up a prayer to her wife to help her win. She felt like she was intruding on a private moment.

The stagehand came again to fetch them and Rhea's stomach clenched as they returned to the set where they stood in front of the judges. Rhea's stomach was practically in her throat and electricity seemed to ricochet through her body. She had an urge to jiggle her legs, but she willed herself to stay still. Anya, standing next to her, seemed just as anxious.

After hearing the evaluations of their desserts, it was the moment of truth. One of them was about to become $20,000 richer. Rhea's lungs compressed, sweat dripped down her temples, and her nails cut into her palms.

"Thank you, both," the hostess finally said. "It's time now to find out who's been sliced and diced." She put her hand on the lid and held it for a long, dramatic moment. To Rhea, it may as well have been an hour.

Finally, she lifted the lid. It seemed as if it were in slow motion. First, Rhea saw the rim of the white plate. Then, a hint of food, but still indistinguishable. Then, the whole lid was off and the entire plate revealed the tatin.

It was Anya's. She'd been cut. For a moment, images became a blur and sounds became echoes. Rhea was vaguely aware of Anya walking offstage, and she might have said, "Congratulations," but Rhea wasn't sure.

She snapped back to reality when the judges applauded and one of them asked her how she felt.

"Amazing" was all she could think to say. She shook the judges' hands, thanked the hostess, posed for the obligatory photo op, then headed to the green room to collect her things.

Anya was still there, packing her things.

"You're still here," Rhea said.

"Yeah, I wanted to see you before you left."

Rhea's spine tingled. "Yeah?"

"I wanted to congratulate you again and tell you that I think you really deserve it."

"Thanks. That's really gracious of you."

Anya seemed to hesitate for a moment before speaking again. "How about a celebratory drink? On me."

Rhea thought about it and decided it sounded fabulous. "Sure, I'd love to."

They walked over to a local lesbian bar and ducked in, happy to be out of the unusual April chill. The bar was packed, but after a bit of maneuvering, they nabbed a spot in the corner, where a couple had just vacated.

"Hey, Mira. What's up?" Anya said to the bartender.

"Anya. Long time no see." Mira's smile disappeared as she said something that Rhea couldn't hear. Anya and Mira both leaned in and met over the bar in a hug. Rhea figured it had to do with Anya's wife.

When they had disengaged, Anya turned to Rhea. "What'll you have?"

Rhea quickly glanced at the list on the board. "Celestial Cider."

Anya smiled, then turned back to Mira. "Two Celestials."

While Mira got their ciders, they sat on the stools.

"You have good taste," Anya said.

Mira placed their ciders in front of them.

"People think I should, since I'm a chef," Rhea said. "But, quite frankly, I'm often happy with a pizza, or burger and fries."

"Me too." Anya held up her bottle. "Congratulations. The best chef won."

Rhea picked up hers and tapped Anya's. After they both tasted, Rhea said, "Well, I don't know about best. I won by a hair."

"C'mon. You rocked it. Own it."

"We both rocked it."

Rhea sipped, struggling to think of something to say, though Anya didn't seem bothered by the silence. Rhea didn't want to pry but decided to take a chance. "Um, I hope you don't mind my asking this, but how did your wife pass away?"

Anya smiled softly. "It's okay. I don't mind." She took a sip of cider. "Pneumonia."

"I'm so sorry."

Anya nodded. "Claire was such a healthy person. Really took care of herself. But a fucking infection took her out."

Rhea drank and let Anya continue when she was ready. She glanced down into her bottle.

"She was so excited for me when I was thinking about applying for *Sliced and Diced*. I wish she could've been around to see me on the show."

The cider turned sour on Rhea's tongue. No way could she compete with that. "Well," she said softly as she got up. "Thanks for the drink."

Anya looked at her, surprised. "Oh. I thought maybe we'd grab a bite to eat."

Rhea had lost her appetite. "Thanks, but I should go."

Anya's brow furrowed. "Can I give you a call sometime?"

Rhea wanted to say yes, but getting involved with someone in Anya's circumstances held so many questions. Against her better judgment, though, she gave Anya her number. She rattled it off quickly, hoping that Anya wouldn't remember it. So, before Anya could reply, Rhea grabbed her bag and said, "Take it easy," and picked her way through the crowd. At the door, she looked back at Anya, who had a stunned look on her face. Rhea wished the circumstances were different.

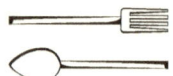

A few days later, Rhea put her cell phone on the table and saw that someone had left a message, so she checked her voicemail. Anya. Damn, she'd remembered Rhea's number.

"Hi, Rhea. Um, I got the feeling that something went wrong the other night. I'm not sure what it was, but I'd really like to talk to you. Would you call me?" She left her number, and Rhea sighed, feeling obligated to call her back. She did, and agreed to meet Anya the next day. It was the least she could do.

They met in front of House of Cupcakes. Anya was waiting for her with two cups of coffee and a bakery bag, which they took across the street to the park. They sat down on an empty bench. Anya handed Rhea her coffee and reached into the bag for a handful of sugar packets. Rhea took two, plus a stirrer, and fixed her coffee.

"Did I do something wrong?" Anya asked, finally.

Rhea's stomach flopped. The only thing Anya had done wrong was to be exceptionally attractive and noble. "Noble," she said.

"Excuse me?"

A dog walker went by, being pulled enthusiastically by two Yorkies and a Dalmatian. When they'd passed, Rhea said, "You're noble."

"I'm sorry, but I don't know what that means."

Rhea stirred her coffee while she pondered what to say. It wasn't just that Anya had competed for her wife, it was that Anya's actions spoke of an underlying selflessness that Rhea felt she neither matched nor deserved.

"You competed for your wife. That was noble. It's a bit intimidating."

Anya looked at Rhea a moment, visibly surprised. "I just did what she wanted me to do. There was nothing noble about it. I just loved her."

"Yeah, and that's the other thing," Rhea said. She tasted her coffee and smoothed out the little paper sugar packets on her thigh. How could she say this without sounding like an asshole?

"I don't think I want to compete with…" Rhea couldn't say it. It sounded awful.

"A dead woman?"

Rhea looked down into her coffee and shrugged.

Anya grinned sardonically and turned to look at a passing jogger. "Wow. I didn't take you for one of those."

Rhea looked up at her. "One of those what?"

"One of those insecure women."

"I said at the studio that I've never won anything in my life. Didn't that clue you in on what a fucked-up, insecure person I am?"

"No. Because you competed like a demon. You plowed through those rounds and you won." She leaned back slowly. "That told me that you're fearless, and you take no prisoners. You're a badass."

Rhea laughed. "I actually debated throwing the challenge for you."

"What? Why would you even think—"

"Because what you were doing—the reason you were competing—was noble."

Anya stared at her then smiled. "Well, I think *that's* pretty noble. I'm glad you didn't. You're a badass."

"I've never thought of myself that way before."

"Well, you should. Don't let the failures of the past keep you from accepting success. In fact, don't even look at them as failures—look at them as prep sessions for success. Because, you know—" she leaned into Rhea's ear and whispered, "You won."

Rhea had been appreciating her victory over the past few days, but with Anya telling her she'd won, it was almost as if she was being given permission to fully enjoy it. She smiled. "Yeah, I did. I still can't believe it. I don't think I've fully processed it."

"Well, process, because you deserved it." Anya sat back again and sighed. "Look, I've been thinking about you since that night. Not just because I didn't know what the hell happened, but also because I really—" She paused, closing her eyes for a moment. "I'd really like to see you again. I mean, if you're single." She cleared her throat. "If not, no problem. I'll back off."

"I'm single."

"Okay, then. So can I see you again?"

Rhea thought for a moment, every inch of her screaming *yes*! But her insecurities extended to women too. She didn't usually get the girl. Not for long, anyway. Then Anya's words kept repeating in her head, like a loop—*you won, you won, you won!* "The thing is, I could really fall for you," she managed to say.

Anya's rose-red lips curled up slightly. "And what's wrong with that?"

"I—I—"

Anya put her hand on Rhea's and moved her forefinger softly against her skin. "You just won $20,000. Why can't you win somebody's heart too? Maybe even mine?"

Holy crap, Anya sure knew the right words to say. The burning in her nether regions was edging out the controlled, cold reasoning of her mind, and the fear in her soul.

"Can we go to my place?" Anya asked. "It's close."

Rhea nodded and followed her home.

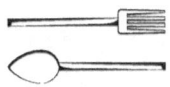

Anya led Rhea to her third-floor walk-up. She had the accoutrements of a chef in the kitchen, but the rest of the house still had remnants of a couple's life. Colorful knick-knacks told of trips taken, and photos showed the smiling faces of Anya and, Rhea assumed, Claire. It made her anxious.

"Relax," Anya called from the kitchen. "I want you to try my new recipes."

Well, if nothing else, Rhea would get some delicious food from a fabulous chef. A few minutes later, Anya emerged from the kitchen. Rhea put down the kiva-shaped incense burner that had "Santa Fe" painted on it and went to the dining table, where Anya had placed a serving tray. On it were two martini glasses, rims beautifully garnished with what looked like toasted coconut. Round white balls on lollipop sticks rested next to the glasses on a separate plate.

"*What* are those?" Rhea asked, her salivary glands reacting.

"First, the drinks." Anya picked up the glasses and handed one to Rhea. "Cheers."

Rhea sipped the drink and thought her taste buds had burst. "Oh, my God. This is fantastic." She licked bits of coconut off her lips and savored their texture between her teeth. "What is it?"

"I call it Coconut Orgasm."

Rhea laughed. "I can see why. I think I'm having one right now."

Anya's eyes glinted with mischief. "Well, let's not rush things."

She gestured toward the sofa, and Rhea sat down with her drink. Anya brought over the tray and set it on the coffee table.

"Okay, now try these."

Rhea felt like a kid getting a special treat. She picked one up and turned it around to admire it. Then she bit into it. Instantly, she tasted coconut, chocolate, raspberry, and hazelnut. She closed her eyes and swirled the flavors around in her mouth.

"Mmm," Rhea said, afraid to open her mouth, lest the tiniest crumb fall out. Before she could open her eyes, she felt warm lips against hers. They were soft and tasted like coconut rum.

Rhea moved closer and let Anya's tongue into her mouth. She slid her arms around Anya's shoulders, careful not to get the stick on her shirt.

The kiss was melting her, so Rhea pulled away. Breathless, she opened her eyes. Anya, gazing at her, face flushed, had a piece of coconut near the corner of her mouth. Rhea leaned in and with the very tip of her tongue, licked it off.

A new kind of hunger appeared in Anya's eyes, and since it was every chef's goal to feed and nourish, that's what Rhea would do. She didn't know if she measured up to Claire in any way, but she didn't want to fight this. Every inch of her ached and burned for Anya. Even if they never saw each other again, she'd at least have a taste. Anya's words about winning her heart had sounded lovely enough, but in the end, Anya might be disappointed. But for tonight, Rhea could feel worthy.

"You have nothing to be afraid of," Anya said, stroking Rhea's face, her voice throaty, desperate, and thirsty.

Rhea set the stick on the tray, then put her arms back around Anya's shoulders. Their lips met in a delicate, light peck and Rhea whispered, "It seems that I'm a fierce competitor."

"There's no competition here."

Rhea looked into Anya's eyes, and believed her. Anya picked up Rhea's glass, took her hand, and led her to the bedroom. Rhea hesitated for a second. Her body was on fire, but her heart was about to be on a platter.

She sat on the bed while Anya rested the glass on the night stand. Rhea chastised herself for not anticipating this and ensuring it would happen in her place, because now she was on *their* bed.

Anya sat next to her and took her hand. She brought it up to her lips and kissed each fingertip, then the palm and inner wrist. Rhea's concerns dissipated in a sea of other sensations.

Anya kissed her way up Rhea's arm, leaving warmth and electricity, and Rhea's stomach clenched in pleasure.

"I'll be honest," Anya said. "I've been out with a couple of women since Claire died, but only a couple of dates."

Rhea braced herself.

"But this is the first time I've felt like it might be something more than that. I hope that doesn't scare you."

Scare her? Being the first person to make Anya feel anything since her wife died? Oh, no pressure. But despite Rhea's fears, she wanted to continue. "I'll be honest with *you*," Rhea said. "I'm scared. I've never been so attracted to anyone in my life. Maybe it's because you're a chef and you get me. No one ever really got me."

Anya smiled. "I know. I feel the same way. And since that's the case, why don't we do some cooking together?" She leaned in and kissed Rhea, deeply and intensely.

Rhea pulled away, teasing. "Like make a pot roast together?"

"I'll make a pot roast with you any time. But right now, I want to give you another coconut orgasm."

Rhea looked at the drink sitting on the nightstand. Anya turned Rhea's face back with her index finger. "A slightly different one." And then she kissed Rhea again, and it felt so good that Rhea wasn't sure how precisely they both ended up naked, but she wasn't complaining.

"Hold that thought," Anya said and she left only to return seconds later with the plate of coconut pops, which she placed on the bed. She cracked one open as if it was an egg and scooped out some of the hazelnut cream, which she dabbed on Rhea's nipples. But instead of sucking it off as Rhea expected, Anya spread some on her own nipples, then applied some of the toasted coconut from the outer shell. She straddled Rhea and leaned over her and Rhea just about lost all coherent thoughts.

Anya's hazelnut-and-coconut-coated nipples hovered over Rhea's face. She never wanted to taste anything so much in her life. She took a nipple in her mouth and the flavors mingled with the sound of moaning, only she wasn't sure if it was Anya's or her own.

One of Anya's thighs ended up between her own and it was then that Rhea realized just how wet she was, and how ready. But she endured the time Anya spent kissing her shoulders and caressing her breasts. Finally, Anya traveled down Rhea's body and put her lips where Rhea most needed them and it didn't take long for Rhea to gasp in release.

"Mmm," Anya whispered. "Beautiful."

Rhea rolled her over and placed herself on her knees between Anya's legs. She leaned over and grabbed her drink. Carefully, she tipped the glass so that some of the liquid ran across Anya's stomach. Anya hissed from the cold and giggled, which was adorable. Rhea brushed the coconut bits off the rim of the glass and let them fall randomly over Anya's belly.

She leaned in and licked the liquid off of Anya, who shivered, before she gently used her tongue to get the coconut.

"You're delicious," Rhea said, smiling.

Anya chuckled. "That's the Orgasm."

Rhea moved back down Anya's body and positioned herself between her thighs. "No," she said, hearing her own voice thick with longing and need. "*This* is the orgasm." Her tongue slid smoothly through Anya's wet folds, but she took her time to savor Anya's salty sweetness. Whenever Anya seemed ready to come, Rhea pulled back and moved to a different spot. Anya whimpered and moaned each time.

Rhea smiled and continued Anya's torment, her own need building again, and as she licked and tasted Anya she began to throb. Anya writhed and lifted her backside off the bed. "Please," she managed. "Please."

Rhea waited a few seconds longer, then slid the flat of her tongue over Anya's clit. Anya arched her back and trembled. She gripped Rhea's hair and let out a long, throaty groan. At the sound of Anya's release, Rhea let herself go and shook as another orgasm ripped through her belly, but she kept her tongue on Anya's clit. She didn't even need to be touched. When they'd both stopped shaking. Rhea collapsed next to Anya and let out a satisfied sigh.

Anya rolled over to face her. "That was amazing."

Rhea smiled. "I take my work seriously. Sometimes." She brushed Anya's breast lightly, making her shiver again. "I really, really like that drink."

Anya smiled. "There's plenty more where that came from." Her expression softened. "And maybe we can make a pot roast together."

Rhea nodded. She knew that they'd be doing a lot of cooking together. She draped her arm over Anya's stomach and fell asleep, thoughts of pot roasts and coconut in her head.

COCONUT ORGASM

¼ cup toasted shredded coconut

1 ounce coconut rum

1 ounce coconut milk

2 tablespoons lime juice

1. Wet rim of martini glass and dip in toasted coconut.
2. Place remaining ingredients in a shaker with ice. Shake well and strain into glass.
3. Drink cocktail.
4. Lick coconut flakes off your partner's lips and other body parts.
5. Have an orgasm.

CLINCH IT WITH COLESLAW

CHERI CRYSTAL

VIV HEADED NORTH OUT OF Brooklyn for a summer respite after a really tough teaching year and what felt like constant carpooling and supervision of her children's homework. Jared, nearly five, and his seven-year-old sister, Jorie, were great kids, but could be a handful, especially if Jorie was in one of her moods. Fortunately, they arrived at their Catskills summer home without killing each other. With a sigh of relief, Viv made the sharp left toward the parking field, kicking up gravel as she searched for a spot.

Once inside the bungalow, Viv opened all the windows to air it out. Jorie and Jared ran outside to play at the nearby playground. Viv checked on them, then glanced past the playground and noticed somebody moving into the Schwartz's bungalow. She forgot about that as she watched a woman wearing a short white tank top that exposed her sculpted arms and ripped midriff. From what she could tell, the newcomer had razor-short brown hair, rugged good looks, and mesmerizing lips. Her cut-off shorts flaunted solid thighs and a shapely butt. Two sullen-looking adolescents sat idle on the bottom step of the porch.

Curious, Viv walked over and the teens left as she approached.

"Hi there," Viv said to the woman. "Need a hand?"

Up close, the newcomer possessed flawless skin, huge blue eyes, and a generous mouth. When she smiled, Viv warmed up right away.

"Hello. I'm Steph."

"Viv. You with the Schwartzes?"

"They couldn't make it and they offered their place, so here we are."

"Welcome. Anything I can do?"

"If you don't mind taking one end of this ice chest, I'd appreciate it." Steph winked and Viv's temperature increased as she flushed, an unexpected reaction.

"It's over here," Steph said.

"What is?" Viv flushed again, embarrassed this time. She'd been caught staring.

"Ice chest."

"Of course. Sorry." Viv wanted to crawl into the chest to cool off before she combusted from the strange heat. "So how old are your kids? They're yours, right?"

"Yes. Jessica's sixteen and Todd's twelve. They've entered the teen years. Jessie's sulking because her best friend is going to Greece. Imagine choosing the Greek Isles over the Catskills." Steph smiled.

Viv chuckled. "I've never been, so I wouldn't know."

"Me neither." Steph gazed into Viv's eyes, and Viv cleared her throat, nervous.

"Husband?" Viv asked, but kicked herself silently for prying.

"Nope. No men. Nothing against them, but I love women." Steph grinned this time, and butterflies flitted around Viv's stomach. "It's just me and the kids," Steph finished.

Viv smiled back. It didn't matter that her new neighbor wasn't straight, but it was refreshing she didn't hide it.

"How about you? Husband?" Steph asked. "Or perhaps *wife*?"

"No, neither, actually. My husband passed away."

Steph's smile faded. "Oh, shit, I'm so sorry."

"Thanks, but I'm fine." That was only half-true because whenever she thought about Matt, guilt ate away at her gut. Maybe it would have been less painful if instead of dying he had simply left her to marry a woman who desired him.

Viv cleared her throat and switched topics. "If the kids are yours, then how did—? Oh, God, never mind. I'm—I don't usually pry."

"It's okay. People ask. Turkey baster with donor sperm. Their dad's a close friend and an awesome father."

Viv didn't know how to respond to someone so candid, so she stayed quiet. As they carried the heavy chest into the kitchen, Steph shot Viv another captivating smile, which flustered Viv. She tried not to show it.

"Thanks. This is good, for now." Steph surveyed the room. "Phyllis warned me it was small, but this kitchen's a joke. I prepare affordable oven-ready meals for busy moms. Good thing I planned ahead." She patted the ice chest. "This will have to do until I can rent a spare refrigerator. Hopefully the electrical system can take it." She handed Viv a bunch of brochures off the table. "Here. Feel free to spread the word. I have a following back home and even cater parties. Judge for yourself."

Viv scanned them, trying not to look at Steph's eyes, which were both unnerving in their intensity and arousing. "I have plenty of room in my fridge," Viv said, "freezer too, if you need more space."

"Are you sure?"

"Matt—my late husband—was the chef. Barbeques and homemade coleslaw are my claim to fame. Convenience items don't use much room. Besides, I shop often rather than stock up."

"There's nothing wrong with that." Steph held her gaze. "I think I need to taste your coleslaw."

Another strange wave of heat hit Viv's midsection. "It's easy to make," she managed.

"If the cabbage is crispy and the dressing is creamy and subtly sweet with a tangy bite, then it's right up my alley. I'd love to see how yours measures up." Steph grinned again, and Viv almost forgot to breathe.

"Oh," she managed. "You would?"

"We should have each other over for dinner."

"That would be nice, but can I have you first? Otherwise, I'll suffer performance anxiety if I have to follow a professional caterer."

Steph chuckled. "Don't underestimate yourself. I'm sure I'll love whatever you serve."

"I can take some food now if you want. No need to buy ice—the closest grocery store often runs out, unless you want to drive a ways to the superstore."

"Perfect." Steph gathered meats and homemade food in jars and plastic containers, filling a few shopping bags. "If you don't mind taking these—" she handed them to Viv. "I'll carry the rest. Lead on." Steph waited for Viv to go, then followed close behind, and Viv tried not to think about Steph watching her walk, but it was impossible. She hoped she didn't trip. She paid extra close attention to her feet, acutely aware of the elastic of her panties riding up her crotch, and the moisture between her thighs.

"This place is cute," Steph said as they entered Viv's house. "You've updated your appliances too. Sweet."

"Would you like a tour?"

"Love one."

Viv obliged, but each time Steph's arm brushed hers, chills raced along her skin and stirred things at her core. She had never been this turned on by anyone, including Matt, and certainly not by a woman, though she wasn't completely inexperienced in that regard, but those were feelings that would have driven Matt away had they discussed it.

"Your wallpaper is nice. Cozy and bright," Steph said. "I like the cornflower blue with yellow and white daisies. It's you."

"Thanks," Viv said, glad for the new topic as they returned to the kitchen.

"Are you staying all summer?" Steph lifted an eyebrow. She moistened her lips, and her eyes seemed to undress Viv. Or maybe she was imagining it.

"Yes."

"Lucky me, then."

"Excuse me?" Viv stopped to regard her.

"You're a stunning woman, Viv. I bet everyone sings your praises."

Viv flushed yet again. "Not really."

Steph tentatively reached out and touched Viv's hair. "Then they're blind." She stepped away and Viv trembled, though it was hot enough in the kitchen to grill a steak without the barbeque.

"So you cook first," Steph said. "A barbeque would be great."

"Okay." Viv's barely detectable voice sounded unfamiliar even to her own ears.

"Good. These steaks are Porterhouse. I prefer fresh but in a pinch, frozen will do, and I had no idea about butchers around here."

"I'm sure they're delicious."

"They'll do. I'll put them in the freezer and the condiments in the fridge and be off to let us all get settled. Thanks again, Viv. Really appreciate this."

After a wave and a confident smile Steph left Viv staring after her, until she summoned the wherewithal to fill a tall glass with water, though it didn't do anything to quell the throbbing between her thighs or the thoughts of Steph's muscular arms around her, hands on her breasts—

"Stop it," she muttered aloud then set to work unpacking the food she'd brought. After she'd put everything away, she picked up one of Steph's jars, each labelled and dated. She'd never tried homemade ketchup or mayonnaise, and she'd rarely sampled homemade pickles, and Steph had a jar of each. The ketchup and pickles had been opened. Would Steph miss the tiniest smidge if Viv tasted it? Probably not.

She took a butter knife out of the drawer and opened a jar. The label said ketchup, but how could it beat Heinz? Nothing could do that. At least not until Viv took her first taste. "Oh. My. God," she said aloud, just as Jorie and Jared barged into the kitchen.

"What's that?" Jared asked. Viv attempted to close the lid before Jared could stick his finger inside the jar. Nothing edible was safe around him.

"Oh, no you don't, mister. Go wash your hands and face. Now, please."

"Do I have to?"

All it took was a stern look and he obeyed. He hadn't picked up the sass of his big sister yet.

"Who was that funny-looking lady?" Jorie asked.

"Excuse me, that's not a very nice thing to say." Viv gathered the flyaway hair off Jorie's face.

"I thought you let a man in the house, but she had boobs."

"Jorie—"

"She *does* look like a man. And walks like one too."

"Just because a person is different doesn't make it okay to make fun of them."

"Whatever." Jorie huffed dramatically.

"What happened to my sweet little girl?"

"I'm all grown up."

Viv sighed. "Well, nice grown-ups don't make fun of people like that. Now please go wash up. We're going food shopping after I make coleslaw for tomorrow."

"Can we buy Twinkies, please?" Jared called out from the bathroom. He emerged, wiping his hands on his shorts.

"We'll see." Viv rewashed and then dried Jared's hands. "Jorie, take Jared onto the porch. Maybe you can play *Trouble* or something. I won't be long."

"The Pop-O-Matic sticks."

"Then use real dice or play something else, please. I'm busy and you're both in the way."

"Chutes and Ladders!" Jared said.

Jorie grumbled, but she took Jared outside, with a board game under one arm and Jared's hand in hers.

Viv eyed Steph's pickles, trying not to be tempted, but it didn't work. She hoped Steph hadn't counted them. The moment she took a bite, flavor exploded in her mouth. Before she ate another, she sealed the jar and placed it at the back of the fridge. It was everything a sour pickle should be: crisp and succulent. And they would taste incredible in Viv's coleslaw. She set to work, but ended up shredding the cabbage finer than usual, and the carrots didn't fare better. At this rate, the store-bought pickles would be mush. At least the commercial dressing was foolproof. In record time her coleslaw was safely out of sight in the fridge beside Steph's pickle jar. Viv and the kids were soon out the door, walking past Steph's on the way to their car.

"Something smells good," Jorie said.

"I think she's baking cake." Viv thought about Steph's strong hands, working on that cake, and hoped her reddened face wasn't obvious.

"Now can we get Twinkies?" Jared said, and Viv smiled.

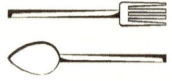

Viv prepared her sticky-chicken recipe for dinner, which involved chicken parts slow roasted in a mixture of apricot preserves, ketchup, and onion soup mix. She served it with potato pancakes she just had to bake, applesauce, and steamed string beans. No fuss. The kids ate most foods drowned in ketchup, and Viv knew her sticky-chickie would burst with flavor doused in Steph's. Maybe she'd ask for the recipe, or better yet, buy a few jars from her, if she sold them. Another good reason to see her.

After the kids were asleep, Viv retired to the porch swing to enjoy the evening. Steph sat on a step next door, taking a drag on a cigarette, blowing smoke rings. She'd changed into cargo pants and a sleeveless white t-shirt. With her legs spread wide, she looked imposing, but inviting. Way too inviting. Viv rose, smoothed her slacks and headed over. Steph met her halfway.

Steph blew smoke away from Viv. "Evening."

"Hi. I didn't know you smoked."

"I don't, but once in a while, I get the urge. It usually passes." She stubbed the butt in an ashtray she was holding. "Technically, I quit years ago." She didn't elaborate. "Kids down for the night?"

"Yes. They played hard today."

"Mine are miserable without electronics. Camp doesn't start soon enough."

"Amen to that."

"Mind if I join you? I have a nice cabernet sauvignon. A gift from a client after I catered his business dinner. Want some?"

The thought of more time with Steph made Viv's heart race. "I'd love some."

"Be right back." Steph left and returned with two glasses and a bottle. She had an army knife attached to her belt and looked every bit ready for anything.

"Sometimes I crave a cigarette with a fine wine," Steph said as she followed Viv to the swing.

"I pegged you for either beer or spirits."

"In my profession, it's handy knowing which wines suit a particular meal. I enjoy beer, but I don't get much opportunity for the hard stuff. Want a cigarette?"

"No, thanks. I quit after I got pregnant."

"Smart. I don't know why I bother." Steph poured the wine and handed Viv a glass.

"Because you like the way it makes you feel."

"There are plenty of other things that make me feel better than nicotine." Steph set the bottle on the floor next to the swing.

"Like what?"

"Like sitting next to you, talking just like this, enjoying the moon and how bright the stars look."

Steph's words made Viv ache. "It's a perfect evening." She took a sip, heart still pounding. "I like sitting here with you too. And maybe this is strange, but I feel like I've known you much longer."

"I'm flattered." Steph sipped her wine. "The feeling's mutual."

The air between them seemed charged, and Viv rushed to fill the space with words rather than something else. "I have a confession to make."

"Oh? What?"

"I tasted your ketchup."

"What? Who said you could?"

Viv started. "I'm sorry. I really, truly am. I couldn't resist."

Steph laughed and patted Viv's thigh, nearly knocking Viv off the swing. "I'm kidding. I'm glad you did. What'd you think?"

"Beyond amazing. You have to sell it."

"I do."

"I'll take six bottles. Your pickles too. And if those are any indication of how your mayo tastes, add a jar to my order."

"You ate one of my prized pickles? I grew those cucumbers in my garden from seeds. And now I see I'm going to have to keep a sharp eye on you, you pickle thief." She grinned.

Viv's throat tightened. She had an overwhelming desire to kiss her. No, more than that. She wanted to get naked with Steph, plain and simple, down and dirty. She took a gulp of wine and glanced at Steph, and the expression in her eyes told Viv that the feeling was mutual. But was Viv ready for that? Steph took her hand and Viv forgot how to breathe for a few moments. She recovered nicely.

"I'm making a barbeque tomorrow night," Viv said. "The coleslaw's ready too. Would you and the kids have dinner with us?" It seemed like ages before Steph slowly withdrew her hand.

"Definitely." She clinked glasses with Viv, swallowed the last drop, and stood. "Good night."

Viv reluctantly handed her the empty glass. "Good night." She watched Steph leave, and practically floated to bed.

The next morning, Viv marinated chicken breasts in barbeque sauce, stirred the coleslaw, sampled some, and was pleased with the results. She husked six ears of corn and by nine-thirty a.m., all she had left to do was cook, serve, and entertain her guests that evening. She and the kids finally managed to agree that the pool, with its new waterslide, was where they would spend the majority of their day.

Viv fretted while putting the finishing touches on her barbeque, and her hard work paid off. Everything from the barbecue chicken, hamburgers, and franks to the coleslaw tasted delicious.

"I have to admit, this coleslaw is excellent," Steph said as she helped Viv clean up. "Care to share your recipe?"

"It's a secret," Viv teased. What would Steph think if she knew about the store-bought ingredients?

"You know I'll get it out of you before the summer is over. Trust me. I'm very persuasive."

Viv smiled and heat raced up her spine. "I have no doubt. But my lips are sealed."

Steph returned the smile, and it was full of promise. "We'll see."

Viv hoped they would, but Steph had to leave to get her kids ready for camp on Monday and Viv had to do the same.

"Thanks for coming over," she said as Steph was leaving.

"Thank you for inviting us." She held Viv's gaze, and Viv saw a lot more than appreciation for dinner there. "See you soon." She squeezed Viv's hand and left before Viv could say anything else.

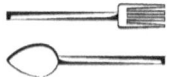

"Hello? Viv?" Steph called from the kitchen. "You decent?"

"Hold on." Decent was a loaded word. Viv wasn't naked, but stepping out of the bathroom wearing an old towel over her shoulders, a ratty T-shirt and capri leggings that were threadbare in the seat might not be decent in some company. She'd have to dye her hair later, clearly.

"Hi." Steph smiled when she saw her. "What've you got?" She snatched the paper out of Viv's hand. Steph glanced at the directions then looked at Viv. "Dyeing your hair? Don't you dare touch a hair on that beautiful head. Your natural color is perfect."

Viv reached for the dye instructions but Steph held it out of reach. "I have some grey hair to take care of."

"A few greys are testaments of a life well lived. And extremely sexy." Steph moved closer. She smelled faintly of cinnamon and before Viv could say anything, Steph's fingers combed through her hair, filling her entire body with sensation. Viv took an abrupt step back and hit her back on the refrigerator door handle.

"Ouch," she yelped.

"What happened?"

"I hit my back on the—"

Before Viv could move away, Steph closed the distance between them and gently rubbed her back. The intimate gesture was unnerving, but wonderful.

"Better?" Steph asked, her breath brushing Viv's face. Oh, God. All she had to do was turn her head and she could kiss her...

Surprised by her reaction, Viv mumbled, "Yes, much better. Thanks."

"I'm serious, Viv," Steph said, still leaning into her. Promise me you won't dye your hair."

"I'm not sure—"

"Please. You don't need to. You're gorgeous."

"I am?"

"Very." Steph smiled, her lips perilously close.

"Well, I was wrestling with the decision when you barged in." Viv smiled, struggling to retain control.

"Sorry." Steph moved away and Viv missed her immediately. "The door was open and I needed a few steaks out of your freezer."

"Oh, of course." Viv opened the freezer, but Steph sidestepped her, draped an arm over her shoulder, and proceeded to point at what she needed. Viv's skin tingled where their bodies touched, and she struggled not to react, a little scared of the effect Steph had on her.

Viv shoved the frozen meat into Steph's chest. "Sorry, but I have to—um, I have to finish some things." And she regretted saying it, because as scared as she was, she also ached to pull Steph against her, and leave the restrained woman she was behind.

"No problem. I have work to do too. Please don't ruin your hair." She said it plaintively, which made Viv smile.

"Fine. I won't."

"Thank you." Steph started to turn away, but stopped. "How about dinner at my place tonight? Are you and the kids in the mood for steak?"

"Um…"

"Come on," Steph coaxed. "It's the least I can do to thank you for the use of your freezer and for the outstanding barbeque. I enjoyed myself last night." Her tone caressed Viv, and there was no mistaking the signs of their combined desire.

Viv stared, not sure what to do. Should she say something about how she felt?

"Hello? Viv?"

"I'm sorry. What?"

"Where'd you go?" Steph frowned, looking concerned.

"Just thinking. Sure. Dinner tonight sounds wonderful," Viv said, her mind made up. "What should I bring?"

Steph smiled, and it lit up her eyes. "Coleslaw, of course."

"Really? Again?"

"I told you I liked it. And I'm going to get the recipe out of you somehow."

"We'll just see about that."

"Yes, we will. How about seven tonight?"

"Perfect," Viv said, surprised at how calm she sounded despite the desire raging through her veins.

"See you then." And Steph left, cinnamon lingering in the air behind her.

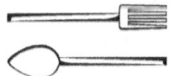

When Viv told Jared and Jorie they were having dinner at Steph's, Jorie clapped, excited. Steph's daughter, Jessica, turned out to be a camp counselor and Jorie liked her, so she washed up without being told, and she even set out a snack of cookies and milk for Jared. She then swept up the crumbs as she told Viv all about their first day at camp.

Unfortunately, Jared fell asleep at the table, leaving Viv disappointed and a little frustrated. She was debating cancelling dinner when Steph came by to collect a few more items from Viv's fridge.

"Uh-oh," she said when she saw Jared. "Camp wore him out."

"He'll be fine for dinner."

"You sure? Jessica can babysit."

"That's too much to ask after she worked all day."

"I'm sure it'll be no problem." Steph said with a smile. "She adores kids and money."

"Let's see what happens first. And Jorie really likes Jessica, for the record. She gushed about her."

"That's nice to hear. And, yes, if Jared's out for the count, let me know if you need her. I'll be off—as it turns out, my brochures for oven-ready meals have taken off. It'll be good to cook steaks tonight because as of tomorrow, I'm going to be up to my eyeballs in preparing Texas-style barbeques. I've already jarred the sauce and wondered if you'd supply that fantastic coleslaw of yours." She winked. "Unless you'd rather divulge the recipe."

"Oh, no you don't. I'll make it, but only if you stop trying to pry it out of me."

"But it's more fun to pry."

Viv playfully swatted her arm and Steph laughed.

"See you tonight. Come hungry."

"I will." In more ways than one, Viv mused as she watched Steph walk. She quickly banished that thought as she had to get some things ready before dinner. At seven sharp, seated at Steph's kitchen table, Viv imagined her and Steph in a fancy steak house. And, oh, Steph's tempura vegetables were to die for, served with chili dipping sauce and delicate lightly dressed greens. Steph grilled Viv's Porterhouse to perfection, and her fries were delectable—dipped in Steph's homemade ketchup, it was a match made in heaven. Even Viv's coleslaw tasted better than usual.

Dessert consisted of Steph's excellent apple tarts, and homemade caramel ice cream.

"To a memorable evening," Viv said as she raised her wine in a toast.

"And many more," Steph added, and Viv really hoped that was the case.

"Let me get Jared and Jorie home. It's been a long day."

"Sure." Steph stood. "We'll eat earlier next time."

"I like that idea. Thank you so much for having us over."

"The pleasure is all mine." Steph gave her a look and Viv took the kids home before she exploded with lust. Though Jared and Jorie went straight to bed, Viv knew she'd be up for hours thinking about Steph. Maybe some rounds of solitaire would make her tired.

Viv's third game was interrupted by a tap on the door. The oven clock read 10:05. Puzzled, Viv padded to the door, and caught her breath. Even through the screen, Steph looked breathtaking, framed by the full moon overhead.

"Hi. What a nice surprise." Viv unlatched the door. "Come inside."

Steph's smile was as bright as the light from the kitchen. She held up a flashlight. "Actually, I hoped you'd join me in a stroll to walk off dinner. Jessica agreed to babysit free of charge."

Viv hesitated. Could she trust herself not to do something rash? And then she suddenly didn't care. "I'll grab sneakers."

"Perfect. I'll get Jessie."

Viv watched her go, heart pounding.

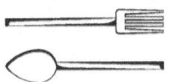

Barely ten minutes into the walk, Steph turned the flashlight off and put it in her back pocket then gently grasped Viv's hand.

"You're shaking. Are you cold?" Steph asked.

"No."

"Scared of the dark?" Steph teased.

"Not at all. You?"

"Nope."

Viv squeezed Steph's hand. "If you are, don't worry, I'll protect you."

Steph laughed, and then silence fell between them, and the air heated with anticipation. Viv stopped abruptly.

"You okay?" Steph asked, turning toward her.

Viv stared at her, the moon brighter than the flashlight, it seemed. And then she moved closer, her desires driving her next actions. Before she could talk herself out of it, Viv leaned in and kissed Steph with an urgency she'd never felt before. Steph tasted of sweet dessert wine, and their kiss deepened until Viv's breath caught as Steph slid her tongue between Viv's lips. She had an aching need for more of Steph's touch, but too soon, Steph paused and it drove Viv crazy.

She was about to beg for more when Steph asked, "What did you enjoy best about tonight?"

"This," Viv replied, breathlessly. "Please continue."

"Gladly. Let's find a more secluded spot." She pulled Viv with her until they came to the barn that served as the camp recreation center, bathed in moonlight. The door was unlocked, and Steph shined her flashlight around the interior.

"Empty. What do you think?"

"Perfect."

Steph placed the flashlight on a table facing the ceiling for an enticing glow as Viv shut the door. Steph pulled her close and Viv sank into the feel of her mouth; arms, and breasts against hers. Every part of her was on fire. But she wanted more. She stepped back and lifted her arms so Steph could pull her shirt off. With a slow smile, Steph then removed Viv's bra and let it drop.

"Oh, God. You're more gorgeous than I imagined," Steph whispered as she stroked and teased Viv's nipples.

"More," Viv said between clenched teeth, her need making her greedy for all of Steph, who fumbled out of her own clothing and in one fluid motion, Steph lifted Viv off her feet and placed her carefully on the paper sheet that covered the arts and crafts table. Steph nibbled along her neck, then lower, covering her nipples with wet kisses.

Viv gasped and shuddered and Steph stopped.

"Are you okay?" Steph asked. "I can stop."

Viv most certainly didn't want to stop, but she had to say it aloud for her sake as well as Steph's. "No, don't. I want this. More than anything." She brushed her lips over Steph's and smiled.

"Me too. You have no idea."

"I think I do." Viv kicked off her sneakers and Steph slid Viv's pants off.

"Oh, my God," Steph said, wonder in her tone. "Beautiful." She slowly removed Viv's damp panties, her fingers trailing along Viv's skin. Viv thought she'd die from want. She held her breath and bit her lower lip to keep from exploding before Steph had a chance to touch her.

"I've been dreaming about this," Steph said, her voice rough and low.

"Touch me," Viv pleaded.

Steph parted her swollen labia, and Viv thought she'd pass out. And then Steph's elaborate, well-placed touches brought waves of ecstasy.

"You're so wet," Steph said, voice husky. "So hot."

Viv had no idea her body was capable of making this much natural lubrication. And then Steph leaned down and went to work with her mouth, combining fingering Viv's G-spot and licking and sucking her clit.

"Oh, God," Viv said with a gasp. She thrust against Steph's mouth, pleasure building, but Steph slowed a little, drawing it out. Fractions of seconds felt like minutes. And then Steph sped up, and by the last surge, aware only of Steph's hot breath, tongue, lips, and a clit about to burst, Viv could barely breathe. "Oh, God—I'm coming," she managed.

Steph slid two fingers deep inside and Viv's orgasm tightened. It felt too damn good to let go just yet. Steph's fingers pumped her and again, Viv's orgasm built, waves of pleasure roaring through her body. Steph replaced her tongue with her thumb and the synchronized movement of her thumb over Viv's clit and her gentle but rhythmic pumping against her G-spot made it impossible for Viv to hold out any longer.

Viv came with an unsurpassed intensity, wrapped around Steph's fingers, crying out her name. When her body stopped shuddering, she collapsed onto the table.

"Oh, my God, Steph, you're incredible."

Steph chuckled softly. "I think you are."

Viv leaned on her elbows and smiled. "I needed that."

"Almost as much as I did." Steph brushed Viv's cheek with the backs of her fingers.

"I doubt it. You had me at first glance."

"I came three times the night we met," Steph said with a grin. Bet you didn't know you've been spending every night with me since then." She pulled Viv into her arms.

"Your homemade ketchup was enough to make me come. And your pickles are orgasmic."

"Pickle thief," Steph said near her ear, in that endearing teasing way that turned Viv on.

"What *really* clinched it for you?" Viv asked.

"Hands down, your coleslaw."

Viv laughed. What a difference it made to follow one's heart. And to think she only had to whip up her coleslaw. Nothing could be more delicious.

VIV'S COLESLAW

Salad Ingredients:
1 head cabbage, shredded
2-3 carrots, peeled and shredded
4-5 sour pickles, diced

Dressing:
½ cup Hellmann's Real Mayonnaise (this is important!), more or less depending on desired creaminess
4-6 ounces of your favorite Italian dressing
Pepper, to taste

Prepare the cabbage, carrots, and pickles as stated above. Set aside in a large salad bowl. In a small bowl, prepare the dressing using a fork or whisk to whip up the mayonnaise and Italian dressing until well blended. Add pepper to taste. Mix the dressing, cabbage, carrots, and pickles until well blended. Cover with plastic or foil wrap. Refrigerate overnight for best flavor or serve right away. Enjoy.

Serves 5-6.

DADDY'S HOT APPETIZER

CK COMBS

I LET MYSELF INTO MY girlfriend's apartment and put my wardrobe bag in the bedroom before stepping into her kitchen. Maureen said hello without looking up from the cookbook she was intently consulting. There was a pile of vegetables next to her cutting board. A roasting pan sat on the stovetop, a gleaming slab of meat in the center, awaiting its plant-based companions. The oven was ticking as it came up to temperature.

She was wearing a brightly colored patchwork apron, which covered her front while her backside was adorned in nothing but a pair of tiger-striped boxers and the apron ties. I thought she'd never looked sexier in the three years we'd been dating. This was an observation I made often, probably every day. She turned to look at me over her glasses, hand on her hip.

"I know exactly what you're thinking and I don't have time for it. Come here and give me a kiss and then get out of my kitchen." She drew me in for a hug and a quick, deep kiss.

Her no-nonsense, bossy tone was supposed to cool me off, but it had the opposite effect. With every finger wag and steely look, I wanted her more. However, my attempt at another kiss was rewarded with a sharp rebuke delivered against an erect nipple. Though normally that would have done nothing but encourage me, I knew better than to push it.

I watched her make quick work of the veggies, piling them into the roasting pan, anointing all with olive oil and red wine. After a quick dusting of seasonings and some garlic cloves tossed into the pan, the roast was ready for the oven. My stomach growled in anticipation. More anticipation was steadily building south of my stomach, with every moment I spent looking at her exposed skin and the way my lover's perfect bubble butt moved inside her boxers.

I needed to watch myself, though. Any other day, I'd be right in the kitchen behind her, pressing her up against the counter and yanking her drawers down. But not today. Today was absolutely not the day to bother her, tease her, or distract her. She'd made that clear when I'd called before I arrived. I could hang out at the house before the dinner party only if I helped and stayed out of the way. As if reading my mind, she gave me a stern look. "No hanky-panky. Plenty of time for that later." Though her voice was playful, she took her hosting duties seriously and I knew better than to interfere with her plans.

A couple of our friends were coming over for dinner and cocktails. One was an ex of mine; both were part of the area kink scene. The last time we'd all been to a play party, the night had ended with the four of us piled on a couch, hatching plans to get together. The dinner party tonight was the first of our ideas to come to fruition. The theme was *'50s Suburban Dinner Party* and we were dressing up for it. My sweetheart and I were going to butch it up along the lines of *Mad Men*, having haunted second-hand stores all over the area for months looking for the right suits and accessories. Our friends were a butch-femme couple, and I was especially looking forward to seeing what my ex—a high femme and retro aficionado—would pull together for the evening.

I busied myself putting the bar together, stealing glances at Maur, who always looked good, but was even more enticing because I couldn't touch her. She caught me in one of those illicit glances, then wagged her finger and pursed her lips while shaking her head. That look said, *I know exactly what you're thinking and you'd better not.* I blushed and looked away, returning to my preparations.

Though martinis would be appropriate, we weren't particularly fond of them, so instead I had acquired supplies for Tom Collins drinks, whiskey sours, and manhattans. From one of the bags I'd brought, I pulled recipe cards and a vintage shaker I'd found at an obscure place on the coast. The gleaming stainless steel shaker took its place with the bottles of booze and mixers, and small containers of garnishes. I had to go back into the kitchen for the garnish sticks. I stood for a moment, waiting for an opportunity to get into the cupboard, admiring the curve of her breast visible under the side of the apron. She turned and gave me a questioning look.

"I need to get the little swords out of that cupboard." I lifted my chin to indicate which one. She stepped aside and I retrieved the box, giving her a light kiss on the cheek.

I set up the bar on the top shelf of her low bookcase, which had been cleared for the occasion. That task completed, I turned to her again. "Babe? The bar is set up. Should I do the music? Or do you need help with something else?"

"Sure... uh, yeah." She was distracted, leaning down to pull a salad bowl out of the cupboard. I had the good sense to keep watching as it afforded me a lovely view of her legs and the way the boxers framed her ass. I had a sudden vision of the night before, when I'd pressed her up against a car on our way from one bar to the next. She'd been worried the owner would discover us debauching their vehicle. I'd told her the best thing to do would be to come quickly before they returned. I'd lifted her dress to discover that she hadn't been wearing panties all evening.

"Surprise!" she'd said before filling my mouth with her tongue while I filled her hole with my fingers.

I must have sighed or let out some other noise while reminiscing because she looked up from cutting salad veggies with her eyebrow raised. I grinned and winked at her, licking my lips elaborately. She scowled at me and turned away but not before I saw the blush spread from her chest to her cheeks.

"What's wrong, baby? Getting too hot in here?" I teased.

"You're a stinker and you'd better stop it before I have to kick your ass," she countered. It wasn't an idle threat—the last time she'd kicked my ass, I had trouble sitting down for a week.

"Hey, I'm sitting way over here, what can I possibly do to you?" I served up my response with a rakish grin and she returned a scowl. I was so turned on by her, by the way her eyes flashed and her jaw tightened when she was perturbed. Besides, I knew she loved this game as much as I did. This was foreplay.

Thinking I should avoid trouble, at least for a little while, I turned my attention to music, figuring out where to place my mp3 player and speakers for best effect. Soon my selection of Miles Davis, Sinatra, Nat King Cole, and '50s pop was filling the apartment. I grinned when Eartha Kitt's distinctive nasal voice came through the speakers with "My Heart Belongs to Daddy." Maur looked at me when the chorus started and smiled. I grinned back and reached down to stroke the crotch seam of my Levis. She narrowed her eyes.

"You are going to get it tonight. I'm gonna make you pay for every distraction," she threatened, sweeping veggie trimmings off the counter and into her waste bowl.

"God, I hope so." I responded with an even bigger grin. Smiling to myself, I picked up my phone, thumbing through social media and email accounts and entertaining her with my dramatic readings of status posts by our mutual friends. I watched as she prepped the second appetizer, shrimp cocktail. The pile of dirty dishes and utensils in her sink was growing.

"Is there anything I can do to help you, honey?" I knew her plan was to have the roast and mashed potatoes finished and staying warm in the oven while she dressed. The shrimp would join the other appetizers and green salad in the fridge, and dessert would go in the oven just before we sat down to dinner.

"Um, yeah, you can peel the potatoes and cut them up for me while I mix the cake batter."

Her apron was hanging from her shoulders and tied loosely at her waist. I had a brief daydream about being that piece of protective clothing, my arms around her shoulders, legs wrapped around her waist. That fantasy shifted to using the apron ties for something more restrictive. The heat rose from my crotch to flush my cheeks. If she'd looked at me right then, I'd have gotten reprimanded again for having impure thoughts. Luckily, she didn't look.

"Can you do the potatoes at the table?" she asked. "I don't have much room in here." She'd begun working on the dessert, pineapple upside-down cake. I took the cutting board, peeler and knife to the table and returned for the bag of potatoes, making sure to brush against her nipple with my elbow. A sharp intake of breath told me I'd gotten to her.

I pulled the garbage can over and began peeling. I barely avoided peeling my fingers a couple of times, since I was watching her more than I was watching what I was doing. Her boxers were large on her and had drooped down in the back, revealing a tantalizing bit of ass cleavage. My mouth watered as I remembered bending her over the night before and licking that very spot.

"Babe, I'm thirsty, do I still have some beers in the fridge?"

"Mm-hmm." She remained focused on measuring the dry ingredients.

I got up and stepped past her to the fridge, reaching around the plate of deviled eggs to get a bottle from the back. As luck would have it, she was standing in front of the drawer with the bottle opener. I leaned lightly against her back and slid my arm around her waist, reaching for the drawer pull. She reacted by stiffening her spine and giving me a sharp glance.

"Just need something from the drawer, babe," I responded with a grin.

She pulled away from the drawer, pressing into me with a sigh. I angled my hips up and she pushed her ass back. I momentarily forgot there was another reason to be there and enjoyed the feeling of her warmth against me as I nuzzled her neck.

She reached into the drawer and handed me the opener over her shoulder. Brows drawn together in concentration, she cracked eggs into her bowl. I flipped the bottle cap off and took a sip, then put the bottle, lid, and opener on the counter behind me. I leaned lightly against her back and watched over her shoulder as she folded more ingredients into the batter. She turned and threatened me with a spatula covered in goo. I kissed her neck, picked up my beer, and returned to my task.

We focused on our work, listening to the music, sometimes singing along. "All Shook Up" came on and I cracked her up with my Elvis impression. She had finished prepping the cake, which she had set aside with plastic wrap over it by the time I finished cutting the spuds. Soon they were in a pot on the stove, warming up.

She had her back turned, consulting her menu. I lightly caressed her spine, tugging on the apron strings on my way down. She leaned back into me and shuddered.

"Oh love, you have no idea how turned on I am," she said.

"I have some idea." I slid a hand up from her thigh to the curve of her waist, enjoying the way she shivered against me.

"Baby, if you don't stop now, I won't want you to, but I'm not quite done yet and I still have to clean up and get dressed... "

Her voice trailed off as I caressed her hips and waist, one hand rising up from her belly to her breasts, the other dipping lower. It was hot like a furnace between her legs and I felt the telltale slipperiness of her arousal through her boxers.

"We've got time," I purred into her ear. "The roast has about 30 minutes left and you can't do the gravy until it's done." Her nipples hardened under my insistent fingertips. "Once the potatoes boil, they can sit for a moment before you mash them." I slid my other fingers inside her boxers. "You watch the pot, and make sure it doesn't boil over or something. Think of this as a form of invisible bondage."

She bit her lip, breathing hard. "I enjoy a good challenge, but if I burn something, it's on you."

"Oh, is that what you think?" I spoke softly into her ear. "I think if dinner burns, it's because you weren't paying attention." I spoke in my "Daddy" voice, hoping she'd want to play.

She gritted her teeth and gave me a dirty look, which made me laugh. Since she didn't give her safeword, I knew the game was on.

I chuckled and kissed her lightly across the shoulder, pulling on the neck strap of the apron with my teeth. Meanwhile, my fingers slid between her wet lips, finding a swollen clit waiting for me. She clung to the counter between the fridge and the stove, eyes fixed on the pot of potatoes.

I stroked her slowly at first, dragging moisture from her hole upward. Every time I brushed by her opening without entering, she whimpered. I chewed the skin of her shoulders and neck lightly, and she moaned as I tweaked and pulled on her nipples.

Squatting down behind her, I pushed my nose into the space between her ass and cunt, inhaling deeply. I never got over how good she smelled, like salt water and honeysuckle. "Mmm, you smell so good, lover."

She moaned in response.

I pulled her boxers down and spread her buttocks open. She tilted her hips to give me easier access. I buried my nose into her cleft, licking her from one hole to the other. She groaned and whimpered while widening her stance.

"Daddy, please. I need you inside me, please!"

I looked up at her face. Her eyes were pressed shut.

"Don't forget the potatoes, love," I teased. Her eyes snapped open, though I wouldn't place bets on her seeing much at that moment.

Nuzzling and licking everything I could reach, I slid my hands up the backs of her legs, keeping my touch firm, then running back down with my fingernails. She gasped. Her knuckles were white as she gripped the countertop. Pulling my face out of her crotch, my tongue repeated the path my hands had taken, lingering every few inches to graze her with my teeth or suck on a bit of her sweet skin. She squirmed a little but stood firm. My hands came up the front of her legs, sliding up until my fingertips rested in the creases where her thighs met her mound. I kissed my way up the backs of her legs, then pushed my nose between them again.

"Oh, Daddy, that feels so good. I want you so badly but I don't want to mess up dinner for our friends. I want to make you proud." She was using her little girl voice, the stern tone completely gone. My arousal doubled in an instant and a rush of moisture surged between my own legs.

"You will make me proud, baby." I nuzzled between her buttocks and used my fingers to torment her clit. "You keep doing your work while Daddy has fun."

"Oh, fuuuuck," was her hoarsely whispered response.

I stood up, leaning against her, pressing my hips against her ass. She pressed back, and reached out to turn the boiling potatoes down to a simmer. My lips were against her ear. "That's a good girl," I whispered. "You always make me very proud, baby."

"Daddy, please fuck me. Please, Daddy, I need it!" Her voice was urgent and rough with desire.

I reached an arm around her belly to hold her against me while I slipped two fingers into her wet hole. She shuddered and gasped, pressing back against my hand. I fucked her hard and fast, rutting my mound against her leg and lightly biting her shoulder. My other hand slid up to pinch her nipples again. We came within seconds of each other and then started again. Once was never enough with us. We were both insatiable for each other. After she came a third time, she opened up so much, I was able to get all four fingers inside her, while my thumb stroked her anus.

That last orgasm weakened her knees and I caught her before she fell. We took a moment to catch our breath. She turned around, grabbed my face and pulled me into an enthusiastic kiss.

"Fuck, I love you." She stared into my eyes, and the heat between us could have fried eggs. "Your turn, Daddy."

Then the timer went off, and we both looked at the oven.

I smirked. "I don't know, baby, are you sure this is the best time?"

She turned the oven off and grabbed me between the legs. "Do you really want me to change my mind right now?"

I sucked in a deep breath as her fingers expertly broke down the feeble resistance I had thought to offer. "Oh, fuck, no, please don't change your mind."

"Hold that thought," she said, pushing me out of the way so she could pull the roast out and set it on the stove. My stomach growled again as the rich, meaty scent of perfectly cooked beef filled the room.

Turning back to me, she pressed me up against the counter and stroked my hardened clit through my Levis, eyes locked on mine. I was ready to climax again when she suddenly stopped and dropped to her knees in front of me. The look she gave me was full of heat and need.

"Yes, baby, please," was my answer to her unspoken question. She unzipped my pants, pulled my briefs and jeans down and pressed her face between my legs. I kicked off a shoe and stepped out of one pant leg, spreading my feet to make more room for her. Her tongue circled my clit and she sucked me into her mouth. My fingers were on the back of her head, petting and gripping her short, buzz-cut hairs. I was lost in sensation, thrusting against her face. Her tongue flicking the underside of my clit hit me like an electrical shock. When she buried her nose in my pubes, I groaned and pressed her against me with a hand on the back of her head.

She knew just how to blow me, licking and sucking, occasionally pulling my swollen lips into her mouth, using her teeth to stretch and pull. Her fingertips stroked my wet hole, and I was overwhelmed by the need to have her inside me.

"Yes, please, fuck me, do it, yes!"

She hit my G-spot with two fingers, sliding in fast and hard, continuing to suck and chew on me. Orgasm hit me and I saw stars, almost falling down, lucky to get my hands on the countertop before my knees gave out.

She pressed her face against my thigh while catching her breath, and I absently played with her hair. She stood and wrapped her arms around me. I gave her a sloppy grin and she slapped my ass lightly.

She glanced over at the clock on the stove and yelped.

"Shit, shit, shit. They're going to be here in less than an hour and I still have stuff to do. And I have to get dressed."

"Let me help you. We'll get it all done together."

She gave me a kiss on the cheek. "Thank you, honey."

Working together, we finished the mashed potatoes and made the gravy. With everything staying warm in the oven, I cleaned up the kitchen while she went to get dressed. I was finishing up when she stepped out of the back room and took my breath away.

Her hair was slicked back and she'd darkened the blond hairs on her lip into a thin mustache. The charcoal grey suit she'd liberated from a vintage clothing store in town sported a crisp white pocket square and her tie was pewter with black diagonal striping over a white shirt. In a word she was gorgeous and my heart was beating wildly in my cunt. A glance at her crotch confirmed she was packing for the occasion. To my eyes, she looked like the hottest drag king ever.

I could do nothing more than stand there with my mouth open like a dumbass, words having vacated the premises at the sheer impossibility of saying anything meaningful.

She looked at my expression and bit her lip, a blush creeping up from her collared neck. "Do I look okay?"

"Oh, fuck, baby, you look... mmm-mmm-mmm. You look so good I can't even find the words."

That made her smile. Then her eyes widened.

"You need to get dressed. They'll be here any minute."

I hustled my butt into the bedroom and got myself suited up and primped just in time for our guests' arrival. Everything went wonderfully, with food, drink, and conversation served up and enjoyed by all. It was very late when we said our goodbyes. I removed my jacket, loosened my tie, and rolled up my sleeves to begin cleaning up.

"Oh, no you don't." She said from close behind me. She turned me around and grabbed my tie. "You're coming with me to finish what you started earlier. Besides, I have to punish you for all the distractions this afternoon."

I smiled as an anticipatory shudder worked its way through my body. What is it about her punishments that makes them seem like rewards?

DADDY'S HOT APPETIZER

One kitchen
Not enough time before a dinner party
A horny Daddy
An aroused and busy cook

Pour together and stir well with fingers. Serve hot.

HONEY AND LEMON

JOVE BELLE

BY THE TIME SHE MADE it home, all Rachel could think about was the blister that had reached epic proportions on her left foot—goddamn new shoes; happened *every* time— and the cavernous ache in her stomach. It was day three of her cleanse. That meant three days of nothing but that damn drink—water with lemon juice, honey, and cayenne pepper—that Juliet had promised was good for them. Three days of watching everyone else eat like normal people while she held up her drink container and said, "Nope, I'm good."

Who was she fucking kidding? She wasn't good. She was starving. And not in the normal, I'm-totally-craving-pizza-with-a-cupcake-chaser kind of hungry. No, there was nothing normal about the way her stomach felt as though it had folded in on itself and was steadily munching on every organ within reach.

It's a good thing she loved Juliet so damn much because this diet inspired all kinds of hate. All she wanted—more than she wanted to take off her shoes and more than she wanted to drag Juliet to their bedroom and work off some of the frustration crawling over her skin like a colony of ants— was to put *something* in her mouth. She wasn't picky. A stray ball of lint from beneath the couch sounded good right now. So long as it had more substance than the damn "lemonade" Juliet had handed her with a smile that morning, she would be happy.

As soon as she cleared the front door, Rachel stepped out of her shoes, dropped her briefcase and keys on the side table, and shrugged out of her overcoat. She let it fall to the floor next to her shoes and stalked toward the kitchen. Juliet was home and cooking something.

Food.

Steak.

And oh, God, those cheesy-bacon potatoes that made her ridiculously pliable. No matter where the conversation started, if Juliet stuffed a forkful of those potatoes into her mouth, Rachel would agree to anything.

A thirty-foot-long trench in the backyard to set ornamental lighting around the planting beds? Yep, she'd agreed to that without a second thought. Until Juliet handed her the shovel, that is.

A trip to her home town in southern Spain because Juliet wanted to meet Rachel's family no matter how many times Rachel told her it would be better to enjoy the sun in Greece instead? Yep, agreed to—and regretted—because Juliet's potatoes made Rachel's common sense depart for regions unknown.

She'd done that and much, much more over the years, for those potatoes, and she hadn't been starving. So, either Juliet wanted something big, or she'd fucked up her cleanse today. Which meant, if Juliet was cooking them, they were guilt potatoes.

Rachel was okay with that.

"Jules?" Rachel called out. Their apartment was enormous. If Juliet was engrossed in what she was doing, she wouldn't have heard Rachel coming in. "Are you home?"

"Mmph-hmm," Juliet said by way of muffled reply.

That bitch has her mouth full. I'm so making her pay. Rachel contemplated all the ways she could torture Juliet for forcing her to do this damn cleanse in the first place. *I'll tie her to the bed and leave her there for hours. I'll read a book,* War and Peace, *and dare her to complain.* She rounded the corner that separated the living room from the kitchen and the aroma hit her viscerally. *But first I'm going to put some of* that *in my body.*

Juliet stood at the stove holding a plate piled high with steak and the cheesy potatoes Rachel loved. A bowl of cucumber and tomato salad sat on the counter next to her. Something Rachel hadn't identified yet sizzled in a pan on the stove. Juliet turned toward her, wooden spoon in her hand, mouth so full her cheeks bulged, and a guilty look on her face.

She set the plate on the counter and swallowed hard. "Hi," Juliet said weakly. "I fixed you some dinner." She gestured toward the plate.

Rachel tried to be stern, but it was so hard to focus on looking like an angry schoolteacher when her body was being drawn forward as if a string ran between the plate and her stomach. She managed to glare at Juliet convincingly enough, but found herself moving forward completely against her will.

The timer dinged just as she pushed Juliet hard against the counter, pinning her body in place with her hips. Juliet whimpered and waved her hand toward the oven, but opened herself willingly to Rachel's kiss. Rachel held her there for a few seconds, one hand resting easily on her hip, the other wrapped tight in Juliet's long dark curls, as she took her mouth in a way that telegraphed her plans for the rest of Juliet's body.

After she ate.

The lingering taste of basil, fresh tomato, and just a hint of garlic in Juliet's kiss brought up a wanton moan from deep inside Rachel. She ended the kiss with a light nip of Juliet's bottom lip and stepped back. Juliet slumped against the counter, her eyes closed, body lax, hair ruffled. Her earlier composure was officially wrecked. Rachel smiled smugly.

"What's in the oven?" Rachel asked as she casually snatched a bite of the potatoes Juliet had made special for her. *God, so good...* This, Juliet's way of feeding every single one of her hungers perfectly, was exactly why she loved this woman so damn much. She took another forkful and held back the groan of appreciation that threatened to escape. She refused to show how much the damn cleanse had affected her.

"Hmm?" Juliet opened her eyes. Her pupils were blown wide, blocking out all but the outer ring of brilliant blue that had initially drawn Rachel to her all those years ago.

Rachel poked her fork at the oven. "What's in there?"

"Oh." Juliet's eyes cleared and she stood up straight. "Shit."

She smoothly slid the sauté pan off the burner and opened the oven door at the same time. She pulled a batch of twelve perfect chocolate cupcakes from the rack and set it on the granite counter.

"So... I take it the cleanse is over?" Rachel asked, no longer trying to hide her pleasure. The food was too delicious, and Juliet looked too perfect as she tried to pull herself back together.

Juliet had the grace to give her a sheepish smile as she popped the cupcakes from the pan and placed them on the rack to cool. "I'm sorry. I just couldn't take it."

When Juliet had proposed the whole idea, Rachel had known then that her wife had lost her mind. Juliet loved three things in life—Rachel, food, and the cabin her grandmother willed to her when she died. Juliet was a chef, for Christ's sake. How she'd expected to avoid food for ten whole days was a mystery.

Instead of laughing outright, Rachel arched an eyebrow—a practiced move developed over years of living with Juliet—and said, "Oh, really?"

She slid another forkful of potatoes into her mouth and then, before she finished properly chewing, added a bit of salad to the mix. Normally, Rachel prided herself on her table manners. She was an executive with an image to uphold. At the moment, however, she pushed food into her mouth at a gluttonous rate.

Juliet spooned mushrooms in brown sauce over the steak, then started cutting it into bite-sized pieces. As she worked, she nodded. "I don't know how people do it. I mean, it's *food*. How am I supposed to say no to this?" She slid a generous portion of steak and mushroom into Rachel's mouth.

A large part of their initial attraction to one another had been food-based. Juliet loved to cook and Rachel loved to eat. Early on, Juliet had learned the power of food in their relationship. No matter the sin, all was forgiven when Rachel ate. She was simply too happy to hold a grudge. Fifteen years later, that still held true.

Rachel closed her eyes and savored the complementary flavors of steak and mushroom as they blended with the remnants of bacon and cheese from the potatoes. God help her, she'd need an extra hour at the gym after this meal, but she didn't care. When she finished, swallowing with a decadent moan, she opened her eyes. Juliet was staring at her, bottom lip sucked between her teeth, eyes dark and filled with illicit intentions.

First, Rachel checked the stove to make sure everything was turned off, then she pulled Juliet to her for a bruising kiss. She'd missed this—the all-consuming buzz of electricity that arced between them—as much as the food. Maybe more. Their passion for one another had ebbed by degrees every moment they continued Juliet's damn cleanse. Rachel was glad to be done with it, and done with holding back her longing to hear Juliet moan her name as she fell apart under Rachel's touch.

She squeezed Juliet tight, letting her fingers dig into the soft flesh of Juliet's ass. Juliet moaned, a desperate, wanting sound that Rachel associated with gloriously naked, sweaty skin. Because she couldn't do everything she wanted in the kitchen, Rachel broke the kiss. She grasped Juliet by the wrist and tugged her in the direction of their bedroom. "Come on." She kissed Juliet again because she couldn't *not* kiss her. "Bring the food."

On her way past the fridge, Rachel grabbed the bottle of "lemonade" that she'd survived on for the past few days. She was glad for the return to real food, but that didn't mean all was forgiven. In the bedroom, she activated the accent lighting only. The wall sconces provided a soft, diffuse glow that provided just enough light to move easily through the room. And, because she didn't want the neighbors to be a part of their afternoon fun, she closed the blinds.

Rachel set the bottle on the chest of drawers with a careful, decisive movement and turned to face Juliet. Her hands filled with plates, Juliet stood just inside the doorway. With a contrite, yet yearning, expression, Juliet looked at Rachel expectantly. Juliet was so very good at reading Rachel and apparently she'd already figured out that, for the moment, Rachel needed to dictate this encounter. She'd felt completely out of control the past few days, and it caught her by surprise. Who knew something as basic as food could shake her at a fundamental level?

For several long moments, she simply stared at Juliet, giving them both a chance to anticipate what would follow. As expected, Juliet grew more uncomfortable by the second. She shifted restlessly from foot to foot.

Rachel crossed the room to stand before Juliet. She kissed her easily as she unbuttoned Juliet's blouse. When Rachel's fingers brushed against Juliet's stomach, Juliet groaned and tried to deepen the kiss. Rachel pulled away with a disapproving *tsk*-ing sound. "None of that."

Juliet hitched the plates up with a whimper, but she didn't argue. Rachel considered taking the plates from her. Sure, they were only a few ounces each and Juliet spent most of her day holding food in some fashion, but any additional weight, however small, can become unbearable after a while. Instead, Rachel decided to let Juliet hold the plates longer. She wanted them to weigh as heavily on Juliet as that damn cleanse bottle had on Rachel for the past three days.

She returned to the radius of Juliet's arms and traced the defined contours of her abdomen. A shiver rippled through Juliet's body and she closed her eyes for a moment. Rachel placed both palms flat against Juliet's stomach and fanned them out for the pleasure of feeling the smooth softness of her skin. God, she loved this woman. Sure, they had their moments where everything they did put them at odds with one another. Even then, with bitter anger fueling her words, there was an undercurrent of reverence, a respect for what they shared. Their kind of love was rare and meant to be cherished.

Before she gave in to her desire to wrap Juliet in her embrace and hold her close, she peppered her neck and shoulders with light kisses, and then released her. She moved her mouth to Juliet's ear, close enough that the heat of her words would brush over it. "Promise me," she whispered in a tone just dark enough to show a hint of the consequences if Juliet refused, "Promise me that you'll never put me through that again."

"Oh, God." Juliet sounded like a woman on the verge of losing her mind. Rachel only had a few short moments before Juliet's control broke and she dumped the plates in favor of tackling Rachel to the bed.

"No, darling, it's just me." Rachel took the steak and potatoes, along with the salad from Juliet. She scooped a bite of cucumber into her mouth, chewed hastily, then added a bite of steak and mushrooms. "God," she said, mouth full and inelegantly muffled, "is it any wonder I love you so much?"

Juliet abandoned her position in the doorway and set the cupcakes next to the cleanse container. The look in her eyes was enough to make Rachel do the same with the other plate. She swallowed hard.

Normally, Juliet moved with the grace of a dancer, fluid and poised, as if nothing ever rattled her. Other times, like now, she adopted the power of a Neanderthal, impatient and demanding and so goddamned sexy, Rachel forgot everything else around her. Juliet shrugged off her shirt, along with her skirt, bra, and panties, until she stood naked before Rachel, and as she unpinned her hair and shook it out, Rachel's plans unspooled along with it.

"Was the cleanse really so bad?" Juliet asked with faux innocence, and Rachel recognized the trap for what it was. Juliet palmed Rachel's cheek, her thumb barely caressing the edge of her mouth.

As Rachel shook her head, she stared into Juliet's eyes, captivated and unable to look away. Juliet slid her hand lower, stopping at the curve of Rachel's throat. She smiled dangerously, then slanted her mouth over Rachel's in a dominating, overwhelming kiss.

This—Juliet's ability to move seamlessly from bottom to top and back again—took Rachel's breath away every time. When they entered the bedroom, she was sure she was the one in control, the one who would dictate this encounter. Then, Juliet effortlessly flipped their relative positions of power. Rachel wasn't even exactly sure when or how it had happened. All she knew for certain was that Juliet held her future, the possibility of pleasure and release, casually in the fingers barely touching and making her tremble with the promise of what was to come.

Without warning, Juliet spun her around, positioning Rachel so she could see herself, and Juliet looming dangerously behind her, in the mirror hanging above their bureau. She circled Rachel with her arms and pulled her back, melding her body flush to Rachel's as she worked the buttons of her silky blouse free. When she reached the last one, Rachel half expected Juliet to pull the blouse down and tie her arms together with it. Instead, she pushed it to the side and let it dangle open to reveal the red flush of Rachel's chest and throat.

Juliet stared at their reflections, her lips curved sensuously into a predatory smile, and whispered, "Watch." She flicked open the front clasp of Rachel's bra—a sheer, lacy piece that Rachel had modeled for her during a recent trip to their favorite lingerie shop. Impatient, she pushed the fabric out of the way and, without her usual soft buildup, Juliet grasped both Rachel's nipples and gave them a sharp, twisting tug.

Fire pulsed through Rachel, and she gasped and nearly doubled over with the searing pleasure-pain. "Oh, fuck."

"*That* is exactly my plan." Juliet purred, her voice a soft counterpoint to her feet as she roughly kicked Rachel's legs open wide. She hiked Rachel's skirt up and pushed her panties down until they caught somewhere around her calves. All the while, she stared into Rachel's eyes via the mirror. Her eyes, dark and lazy, showed the same gleam they held when she realized a food critic had just placed an order in her restaurant.

Rachel was embarrassingly wet with anticipation. She loved Juliet when she was pliant and willing to be taken. And she loved Juliet when she was dominating and demanding Rachel's submission. Hell, she just loved Juliet. Early in their relationship, she'd waited for the day when she'd grow bored, when what Juliet offered was no longer enough. That moment never came. Juliet matched her, desire for desire and kink for kink.

When Juliet slipped inside her, she closed her eyes momentarily, releasing Rachel from her intense stare. Her expression in that moment, unguarded and completely blissed out, touched Rachel just as deeply as the fingers twisting inside her.

"Oh, God." Rachel couldn't hold back her whimper and had learned long ago it was better not to try. When Juliet was like this, she wanted to hear Rachel. The more noise she made, the better.

Juliet's eyes snapped open and her gaze fixed on Rachel. One side of her mouth curved upward in an almost-smile, and not even a second later, she pulled out and fucked her fingers back into Rachel so hard the furniture they were leaning against shook with the impact. Rachel moaned. Somehow, her body managed to both collapse bonelessly against the bureau *and* stiffen and push back against Juliet.

Without preamble, without warm up, Juliet plowed into her at a relentless pace, driving her body toward orgasm with punishing accuracy. In and out until Rachel's entire existence narrowed to include only the blossoming ache spreading through her. She came with an inelegant grunt as her body shook with the powerful release of lust and pleasure, and her head drooped listlessly against the dark wood of the dresser.

Juliet fisted a hand in her hair and pulled her head up sharply. "I'm not done yet." She nipped at Rachel's ear and ever so slowly pulled back until just the very tips of her fingers remained inside Rachel. She pushed back in just as slowly, just as deliberately. And, God help her, despite the massive orgasm still rippling through her, Rachel's body shuddered in approval. Her cunt clenched and the easing wave of arousal bolted sharply to attention once again.

"Jesus...fuck..." Rachel reached back to clutch Juliet to her. She turned her head to crush their mouths together in a sloppy, wet, open-mouth kiss that ended as soon as it began when Juliet thrust sharply into her again. Rachel gasped.

"That's it," Juliet murmured, her voice soft and low. Rachel thought about every indecent thing Juliet had ever whispered to her in that same soft tone, and a loud moan rumbled through her in response. Juliet nipped at her neck, then sucked leisurely at the juncture where her throat met her shoulder. With every longing pull of her lips, she continued to fuck Rachel until her vision blurred and she came again in wave after wave of body-shaking pleasure.

When Rachel returned to her senses, she was on the floor, slumped against the dresser with a brass pull digging into her back. Juliet had kindly removed her underwear all the way so she was saved the embarrassment of being tangled in her panties on top of everything else. She tried to right herself into a proper sitting position, but her muscles were loose and not ready to work yet. She ended up settling onto her back with Juliet hovering inches above her.

"Well," she traced a finger over the contour of Juliet's jaw, "that was...unexpected."

Juliet smiled in her patently sexy way that said she was far too pleased to have had her wicked way with Rachel. "Glad I can still surprise when the occasion calls for it."

Rachel shook her head and laughed. There was simply no good way to respond to that with words, so she pulled Juliet into a sweet, lingering kiss. Her stomach grumbled loudly, and their kiss turned into a giggly mashing of lips. Not exactly their most elegant moment, but that was also part of the charm in their relationship. They didn't need to be proper at all times.

Juliet retrieved the cucumber and tomato salad and handed the bowl to Rachel, then grabbed the plate of steak for them so share as well. She forked a small portion of meat and added a few mushrooms, then fed it to Rachel, who groaned her appreciation. "So good."

"I'm sorry." Juliet dropped an easy kiss on the tip of Rachel's nose. "I should have let you finish eating."

Rachel's stomach clenched at the reminder of why they'd stopped eating in the first place. As far as she was concerned, it was a worthwhile sacrifice. "Don't be."

Juliet attempted to feed her another forkful, but Rachel redirected her hand gently, urging her to eat it herself. Juliet arched an eyebrow. "You're not hungry anymore?"

"No, I'm definitely hungry." Rachel picked up a chunk of potato with her fingers and popped it into her mouth to prove her point. "But you need to eat. You'll need your strength for what I have in mind for you."

Juliet slipped the steak in her mouth, then quickly followed with another bite. Rachel laughed and thought about how lucky she was to share her life with this beautiful, inspiring woman.

If anyone ever asked, Rachel would deny it emphatically. But the way Juliet decided to end their cleanse *almost* made it worth it. Lemon water, plus cayenne and honey. If three days of the drink was rewarded with a blackout-inducing orgasm, what would the full ten days get her?

CHEESY BACON POTATOES

1. Preheat oven to 425 degrees F.
2. Cube enough potatoes to fill your baking dish three-quarters full (I prefer Yukon Gold, but any potato will work).
3. Sprinkle some olive oil over the top (a tablespoon or two).
4. Add salt, pepper, and basil to taste, and stir.
5. Cover with foil and bake for approximately 40-45 minutes.
6. Remove foil. Add shredded cheese to cover the potatoes (I use cheddar). Add bacon bits.
7. Bake for another 15 minutes (or until cheese is thoroughly melted).
8. Let it cool for a bit, then eat and enjoy!

THE INDULGENT CHOCOLATIER

PASCAL SCOTT

"You eat with your eyes," she tells me.

She's standing behind the counter of The Indulgent Chocolatier, a four-star international chocolate salon in downtown Altamont, our hip, urban dyketopia here in the mountains of North Carolina. I'm standing on the other side of that counter, mentally thanking my editor at *The Blue Ridge Alternative*.

"Valentine's Day is coming up," he said yesterday at our Monday morning staff meeting. "And there's an editorial hole to fill. I need 5,000 words."

Valentine's Day. Love and poetry, hearts and flowers, and chocolate. My hand went up in the air like a bird, flapping *me, me. I can write that.* My deadline is Friday.

She extends a latex glove-covered hand across the glass to offer me a golden truffle. I'm thinking: *If that's true, if you really do eat with your eyes, then I'm eating you up right now.*

This is why. Her eyebrows are shaded black, the line of them drawing me in to notice her eyes, which are so piercingly jade green that they tug at me like a riptide. Her nose is narrow, her mouth a perfect pout of red lips. Her skin is olive in complexion. Her hair is dark, short, and lock-pullably wavy.

I accept the truffle and bring it to my mouth. It feels hard and smooth against my lips. She watches as I open it with my teeth. A core of Champagne-flavored ganache bursts onto my taste buds, buttery and creamy and rich, melting with the chocolate.

"How is it?" she says.

"Hmmm," is all I can manage.

"You won't taste the gold. People swear they can, but it's tasteless. Gold is for the eyes only. We call it luster dust. You see the sheen of it? The drama of the gold against the chocolate background?"

"Yeah," I say. "I see it."

What I see are the flecks of gold in her eyes. I scribble the quote in my reporter's pad. Behind her I notice a wood-carved sign with raised black letters. "Indulge Your Dark Desires," it reads. The taste of chocolate lingers on my tongue.

"How long have you been indulging?" I ask.

Those black eyebrows lift.

I point to the sign. "Your Dark Desires."

A slight nod of her head. "About twenty years. I have a classical education. I studied with Chef Julian Rose at The Chocolate Academy in Paris."

"Wow. *Parlez-vous francais?*" I ask, trying to remember my high school French.

"*Oui.*"

"Two decades. You don't look old enough."

"Thank you." I see the quick dart of a pink tongue against her front teeth. "You're very sweet."

Thinking: *For you, I could be even sweeter.*

"Where are you from?" I ask.

"Sonoma. California."

"Really? A Cali girl. What brought you to Altamont?"

Something slips across her eyes, a shadow.

"A friend," she says. "A friend brought me here. We opened the shop together three years ago. I've been fortunate. Altamont has been good to me. And your newspaper has helped by naming us The Best Chocolate in Town."

She's referring to our annual Best of Altamont poll, the *Alternative*'s comprehensive guide to the city. It takes the whole staff to write it, including me. Too bad I wasn't assigned the Food Section. I got Other Services and had to interview a local crystal-healing psychic who heard voices (Best Schizophrenic?).

"And what *are* your dark desires?" I ask.

A smile, on the lips and in the eyes. I'm thinking: *Girl, do you have a license to use those eyes?*

"Dark chocolate," she says. "Dark chocolate is indulgence, delight, and romance, all mixed together. We use chocolates from six countries—Belgium, Germany, France, Switzerland, Venezuela, and the United States. We blend the chocolates, which is unusual in itself. We don't use preservatives, additives, or vegetable oils. The most important thing is freshness, world-class ingredients, service, and our recipes, which are secret, obviously."

"Obviously," I say. Sounds like she's given this lecture before. "You say 'we.'"

"My staff and I. The other owner is, ah, well—she's gone."

She removes one glove, then the other. They make a slapping sound as they come off. I note what she's wearing: a white chef jacket over white chef pants. She's curvy, even under the unisex clothes, and a few inches shorter than me, which still makes her tall. And just right.

"You must try our Chocolate Experience," she says.

"Your, uh, chocolate experience?"

"It's our private tour. Usually I need more time to make arrangements. But—for you…"

She's looking at me now like I'm a bite of something she might like to taste.

"Why don't you come back tonight after closing? Maybe, half-past six? I'll give you our Chocolate Experience."

How can I say no?

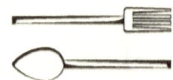

Her apartment is above the shop, one floor up, one of those loft jobs developers rushed in to do a few years back when Altamont became trendy. Downtown used to be the Piggly Wiggly and Charlotte's Wig Center and the musty aisles of the main library. Now it's condos and boutiques and a fresh market where you can pay too much for locally grown organic produce. Inside her apartment the walls are original red brick, except in the kitchen, where builders put up sheetrock and someone painted it this year's shade of neutral. There's tasteful drop lighting and a chandelier in the dining room, and all that bright light reflects back and up from the polished oak floors. The appliances are gleaming stainless steel: a French-doored refrigerator, microwave, and a double oven gas range. There's a black marble countertop on an island that gives guests a place to sit, to watch her as she cooks. The cabinets are chocolate colored. Of course.

She's changed out of her chef clothes, and I'm suddenly feeling very underdressed in my black jeans and white Oxford shirt. Outclassed too. She's wearing a black dress with a wide neckline that shows off her collarbone and neck, and when she turns, I see a low back with the drape at the lower waist. The dress stops a couple of inches above her knee, which is covered by black silk stockings. I glance down to notice her high, top-of-the-line black heels. *Uh-huh.*

She invites me to relax. I pull out a chair, one of three. It's more comfortable than your usual kitchen bar stool. It's a real chair, solid wood and padded cushions. Black leather. *I like this girl's taste.* On the island there's a magnum of red wine and a corkscrew. Effortlessly, as if she's done this a thousand times, she uncorks the bottle. It pops with a sound that seems to please her. She gives me that smile with her eyes. *God help me.*

From a cabinet she removes two wine glasses, sets them on the marble, and pours. "Cabernet sauvignon," she says. "Napa Valley. No disrespect, but North Carolina wines can't compete."

She's right. I did a story on it. We try, and the Altamont Tourism Authority will do its best to convince you otherwise, but our wines just aren't in the same class. The truth is, local vintners import most of their grapes from California. I swirl the wine before I sniff, then taste. I roll it around my mouth with my tongue. It's oaky with an aroma of cherries. She watches me.

"Nice legs," I say. I'm trying to impress her. Can't tell if it's working.

She takes a sip. "Yes. It's...complex." She tilts her head to look at me. "With a lingering, satisfying finish."

Involuntarily, I blush, something I haven't done for as long as I can remember. She lifts her glass.

"To dark desires," she says.

I clink my glass against hers lightly.

"To dark desires."

She brings the edge to her lips, looks me in the eye, and downs the wine all in one swallow. I do the same. She pours us each another glass. Then she turns that beautiful long back to me, and when she turns again, she sets a plate of chocolate truffles on the counter. The plate is brilliant white china with a rolled gold edge. The truffles sit like little dark queens in their dark candy cups inside the golden borders of their protected white queendom. Two smaller matching plates appear, one for each of us. She places three truffles on each plate.

"We'll begin with the lighter, more elusive experience," she says. "Each truffle here is what we call an Ecstasy Truffle. Our Ecstasy Collection is European rather than American in taste and texture."

"And that means?"

"European-style truffles have a center that is lighter and less dense than American truffles. The European flavors are more sophisticated and more subtle."

"Ah," I say. I write this down.

"We'll begin with the Violet Petal."

On my plate, she points a red fingernail at the truffle wearing a fragile flower petal, like a little purple cap.

"You'll find in the dark chocolate center hints of lemon zest, ginger, and saffron," she says. "But first, I must teach you how to savor the experience."

Oh, please do.

"Close your eyes," she says.

I close them.

"Now I want you to take three deeply cleansing breaths."

I do. I breathe in and out. Innnn and ouuuut. Slowly. Innnn and ouuuut.

"Quiet your mind. Let your mind relax. Think of nothing but my voice."

She has a great voice, now that I'm thinking about it. Listening to it. An amazing voice, in fact. I'm wondering why I didn't notice it before. It's a little raspy, gravely, throaty. And I *am* feeling relaxed. Floaty almost. I come back to focus on what she's saying.

"The fourth chakra is the heart, where we love..." that lovely voice is saying. "The fifth is the throat. The sixth, the third eye. And the seventh is the crown chakra. Let your golden rope of energy lift up now out of your crown chakra—up, up, up into the mist, into the thin dark clouds of the night sky. *See* your golden energy there. *Feel* your golden energy there. Now let it rain down on you in golden raindrops..."

I'm picturing those golden raindrops. I can almost feel them falling on my upturned face.

"Now," she says. "Open your eyes."

I open them. I think, *My God, she's pretty.* I'm not thinking about raindrops or chakras or chocolate at all.

"I want you to touch the Violet Petal," she says.

What?

"Lift it out of its delicate cup."

Oh, the truffle. Obediently, I pick it up.

"Run your thumb and forefinger across its surface. Feel how smooth it is."

I do. It is.

"Now bring it to your nose. Cup your other hand around the truffle and inhale deeply."

I follow her instructions. It smells rich and chocolatey and slightly floral.

"Now bite."

I bite. I hear a crisp, clean pop as the truffle snaps in two. The half that is in my mouth slips from my teeth to my tongue. I press it against my palate. It tastes sweet and citrusy with a hint of salt that makes me think of a sea breeze. The chocolate begins to melt in my mouth. She watches me. I finish the second half.

"Wow," I say when I'm done.

"Take a breath," she tells me. I do.

"Now chew on the breath. You should still be able to sense the chocolate."

I can. I can still taste it.

"Did you enjoy?" she says at last.

"I did," I say.

The next truffle is the Dragon. It's a burst of dark chocolate followed by the taste of sesame seed, then a kick of wasabi—but only for a second—before it finishes with the memory of chocolate. The last is Velvet Sin, a creamy ganache enrobed in a deep rich chocolate and drizzled with dark chocolate strings. By the time I finish Velvet Sin, I decide I'm about chocolated out for the night.

"You're familiar with endorphins?" she asks.

"Yeah," I say, "the brain thing."

"Endorphins are the hormones secreted within the brain that give you a sense of pleasure," she says. "Eating chocolate is one way to stimulate the release of endorphins."

"Yeah," I say. "That was it."

"There are other ways."

"Are there?" I say.

"Finish your wine," she says.

The last swallow tastes a little bitter after all the sweetness before.

She stands, eases around to where I'm sitting and takes my hand. And suddenly I'm up out of my chair and being led down the brick hallway into her bedroom. She walks with her shoulders and hips, slowly, everything swaying. I notice the seam on the back of her stockings. Obsessively, I follow the line of her legs to the bedroom. Inside there's more red brick, broken only by the east wall, where windows stretch from the floor to the white crown moulding of the ceiling. There are only a few pieces of dark wood furniture here: a cabinet and two end tables made of glass on which sit black-based lamps topped by honey-colored shades. The lamps give off a soft golden glow.

But the main thing I notice is the bed. It fills up most of the room. It's a king covered by a storm-cloud gray bedspread with two matching pillows resting on two other pillows, these in white pillowcases. Gray on gray, gray on white.

She walks me to the foot of the bed, then turns me by my shoulders to face her. Gives me a wicked smile and pushes me down. My knees bend as my legs touch the mattress, and I fall easily. I'm left sprawling, limbs in the classic X "tie-me-up-now" position. The shoes come off first. She leans in to remove my patent leather Oxfords, black, the best shoes I own, the ones I splurged on. She lifts up the heel of my right shoe, still smiling that smile, pulls it off, and lets it fall. Then the left.

She walks around to the left side of the bed purposefully. I roll over to meet her, raise myself up on one elbow. She stands so close, I can reach out and touch the skirt of her dress. I run my fingers along the hem. It feels satiny and cool. I let my fingers slip under the fabric and I caress her inner thigh with the back of my hand. I can feel the heat between her legs. She makes a slight movement, lifting her skirt just enough to let me catch a glimpse of black lace adorning a garter beneath the fold of her stockings. That's all it takes.

I'm up on my knees, lifting her dress over her head. She's naked now except for the garters, stockings, and heels. My own clothes come off in a heartbeat. I pull her down on top of me as I fall back. I put my hand behind her head and bring her face in close to mine. She smells clean, like soap and water. I kiss her—the most tender, romantic, Valentine's Day kiss I can conjure. When our lips part, she opens those green eyes and looks at me. But she's not looking like a girl who has just been kissed. She's looking like a girl who's pissed. She lifts herself up on her palms so that her arms are rigid and she's balanced over me.

"That all you got?" she says. "*Boi*."

Oh. With one move, I flip her onto her back and I'm on top. I pull her head down by the back of her hair and pin her arms over her head, wrist over wrist.

"What I got," I say slowly, deliberately, "may be too much for a little dicktease like *you*."

Her eyes widen in response. She struggles to get up. I hold her down, my left hand on her wrists, my chest pressing against her erect nipples. I work my knee between her legs, spreading them, pinning the right one beneath me. She kicks once in protest. One of her high heels has come off in the throw-down; now the second shakes free. I let my hand find the scalloped trim of her lacy garter belt then move lower. At my touch her body tenses, then slackens in surrender.

I force my mouth against hers, kissing her hard now, teasing her lips with my tongue before I bite—not at all the gentle lover I was only a few minutes ago. Her breathing comes in short, hard gasps. I part the lips of her pussy, running my finger along the folds, feeling the wetness. I slip a finger inside. Then another. She moans.

"You want more?" I whisper. She nods.

"What makes you think you *deserve* more?"

She draws a quick breath. Several seconds pass before she lets it go.

"Nothing," she says. "I don't deserve you."

I chuckle. I'm still working my fingers inside her, stroking her clit with my thumb.

"Damn right," I say. Her cheeks flush.

"I know your kind. I've been with girls like you. You think just because you strut around in your stilettos and silk stockings that bois like me are going to lose control. *Don't* you?"

"Yes, sir," she says. She struggles to get the words out.

"That's better. A sign of respect. You do respect me, don't you?"

She's nodding as if her orgasm depends on it.

"I'm gonna let go of your wrists now but I want you to leave your hands right where they are. Understood?"

"Yes, sir."

"Good girl," I say.

I let go. She doesn't move a muscle in her arms. I plunge three fingers inside her. She's so wet her juices are running down my hand.

"Is this what you want?" I ask.

"Yes," she whispers.

Her hips lift and the muscles of her thighs contract each time I thrust inside. I'm pumping a steady rhythm, four fingers in now, working her clit. Her pussy is grabbing my fingers, enclosing them like a tight glove. I squeeze my hand into its narrowest shape. I'm wishing I had thought to bring some lube. Wondering if I'll hurt her if I try to fist her now. I'm thinking I'll try anyway when…she comes. Her back arches and she lifts up at the same time that she grabs a pillow and pulls it over her face. I hear her muffled scream beneath the gray pillow case. And I can't help myself. I laugh.

Several minutes pass before she removes the pillow and tosses it aside. And there are those beautiful green eyes: pissed and satisfied, pleased and spent.

"Oh, sweetie," I say. "You know that I could just eat you up."

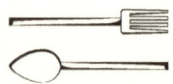

The chocolatier is my girl now, and when I told her I was writing this story, she knew immediately what I was going to ask.

"No," she said, quite firmly, "you may *not* have a recipe."

What followed then was a great deal of untoppish-like begging on my part and an undignified number of *please please please pleases*. She would not be moved.

I was forced to resort to subterfuge. While she was sleeping, I stole into her secret pile of important papers from the past. And there I discovered the following. It is, I believe, from her experimental phase and not representative of her best work. Yet it can rightly be called an Indulgent Chocolatier Truffle.

And so, dearest reader, I share it with you now. And yes, I give you permission: Feel free to indulge *your* dark desires.

AQUAFABA DELIGHT

10 oz. baking chocolate (premium quality, high cocoa content)
1 (15-oz.) can chickpeas
3 tablespoons maple syrup
2 tablespoons good whiskey
Unsweetened cocoa powder

Break the chocolate into pieces and place them in a mixing bowl. Pour off 1/2 cup of the chickpea liquid (aquafaba). Pour the aquafaba into a saucepan. Stir in the maple syrup and whiskey. Bring to a simmer. Pour the mixture over the chocolate and stir until smooth. Chill at least 2 hours. Roll into truffle-sized balls. Dust with cocoa powder.

ABOUT THE AUTHORS

JOVE BELLE

Jove Belle lives in the Pacific Northwest with her partner of twenty years and their many, many children and pets. She's the author of several novels and even more short stories. Learn more about her online at www.jovebelle.com.

CHEYENNE BLUE

Cheyenne Blue has been hanging around the lesbian erotica scene since 2000. Her short stories have been published in around 100 anthologies, including a few with "best of" in the title. She's the editor of Lammie and Goldie finalist *Forbidden Fruit: stories of unwise lesbian desire*, and *First: sensual lesbian stories of new beginnings*. More recently, her longer erotic romances, *Never-Tied Nora* and *Not-So-Straight Sue*, have been published by Ylva Publishing.

She lives on a ridgetop in southeast Queensland, Australia, where she goes camping, bushwalking, and four-wheel driving. She makes bread and cheese, collects bunya nuts in January, and grows veggies. One of these days, the bugs will leave her some.

CK COMBS

CK Combs writes dirty stories, hot stories, stories to seduce you, stories to take to bed... CK is active in the Olympia, WA, community as an activist, educator, and advocate for queer youth and is wonderfully supported and encouraged by their partner of over 20 years, two daughters, and other significant other. CK's thoughts on gender, privilege, kink, polyamorous relationships, and parenting can be found at Butchtastic.net.

CHERI CRYSTAL

Cheri Crystal is a registered dietitian by day and erotic romance writer by night. She is a native New Yorker who has crossed the pond to live in the United Kingdom with her loving wife. Cheri began writing fiction in 2003 after reviewing for *Lambda Book Report*, *Just About Write*, *Independent Gay Writer*, and other e-zines. She has numerous stories on Amazon and in published anthologies. Her solo collection of erotic romances, *Attractions of the Heart*, won a 2010 Golden Crown Literary Winner for lesbian erotica. In her spare time, she enjoys sports, cooking, jigsaw puzzles, and spending quality time with family and friends. *Across the Pond* is her first novel.

Website: www.chericrystal.com

LEA DALEY

Lea Daley has written fiction and poetry while raising children, claiming a lesbian identity, earning a BFA in painting, teaching preschoolers and college students, surviving the death of her only daughter, and heading a nonprofit agency that serves low-income working families. Retired now, she writes full time. Her debut novel, *Waiting for Harper Lee*, was a Golden Crown Literary Awards finalist and received a Lavender Certificate from the Alice B Readers Appreciation Committee. Her second book, *FutureDyke*, won a Goldie Award and was a Lambda Literary finalist.

A hard-core liberal, Lea enjoys animated debates at the dinner table. She travels whenever possible, alternating visits to bustling cities with trips to serene ocean shores. Because baking is another passion, her freezer almost always contains homemade desserts, and she loves sharing her recipes.

Lea resides in St. Louis, Missouri. She married her long-time partner in 2014, the morning after the city began issuing licenses.

N.R. DUNHAM

N.R. Dunham is a writer, a blogger, and a lover of Netflix. She's penned several short stories about sexy women and the women who love them, and hopes to get a longer, novel-length story written one of these days. She lives in Wisconsin, but dreams of traveling the world, taking selfies from exotic locales.

Facebook: www.facebook.com/NRDunham

R.G. EMANUELLE

New York native R.G. Emanuelle spent more than 20 years as an editor, writer, and typesetter. When she was a child, a neighbor called her a vampire because she only came out after dark, so it's fitting that she writes about creatures of the night, which includes her first novel, *Twice Bitten*. She is co-editor of the Lambda Literary Finalist anthology *All You Can Eat: A Buffet of Lesbian Erotica & Romance*, and the Golden Crown Literary Award winner *Unwrap These Presents*. She is also a culinary school graduate, which is what inspired her to write her romantic novella, *Add Spice to Taste*, and *Have a Bite*, the first of *The Vampires of Brooklyn Chronicles* novella series. Her short stories can be found in numerous anthologies.

Blog: www.rgemanuelle.com
Facebook: R.G. Emanuelle & R.G. Emanuelle, Author
Twitter: @Rgemanuelle
Email: rgemanuelle@gmail.com

JAYE MARKHAM

Jaye Markham is a pen name for a former feminist bookstore owner and archivist in a repository of World War II memorabilia. Since her teen years, the Second World War, and especially participation by women, has fascinated her. She has had the privilege of meeting and interviewing members of the WAC, WAVES, Marine Corps Women's Reserve, SPARS, Army and Navy nurses, WASPS, Red Cross and Home Front workers, and British war brides, among others. In addition, she has a story, "Madam Secretary," in the anthology *Hungry for More: Romantic Fantasies for Women* (2014). She may be contacted at jayemarkham@yahoo.com.

ANDI MARQUETTE

Andi Marquette is an editor and award-winning author of mysteries, science fiction, and romance. Her latest novels include *The Secret of Sleepy Hollow* and *The Bureau of Holiday Affairs*. Her co-edited anthology *All You Can Eat: A Buffet of Lesbian Romance and Erotica*, was a 2015 Lambda finalist. Find out more about her work at her website: www.andimarquette.com.

LIZ MCMULLEN

Liz McMullen is a mentor, author, editor, publisher, documentarian, and talk show host. Her debut novel, *If I Die Before I Wake*, is a Rainbow Award Finalist. She is the co-author of *The Finding Home Series*, which she writes with her good friend Shelia Powell, who happens to be a gifted psychic medium. Liz's first romance novel will be published in June 2016; *Unspoken* takes place at her alma mater—Mount Holyoke College.

PASCAL SCOTT

Pascal Scott is the pseudonym of a Decatur, GA-based writer whose erotic and romantic lesbian fiction has appeared in *Harrington Lesbian Literary Quarterly* and *In Posse Review,* as well as the anthologies *Thunder of War, Lightning of Desire,* and *Through the Hourglass.* Her literary fiction and poetry have been published in *Mississippi Review, Beloit Poetry Journal, The Iowa Review,* and other journals.

MARIE STERLING

Marie is a native Midwesterner who now resides in Florida. Her partner would probably describe her as sarcastic, but that's not always true. Sometimes she's sleeping. Marie spent a good chunk of her life in the United States Army, several of those years working in Military Intelligence. She could tell you more, but then she'd have to kill you. This is her first time being published and it will definitely not be the last.

Marie can be quite the little social butterfly, so please feel free to contact her on Facebook at https://www.facebook.com/marie.sterling76, or email her at marie_sterling76@yahoo.com. She promises to be nice, and welcomes breaks from plotting to take over the world.

REBEKAH WEATHERSPOON

Rebekah Weatherspoon was raised in southern New Hampshire and now lives in southern California with her favorite human and their two furry babies. She writes steamy new adult and adult multicultural contemporary and paranormal romance. Her latest novels are *Soul to Keep* and *Treasure.* You can find her, and information about all of her titles, at www.rebekahweatherspoon.com.

EMMA WEIMANN

Emma Weimann knew at an early age that she wanted to make a living as a writer. She knew exactly how and where she wanted to write the books that would pay for her house at the beach and the desk with a view of the ocean.

Even though she has had those dreams for over thirty years, neither the house nor the desk exist. Not yet. But she's making a living producing books, not just as a writer but also as a publisher, establishing Ylva Verlag, and its international pendant, Ylva Publishing, in 2011 and 2012.

She also is the author of *Heart's Surrender*, a 2015 Golden Crown Literary Award Winner for lesbian erotica.

BREY WILLOWS

Brey Willows is the author of the forthcoming Afterlife Inc. series and has been editing lesbian fiction for nearly a decade. Under another pen name, she has published stories in *Me and My Boi*, *All You Can Eat*, *Don't be Shy*, *Women of the Dark Streets*, *Where the Girls Are*, and several others. She lives with her partner and fellow author in the UK.

OTHER BOOKS FROM YLVA PUBLISHING

www.ylva-publishing.com

ALL YOU CAN EAT
A Buffet of Lesbian Erotica and Romance

ISBN: 978-3-95533-224-2
Length: 260 pages (58,000 words)

Chef R.G. Emanuelle and sous chef Andi Marquette locked themselves in the kitchen to create a menu that would explore the sensuous qualities of food and illustrate how the act of preparing and eating it can engage many more senses than simply taste and smell. They gathered a great group of cooks who put together an array of dishes that we hope will whet your appetite and send you back for seconds.

NIGHTS OF SILK AND SAPPHIRE
(Nights of Silk and Sapphire - Book #1)

Amber Jacobs

ISBN: 978-3-95533-511-3
Length: 309 pages (113,000 words)

Dae is rescued from desert slavers by the mysterious Zafirah Al'Intisar and placed as a prize in the Scion's harem. At first, Dae struggles with desires she has never before experienced, but as love and lust collide these two women slowly forge a bond.

DON'T BE SHY
A Collection of Erotic Lesbian Stories
Astrid Ohletz & Jae [Ed.]

ISBN: 978-3-95533-383-6
Length: 350 pages (139,000 words)

From kinky phone sex to unexpected, steamy encounters with the new neighbor. Fun with a love swing and unexpected relaxation techniques. This anthology has it all.

Twty-five authors of lesbian fiction bring you short stories that focus on the sensual, red-hot delights of sex between women and the celebration of the female form in all ist diverse hedonism.

Are you in the mood for something spicy?

HEART'S SURRENDER
Emma Weimann

ISBN: 978-3-95533-183-2
Length: 305 pages (63,000 words)

Neither Samantha Freedman nor Gillian Jennings are looking for a relationship when they begin a no-strings-attached affair. But soon simple attraction turns into something more. What happens when the worlds of a handywoman and a pampered housewife collide? Can nights of hot, erotic fun lead to love, or will these two very different women go their separate ways?

COMING FROM YLVA PUBLISHING

www.ylva-publishing.com

THE CLUB

A.L. Brooks

Welcome to The Club—leave your inhibitions and your everyday cares at the door, and indulge yourself in an evening of anonymous, no-strings, woman-on-woman action. For many visitors to The Club, this is exactly what they are looking for, and what they get. For others, however, the emotions run high, and one night of sex changes their lives in ways they couldn't have imagined.

Order Up. A Menu of Lesbian Romance & Erotica
© 2016

"Not Spam Again!" © 2016 Jaye Markham
"Bunya Bunya" © 2016 Cheyenne Blue
"A Twist of France" © 2016 N.R. Dunham
"The Way to a Woman's Heart" © 2016 Marie Sterling
"The Secret's in the Sauce" © 2016 Andi Marquette
"God's Tamales" © 2016 Brey Willows
"Sweet or Savory" © 2016 Lea Daley
"Cassidy's Anniversary Caper" © 2016 Liz McMullen
"Potluck Club" © 2016 Rebekah Weatherspoon
"Something Salty, Something Sweet" © 2016 Emma Weimann
"Sliced and Diced" © 2016 R.G. Emanuelle
"Clinch it with Coleslaw" © 2016 Cheri Crystal
"Daddy's Hot Appetizer" © 2016 CK Combs
"Honey and Lemon" © 2016 Jove Belle
"The Indulgent Chocolatier" © 2016 Pascal Scott

ISBN: 978-3-95533-658-5

Also available as e-book.

Published by Ylva Publishing, legal entity of Ylva Verlag, e.Kfr.

Ylva Verlag, e.Kfr.
Owner: Astrid Ohletz
Am Kirschgarten 2
65830 Kriftel
Germany

www.ylva-publishing.com

First edition: 2016

Credits
Cover design by Sue Niewiarowski, n-design.com
TOC design/layout by R.G. Emanuelle
Interior text design by Streetlight Graphics

The recipes belong to the authors of the stories in which the recipes appear.

www.ingramcontent.com/pod-product-compliance
Lightning Source LLC
Chambersburg PA
CBHW031553240626
47153CB00002B/486